"Relevant and provocative. We can each learn something about ourselves through the characters in *Afraid of the Light*."
DEBBIE MACOMBER, #1 *New York Times* best-selling author

"Another winner by Ruchti. She never disappoints her readers."
LAURAINE SNELLING, award-winning, best-selling author
of *A Song of Joy*

"Award-winning author Cynthia Ruchti's storytelling captured my heart from the first pages of *Afraid of the Light*. A gifted wordsmith, she's crafted yet another story that keeps readers turning pages as they fall in love with her true-to-life characters. Exploring complicated relationships with realism and sensitivity is what Ruchti does best."
BETH K. VOGT, Christy Award winner and author of the
Thatcher Sisters series

"*Afraid of the Light* holds surprising moments of laughter brilliantly timed to enhance rather than interfere with the moving, weighty themes of this unforgettable story. Cynthia Ruchti delivers it all in this masterful, compassionate tale of redemption. Keeping this one on my read-it-again-and-again shelf for sure."
RHONDA RHEA, award-winning humor columnist,
TV personality, and author

"Ruchti's book shines a light on the realities of hoarding and its impact on those around the hoarder. As protagonist Camille Brooks deals with her own hoard, I was often prompted to look around (both physically and emotionally) to see what I was stashing and where I needed to sort and toss."
BECKY TURNER, international speaker and
nonprofit consultant

"Who knew that a novel about hoarding could hold both quirky romance and redemptive healing in equal measure? Hoarding is a deeply painful and multifaceted disorder, yet favorite author Cynthia Ruchti brings great compassion and finesse to the issue in *Afraid of the Light*. I entered a whole new world as I eagerly devoured the story of Camille and Eli reaching out in different ways (and for different reasons) to those trapped in the prison of their own accumulations. Ruchti's extensive research gave me greater insight and empathy, and the love story is clever and utterly endearing. Ruchti is such a grand storyteller, reminding us all that there truly can be complete (albeit slow) transformation through the healing power of Jesus—the only source of Light."

LUCINDA SECREST MCDOWELL, author of *Soul Strong* and
Life-Giving Choices

"Captivating. Intriguing. Significant. In this page-turner, Cynthia Ruchti once again pulls her readers into a novel that is engaging and entertaining but also filled with personal application for all who engage in this fascinating narrative. You won't be able to put this book down."

CAROL KENT, speaker and author of *Staying Power*

"In her signature lyrical style, Cynthia Ruchti introduces us to multifaceted characters whose stories are refreshingly unique—yet could be our own. *Afraid of the Light* is more than a delightful read. It is a journey from fear to faith, from regret to release. Don't be surprised if you find yourself stepping into the light right along with Camille."

BECKY MELBY, speaker and author of *Hushed October*

"I could hardly wait to open the pages of *Afraid of the Light*. And I wasn't disappointed. Cynthia Ruchti captivated me from the first lines and pulled me deep into the characters—each one filled with quirks and relatable conflicts. Ruchti never disappoints."

KAREN PORTER, award-winning author of *If You Give a Girl a Giant*

"I anxiously await every one of Cynthia Ruchti's hemmed-in-hope novels. With wit, winsomeness, and wisdom she stitches together characters who could live in my real-world circles—folks with longings that resonate with my own heart."

JANET HOLM MCHENRY, best-selling author of *PrayerWalk*

"She's done it again! Cynthia Ruchti is a captivating wordsmith with a talent for telling poignant stories that wrap around your heart, mind, and life in a way that makes you a better person for picking up her books."

PAM FARREL, best-selling author of *Men Are Like Waffles, Women Are Like Spaghetti*

afraid of
the light

afraid of the light

a novel

CYNTHIA RUCHTI

KREGEL
PUBLICATIONS

Published in association with Books & Such Literary Management, 52 Mission
Circle, Suite 122, PMB 170, Santa Rosa, CA 95409-5370, www.booksandsuch.com.

All Scripture quotations are from The Passion Translation®. Copyright © 2017,
2018 by Passion & Fire Ministries, Inc. Used by permission. All rights reserved.
ThePassionTranslation.com.

Library of Congress Cataloging-in-Publication Data
Names: Ruchti, Cynthia, author.
Title: Afraid of the light / Cynthia Ruchti.
Description: Grand Rapids, MI : Kregel Publications, [2020]
Identifiers: LCCN 2020004904 (print) | LCCN 2020004905 (ebook) |
Subjects: GSAFD: Christian fiction.
LC record available at https://lccn.loc.gov/2020004904
LC ebook record available at https://lccn.loc.gov/2020004905

ISBN 978-0-8254-4657-3, print
ISBN 978-0-8254-7692-1, epub

Printed in the United States of America
20 21 22 23 24 25 26 27 28 29 / 5 4 3 2 1

Dedicated to the readers
who have kept me writing,
to the hurting who have captured
my hope-hemmed heart,
and to those who have shaped the time
I spend on my knees.

Many are afraid of the dark.
May we never be afraid of the light.

You gain strength, courage and confidence by every experience
in which you really stop to look fear in the face.
—ELEANOR ROOSEVELT

chapter one

THAT ACRID, CHOKING SMOKE SMELL. Cam caught a whiff of it—or her mind did—every time she walked a path from the curb to a client's home. Paper, cloth, wood, shingles burning. She couldn't let herself consider anything else beyond that.

She rechecked the address she'd been given. It wasn't often she crossed a mowed, relatively tidy lawn when approaching a new client. The address was correct. And the drapes were drawn tight or shades pulled down on all the windows. All of them. It must be the place. Another client afraid of the light.

A frequent guest on Camille's *Let In the Light* podcast—her producer Shyla's favorite—Allison Chase had finally agreed to engage Dr. Brooks's services. From their introductory phone call, Camille suspected what she'd see when Allison opened the door today. If she opened the door.

But that lawn—freshly mowed and tidy. Curious. Empty, barren window boxes hung beneath smudged windows on either side of the centered front door of the ranch-style home. The paint color, faded blue, made it look like tired, bleached jeans. Probably built in the eighties. Probably not updated in the almost forty years since.

Camille tossed the judgmental thought and drew a steadying breath before knocking. *Here we go again.* It wasn't a prayer, exactly. More like a rallying cry. If God was listening, all the better.

She waited. Her stomach growled. She should have eaten lunch an hour ago. Now, depending on how the appointment progressed and what she found behind the door, she might not eat for hours.

The lined drape for the window on the left moved. Others might not have caught the movement. Camille knew to look for it. Her knock had been heard. She'd been observed. Steps one and two in gaining entrance. She adjusted her quilted purse—machine washable, a necessity—on her shoulder. Its bright turquoise and pink pattern should seem less threatening than a black attaché or alligator-print laptop case. It had worked to break down barriers before.

Click. Click. Click . . .

Camille counted five dead bolt clicks before the door opened an inch.

"State your name." The voice sounded more apologetic than demanding.

"Good afternoon, Mrs. Chase. I'm Dr. Brooks. Camille Brooks. I'm so glad to finally meet you." *Tone down the exuberance, Camille. Too much happy can scare off a person in this woman's state of mind.*

"Allison. My first name's Allison."

"Yes, I remember. From our chats. You said I could come over today and talk with you face-to-face. Is that still okay?" Podcast listeners had described Camille's voice as soothing, comforting, that her midnight broadcasts helped them sleep, of all things. She hoped her voice came across as nonthreatening now.

"You won't stay long?"

Camille smiled. Textbook question. "Not today. Not unless you want me to." Textbook answer.

The door swung open a little less than the width of Camille's hips. She turned sideways and shimmied through the space. It closed quickly behind her. Five clicks.

The darkness wasn't unexpected, deeper and thicker than merely stepping from outside to inside. The smell surprised her though. Lily of the valley. Her olfactory system had been prepped for rancid, moldy, or at best, stuffy. It wasn't prepared for lily of the valley.

The diminutive woman stepped away from the door. "Let me turn on another light."

Another?

Allison reached across a tower of mismatched boxes, angled her body to avoid a pile of a dozen or more blankets, and flicked on a table lamp. It stood four feet tall. Only the top of the shade was visible behind the stack.

Camille hadn't expected lily of the valley. Or a client who looked like her mother.

Same pale eyes rimmed in darker blue, the outer corners tilted down as if already halfway to a frown. Same wispy shoulder-length blond hair that seemed unsure of its role on the woman's head. Same—Yes. Same open button-down sweatshirt cardigan. Different shade of gray.

Allison flicked at her hair.

Camille made eye contact and reined in her renegade thoughts. "A pleasure to meet you, Mrs. Chase."

"You too." Allison tugged her cardigan closed. "You'll need a place to sit." She moved through the room without waiting for an answer, surveying the stacks, rejecting several possible options, and moving to the next.

"Where do *you* usually sit, Allison?"

She brightened. "Over here. I keep all my things handy." She pointed to an upholstered glider rocker and ottoman surrounded on three sides by walls of magazines and books. Many of them cookbooks, Camille noted. And well-worn classics.

"You take your favorite chair then, and I'll . . ." This next step wouldn't be easy. She considered moving a plastic tote closer to where Allison now sat—a makeshift place to sit— but for her client's anxiety's sake, she couldn't disturb the disordered order. "Would it be okay if I used this straight-backed chair? I can set these books right over here for now."

"Can't use that chair."

This could get interesting.

"It only has three legs."

"This one then?" Camille rested her hand on the back of another, not a match to the first.

"Three legs. I'm kind of partial to chairs with three legs." Allison shrugged, as if that were all the explanation necessary.

Camille bent to look. Both chairs were propped with piles of bricks where a leg should be. "I don't mind standing for a while."

"That might work." Allison's chin quivered.

"For now."

The woman offered a barely there smile. "For now."

Smoke. Camille smelled smoke again. And that persistent lily of the valley. A candle burned somewhere in the room. There it was. On top of the aged television. Not safe. But a whole lot of trust building would have to come first before Allison would be ready to have Camille warn her of the danger.

Camille shifted her position so she couldn't see the candle's flame and the way it danced awkwardly, mocking her.

One woman's anxieties at a time. Allison's first.

"I suppose you want me to tell you I'm ready to get rid of this stuff," Allison said, gaze fixed firmly on her hands in her lap.

"I'd be surprised if you *were* ready, Allison."

Camille focused on the hands too. Pale and soft, with short, even nails. Like her mother's. Allison's fingernails sported the remnants of what looked like weeks'-old pink polish. The woman picked at what little remained.

"I'm honored you invited me in, Allison."

The woman looked up. "Funny word. *Honored.* Not one I would have chosen."

"What would you have said if our roles were reversed?"

She waved off the question.

"I'd like to know."

Allison surveyed her domain. Camille watched as Allison took note of every tilting pile, every stain, every stack and bundle and nameless bag. One barely navigable path wove through the chaos, and even it was littered with remains of past days. How was there room for tears to form and stay?

"Mortified."

"What?"

The cardigan sides overlapped. "I'd be mortified to step into a place like this."

"It's your home, Allison." Camille tiptoed carefully with her words. Her work with a client like Allison hung on fragile threads of trust.

"Don't know many who would call it that. They'd call it a disgusting mess. It isn't normal."

"Is that why you listen to the podcast? Why you allowed me in? Because you're looking for normal?"

Lily of the valley fought for dominance over a rancid smell wafting from what Camille assumed was the kitchen beyond a sheet-curtained doorway. Waiting for Allison's answer would be easier if she didn't have to breathe. Outsiders assumed Camille had gone nose-blind to the odors in the homes of her hoarder clients. Desensitized, maybe. But certainly not nose-blind.

Something scritched across metal in a nearby room. Cam had long ago trained herself not to flinch.

"Mice," Allison said. "Not proud of that, but what's a person going to do? My cat used to take care of them."

She had to ask. "You have a cat?"

"Had a cat. She . . . disappeared."

Well practiced, Camille kept her facial expression in check. Somewhere in the rubble of a decaying life lay a decaying feline that might never be found.

"Freedom," Allison said softly. "I don't want normal. I want freedom. But . . ."

"But what?"

"No amount of letters behind your name can give me that, Dr. Brooks."

Camille would have argued. But she was right.

"Can I change my answer?" Allison's tears glistened in the underachieving light from two small lamps and one struggling candle.

"Sure."

"My children. I want my children back."

Allison would have no way of knowing why Camille paused so long before answering. No way of knowing what Camille would have given to have heard those words more than a decade ago.

"How old are your children?" she asked, deflecting her own thoughts from where they drifted.

"Mid-twenties. One is forever . . . a newborn," Allison said.

Cognitive issues? Disability?

"Lia lives in Stafford. Ryan's . . . Ryan moved. I'm not sure where. He won't give me his address. He calls at Christmas."

Did Ryan think his mom was going to drop in unexpectedly, a woman who rarely left her house? Why refuse to give his mother his address?

Camille waited again. No more information.

Forever a newborn? Oh. Allison had lost a child. Another piece of the puzzle. Camille stored the information with well-honed memory tools. She'd watched her clients grimace when she scribbled notes as they spoke, as if every sentence were an indictment against their character. Jotting a note had completely shut down communication in the early days of her practice.

"Allison, do you want to talk about your other child?"

"No. Don't ask again." The woman flattened her palms on her chest, as if her breasts ached.

"Okay. You said you want your children back. I assume that means you haven't seen Lia or Ryan for a while. They haven't been here to visit."

"I disgust them."

"Allison . . ."

"Dr. Brooks . . ." Her voice held a tinge of impatience. "Look at me. Look at what I've become. They say I care more about my things than I do about them."

"Is that true?"

"Of course not. But they won't come back until I fix this." Her face registered crippling pain. "And I can't fix it."

"Neither can I."

Camille got the reaction she expected.

Shock replaced Allison's pained expression. "Then why are you here?"

"Because this calls for teamwork. Maybe you and I together can make some progress. That word *progress* makes you anxious, doesn't it?" *Tread carefully.* "Allison?"

"The real problem is that I just don't have enough storage space." She looked like a first grader trying to convince her teacher that a dog really did crave the taste of homework.

"You and I both know storage is a small part of what you're facing."

"I can rent another storage unit."

As she'd suspected. "Another one? How many do you rent now?"

"Four or five. Six, maybe."

Camille tilted her head. "Imagine what you could do with the money that's now being spent on storage rental. Just imagine."

"It's not that much."

"Think about it for a moment. How much per month?"

"I got a good deal because I have so many." Allison shrank into her cardigan.

"Around here, I'd guess you're paying somewhere around a hundred dollars a month for each unit, right?"

"Not quite that much."

"Let's use a hundred as a guesstimate to make the math easier on me. Five or six units means six hundred dollars a month, times twelve months equals more than seven thousand dollars a year."

Allison shifted in her chair.

"What would you do if you had seven thousand dollars?"

"It won't happen."

Camille brushed a feather from her slacks. *A feather?* Maybe Allison hadn't noticed her action. "Play along for a moment please."

"I'm not a dreamer, Dr. Brooks." She rubbed her jaw, as if trying to knead a knot of tension. "Not anymore."

Ah. An opening. "When you did dream, years ago"—she slowed the pace of her sentence—"how would you have answered the question then?"

A lawn mower revved up a few houses away. Camille picked up the sound despite the extra sound insulation a hoarder's house provided.

"Foolishness to think about it." Allison twirled the series of rings on her right hand, two per finger. "I suppose I would have said back then that I'd visit my sister. My sister Charlotte lives in Charlotte. Always thought she moved there on purpose just so she could raise eyebrows when she was introduced at work or parties."

"Seven thousand would allow you to do much more than that." The childlikeness in Allison's eyes made Camille's heart clench. It was as if Allison were peeking through the slats of a fence at a magical world on the other side.

"I'd . . . This is hard."

"I know." Cam would wait however long it took for Allison to give birth to the words.

"Okay. I'd rent a cottage on a beach somewhere warm and host my children and grandchildren for Thanksgiving. All of us together. Laughing and playing games and digging our toes in the sand. I'd watch the littlest ones while their parents took the older ones into the water. And the sky would be a color I couldn't imagine and the sun would feel so good on my skin. Like a brush of angel wings. And the babies would let me hold them however long I wanted. And right after Thanksgiving dinner at a big long table on the patio—dinner that I made for them—with everybody there, my kids would call me Mama and it wouldn't sound like a curse word."

Camille shoved aside the pale statistics of hoarders who fully recover and made a mental note to do everything in her power to help Allison realize that dream.

chapter two

PLUMS. YELLOW PLUMS WITH A *rosy blush hung from the branch that arched over the narrow path. I reached to pluck one past its prime. It didn't count as stealing, though the tree and path weren't mine. Another hour or two longer and the spent plum would join those already decaying at the tree's roots.*

But few dying plums could reach the roots for all the decaying cardboard boxes littering the yard, black garbage bags bloated with rotting unknowns, Jenga stacks of damp newspapers and damper House Beautiful *magazines.*

I rubbed my fingers over the plum's infant-smooth skin, which gave a little under my touch. How had it survived? How had any fruit found the courage to grow in this tangle?

Still holding the plum, I picked my way up the path to the back door as I once did at the end of a school day. Not this back door. Another one, long ago reduced to ashes.

This house, this bungled bungalow on an otherwise normal street, wasn't where I grew up.

I'd had to grow up first before I could think about entering the home of a hoarder and care about who lived—or tried to live—inside.

"That'll preach."

"You know how I feel about preaching, Shyla." Camille closed her iPad and pushed back from the microphone.

Camille's engineer/producer/friend with attitude removed her headphones, drew her enviable micro-braid hair extensions in front of her shoulders from where they'd been exiled behind her ears during taping, and stared at Camille like she'd grown a third nostril.

"I meant," Shyla said, "that's good stuff. Fits with the 'Embrace the poetry of living' theme you've been harping on in this month's podcasts."

"I do not harp."

"Camille . . ."

She mimicked her friend's tone. "Shyla . . ."

"If you'll excuse me," Shyla said, using both index fingers to point to her laptop screen, "I have editing to do before this episode is ready." She adjusted her headphones over her ears and tuned Camille out.

If she weren't so good at her job . . .

And if Camille were paying her what she was worth . . .

And if she weren't doing me a favor by liking me . . .

Okay, tolerating me.

Most days.

Camille waved an overexaggerated goodbye, grabbed her purse, and left Shyla's studio apartment, making sure the woman noticed that Cam had to turn sideways to slide past the monstrous armoire on her way to the door.

As always, Shyla would fake-fume for a moment after Camille left, but nothing would change.

So like my clients.

Occupational hazard. Every home visit required a shower before Camille could call the day done.

She dressed in her standard at-home soft jeans and French terry shirt, toweled her hair dry, and restored the bathroom to order before padding barefoot across the dark hardwood floor to the kitchen.

The refrigerator glowered at her. It accused her of skipping too many meals lately. So she yanked its handle open and squinted at its blue-white interior light, feigning interest. Except for the few staples on the nearly bare shelves, it could have been a display-model fridge. No leftovers. She didn't do leftovers.

In her career, Camille had seen too much of the aftermath of forgotten food.

She checked the expiration date on the small glass container of lemon velvet yogurt. Another two weeks from now. The glass felt cool in her hand, but the inky date glowed as if on fire. Two weeks? Too close. She depressed the foot pedal on the stainless-steel waste can and tossed the jar into its dark cavern.

Her stomach rumbled. *Let it complain. I'm not going out again.*

"Ever heard of takeout?" Shyla would say.

"Ever heard of takeout *wrappers*? The garbage of convenience," Camille would counter. She flicked the switch on her electric teapot and waited for the water to boil for tea.

Allison wanted her children back. Didn't they all? So many with hoarding tendencies or disorders, like Allison's, walled themselves off from their grown children without intending to. The larger the accumulation of things, the greater the distance.

Camille stared out the floor-to-ceiling window of her

eighth-floor apartment at the night-shrouded but blinking city. The bridge over the river was lit with two parallel rows of streetlights crafted to resemble the gas lamps of days gone by. The riverfront section boasted an intentional mix of modern and historic buildings and trim parks that made Camille's view as picturesque as artwork.

It *was* her artwork. The walls—each one—remained unadorned, the expanses unhindered by visual interruptions. No disruptions. As it should be.

I can help you get your children back, Allison. But you're going to have to trust me.

Their connection through the podcast had been a start. But Shyla was right. If they failed to find sponsors for the podcast, it would disappear from cyberspace. Camille couldn't afford to foot the bill forever. And the bulk of her audience wasn't in a position to donate to the cause.

If Adult Social Services got on board . . .

But they were both her supervising entity and her strongest opponents, convinced a podcast was the least effective way of addressing the issue.

If this worked with Allison, her unofficial beta tester, and if Camille could prove the podcast could form a vital trust bond with other hoarders and the people who cared about them, maybe she could make a dent. Maybe she could prevent other families from shattering like hers had.

Redemption. Maybe she could finally know what redemption felt like.

The timer on her counter dinged. The tea had steeped exactly 3.5 minutes.

Okay. So, she'd eat. She opened a single-serving can of clam chowder and poured it into another pottery mug. Two minutes in the microwave, another thirty seconds to wash out the can, dispose of the can in the recycling chute in the hall, then swipe down the interior of the microwave, and she'd be eating.

"Are you happy now?" she said to the silent refrigerator.

Apparently not. It wouldn't stop glaring. Or humming indistinct disapproval.

Minutes later, mug and spoon thoroughly rinsed and in the dishwasher, Camille sat on the charcoal gray couch and opened her laptop.

She scrolled through comments on the podcast page of her website. Last week's episode had touched a nerve. "How Do I Know When It's Time to Tattle on My Parent?" had generated more responses than the previous two months' worth of topics.

The angry comments she could ignore. Especially the ones that quoted Scriptures like "Honor your father and mother," as if that applied to hoarding.

"Forgive me, God. You know what I mean."

Whoa. An out-loud prayer. Bold.

The questioning commenters deserved her attention though. She took the time to give at least a short word of encouragement or a link to another resource or an expression of empathy to each one.

So many families dealing with hoarding issues—Mom, Grandma, son, daughter, friend . . . It no longer surprised her. But that didn't stop her from feeling overwhelmed by the magnitude and the aftershocks—often through whole communities. Generations.

She ought to know.

Overwhelmed. She stuffed the emotion behind a stack of others that screamed for attention she refused to give them. That was what it took to survive.

Camille slapped her laptop shut again and circled the perimeter of her apartment, paying special attention to the kitchen. Teakettle had shut itself off. No burners on.

But she thought she'd caught a whiff of smoke.

Moving wasn't an option right now, with so much tied up in repaying school and grad school loans, endless repairs on her car, the investment in podcast marketing. But as soon as she could, Camille would definitely consider it.

For now, she'd file another complaint with the housing manager about the resident two floors down who persisted in ignoring the *no smoking on the balcony* rule.

Traffic on the street below captured her attention. Several blocks away, the flow of taillights and headlights stalled, like red and white blood cells blocked by a clot in a major artery. The vehicular version of a stroke. She was aware of all the clinical reasons why her clients would let that happen in their homes. But seeing it play out in front of her had given her a new podcast topic.

Her colleagues could rail all they wanted. Just because they hadn't thought of it first didn't mean the podcast was a bad idea. Three million hoarders in the United States, a lowball estimate. And how many specialists to address the issue? How many shattered families did each of those three million represent? Someone had to take it to the airwaves, to cyberspace. Why not her?

"You'll catch more flies with cupcakes than a power bar," Shyla had told her on more than one occasion.

"Depends on the recipient," Camille had responded. Every time. "One person's power bar is another person's guilt-free, calorie-conscious, plant-based cupcake."

Yeah. She didn't buy it either.

She checked her multifunction watch. Still time. Within seconds, she texted Shyla. "Your Cupcake Guy bring home any leftovers tonight?"

Imagine being married to a baker.

Imagine being married. Camille shivered.

"Y?"

"Cuz. What do you mean, 'Why?'"

"Lime in the Coconut w/ toasted Swiss meringue ok?"

"Be there in ten."

Camille grabbed her keys and purse. Her phone pinged.

"Cam, bring a box of tissues, will you? We just lost another baby."

~

She stopped at Walgreen's on the way to Shyla's townhouse. Hoarders kept a stash of one-hundred packs of tissues. Not Camille's style. She held the box—"soft and durable," it said— in front of her like a pan of brownies for a housewarming. She elbowed the bell and waited for the door to open.

Not soft *or* durable enough for a moment like this.

Shyla's beautiful face glistened with tear tracks.

"I'm so sorry. Why didn't you tell me you were pregnant?" Camille said as she scooted past the armoire in the entry.

"Because of this," Shyla said. "Because of having to tell you that I'm not anymore."

"I am so sorry."

"You said that. Have a seat. Jenx is getting your cupcakes from the car."

What kind of friend was she? She'd almost corrected Shyla for pluralizing the word *cupcake*. "How's he taking it?"

"Like always. Sad but supportive. He's a rock."

Imagine being married to a rock.

"Is there anything I can do, Shyla?"

"You know the answer to that. No. Nothing. I could use a hug, but you don't 'do' hugs."

"I will tonight." Camille felt the weight of her friend and something much heavier in the circle of her arms. "I'm just so sorry."

Shyla pushed away. "And I'm still cramping."

"Oh. I . . ."

"Thanks for coming, Camille, but you don't have to stay. I'm going to bed early."

"I understand."

"And for the tissues." Shyla grabbed the box and clutched it to her chest.

"Right. No problem."

With one hand braced on the arm of the couch, Shyla stood, back arched as if she were near her delivery date. But she wasn't. And might never be.

"How . . . how far along were you this time?"

Shyla squeezed the tissue box so hard, its sides collapsed. "Do you think that matters? How long I was able to love this baby, or how short, makes a difference?" She ripped a tissue from the mangled container. "All that schooling. You don't know much about the human heart, do you? Or what it means to lose child after child after child."

The deluxe edition of a pain response. Camille waited, resisted the urge to leave Shyla emotionally bleeding out.

"I apologize."

"Shyla, don't. Everything you said was true. And I've already told you I had to take Compassion 101 twice and barely passed the second time around." Camille took a step back, ready if her friend decided to hurl something her direction.

"Interesting career choice for a woman without an empathy gene."

The falsehood of Shyla's statement didn't need correcting. Not now. Or ever.

Shyla's faint smile faded quickly but lasted long enough for Camille to know it was real. Like the too-brief life of a child.

"You know I care about you, Shyla."

"I know."

Jenx entered the room, a BakedStuff bag in hand. The young man needed a branding coach. The caramel-colored bag hinted at what was inside. But cupcakes had lost their appeal. She couldn't let him know that. He'd gone to extra trouble for her.

"Hey, Camille."

"Jenx. Thanks for"—she pointed to the bag—"that. And I'm sorry about"—she pointed toward his wife—"the baby."

He handed Camille the bag and embraced his wife. "We've been down this road before. It doesn't get easier."

He spoke so tenderly into Shyla's hair that Camille fought back tears.

Imagine being held at a moment like that.

"I'll call you tomorrow, Shyla."

"Okay."

Camille was in her car, heading home, before the embrace ended. Or that was how she pictured it in her mind.

chapter three

IT DIDN'T SURPRISE CAMILLE WHEN the alarm buzzed. She'd been staring at those red numbers most of the night, noting their periodic change but unable to make them stop taunting her with the reminder that, of all nights, she needed to sleep.

When she closed her eyes, though, she saw Shyla's pain as a roaring, seething, child-swallowing monster.

Probably a second cousin to the beast Camille saw in childhood when she dared to fall asleep under her parents' roof.

The cupcakes hadn't helped. Once she'd convinced herself it would have been cruel to ignore them after Jenx's efforts, she ate both magnificent wonders. Hence the alarm set to 5:00 a.m. She'd have to double her workout routine to cover the sugar.

An hour later, Camille had run four miles with hand weights and calculated at least two cupcakes' worth of sweat lost in the process. Shower. Dress. The endless routine before she could begin her workday.

On the day's schedule, another home visit with her client, Chester. Camille rolled the tension—or workout

31

remnants—from her shoulders. Chester would not have show-ered. He would have been happy to . . . if his house's plumbing was in working order. An all-too-familiar scenario.

Their previous visits had often ended abruptly when Camille ventured too close to suggesting Chester consider his core values. What was more important to him—the items that filled his home or the friendships he'd lost, the freedom he'd forfeited, even the freedom to allow a plumber into the house to fix the drains on his shower and sink?

Without a breakthrough, the stalemate in their discussions would redefine the word *stale*.

As Shyla would say, "Shame is nothing to sneeze at." In the case of Camille's hoarder clients, though, it often was. Shame kept them chained in dusty, dank prisons that once served as homes. Sneezing was not out of the question.

"I can't let anybody in to see this, to see what I've done to myself," Chester had said on their last visit several weeks ago.

"You let *me* in," Camille had said, her voice threaded with the practiced, even tone she used to set her clients at ease. Correction, to *attempt* to set her clients at ease.

"Rethinking the wisdom of that," Chester had said, scratch-ing the patchy stubble on his chin.

He'd ended the conversation moments later.

But he'd answered the phone when she called. A good sign. And he'd agreed to open the door if she showed up today.

Every visit required documentation. After two years of working with Chester—the long, slow crawl toward recovery—she hoped to have something more to write than "No progress."

⌇

"Chester, it's good to see you again."

"It's not a good day. Sorry you came all this way." The door opening narrowed from three inches to two.

"I'm not having a great day either. Maybe we could be

miserable together." She mentally flipped through volumes of protocol. She'd gone completely off grid.

Moments ticked by. The opening widened a fraction. Chester stepped back and dropped his arms to his sides. "As long as we stop talking when I say so."

Camille nodded.

"Then come in, if you can get in." He huffed. "Wonder who made up that phrase. A person like me?"

She knew better than to try to throw the door open wide. Few of her clients could throw anything wide. Camille nudged it a few more inches and slid through the narrow space, her mind on the ill effects of double cupcakes late at night.

She was greeted by a scene like so many others. A narrow, debris-strewn path through tottering stacks of debris from which the *strewn* had fallen. As always, she swallowed her initial reaction—*Oh, Chester!*

"What makes this day harder than others?" She steadied herself with her fingertips on towers of plastic totes as she navigated the path and took the office chair he'd pulled out for her.

The man shrugged, the action half smothered by the upholstered brown recliner where he'd perched. "It doesn't take much."

"Is it your health?"

He chuckled. "You'd think, wouldn't you? Living in a"—his eyes surveyed the room—"mess like this. You'd think I'd be flat out with any number of gruesome diseases. No. Nothing's threatening my health at the moment."

She'd disagree with him, in light of his asthma-like wheeze, but how far would that dialogue go? She leaned forward. "Something else then?"

"Landlord was here."

"Oh."

"I didn't let him in, of course."

"Of course."

"But he saw enough. Had a fit loud enough to wake

Benjamin Franklin's dead ancestors. And that's saying something." Chester rubbed his palms on the arms of his recliner.

"What did your landlord say?"

"The usual. Threatened me with eviction again if I don't get the place cleaned up. Gave me a deadline this time. First of the month."

"And what did you say?"

"Told him I'm working on it."

The opening she'd been waiting for. "Are you ready, Chester? I can have a team here in two days if you're serious."

His eyes glazed over.

"Chester?"

"Yeah? I heard you. I guess so. Guess I have to be."

She might not get stronger confirmation than that. "Let's spend a little time talking through the process then."

"Okay."

"The team I work with are top-notch people, Chester. They'll respect you and your belongings."

Chester slammed his footrest closed. "With a shovel. That's respect?"

"We'll take it at the pace you need, but the first of the month is not that far away."

"I need your promise they won't throw out anything unless I've approved it. I know some of this stuff might look like garbage, but most of it has a purpose they might not know about. I don't want them hauling things away that mean something to me."

Not even these dozens of used paper plates, Chester? Not even the spoiled meat, the long-empty eggshells, the unidentifiable liquids-once-solids in plastic bags on your kitchen counters?

"We will involve you in all the decision-making. Your part will be trusting like you never have before and letting us help you make the hard decisions. But you landed on an important point. What among all this means something to you?"

"You've turned to mocking now, Dr. Brooks?"

"No." She leaned farther forward. "No, Chester. That's not what I meant. I sincerely want to know—need to know—what criteria you use to determine an object's value."

"It's all valuable to me. Do you think I would keep it around if it wasn't?"

Yes. "We're looking for *your* definition of 'important to you.' And then, as we've said before, make little conscious shifts in that definition."

He sighed. "Readjust my attachments, my emotional connections to inanimate objects."

"Yes. You *have* been paying attention, even when you sat there week after week with a scowl on your face." She smiled.

His lower lip quivered with the effort to squelch it, but he returned the smile.

Camille opened the notes app on her phone. "I'll keep a record of your answers so we can communicate clearly with the—"

"The dumpster people?"

"With the organizational experts. We use trucks, not dumpsters."

"Nice touch."

"I'm not insensitive to how difficult this is for you, Chester. But I'm also not insensitive to its necessity. I want you to be able to stay here in the place you've called home. Where else would you go?" *Too much?* She held her breath.

He turned his head, as if listening to an unseen person for further directions. Camille was forced to breathe again before he spoke. "I've outlived my welcome with everyone else who was once in my life. They don't want me to come near them if I'm hauling all this with me."

"So," Camille ventured, "you have two strong reasons to tackle the accumulation."

"'The accumulation.' How distinguished a phrase for it."

"Two compelling reasons. You'll get to keep your house,

and you'll finally have a chance to start rebuilding those relationships."

Chester closed his eyes and rubbed the side of his head, as if warding off a headache.

"Would you let me start today?" Camille asked.

"What do you mean?"

Courage, Camille. But tread carefully. "Would you allow me to remove one thing, one item, whose value is no longer as strong as it once was? One item? Can you look around this room and choose one thing you can part with?"

Minutes passed as Chester pawed through the refuse near his chair. "I'm having a hard time—"

"Something broken? Beyond repair?"

"See, that's the thing. I have a particular fondness for the broken."

She risked laying her hand on his sleeve. "I understand. I do too." Something twitched in her chest. Heart. Seat of the emotions. Somehow she'd have to show she cared without . . . showing it.

His eyes fixed on her hand. She withdrew it slowly. "I have an idea," she said.

"You and your ideas."

"Near the door is a basket with dozens of umbrellas."

"For visitors, if they need one."

"How many visitors have you let into the house in the last five years?"

"Two. My brother—but he won't be back. And you."

"May I use one?"

His eyes widened.

She changed tactics. "Borrow. Let's see if you can live with one less umbrella for the next twenty-four hours."

"It's just a game, isn't it?"

"Chester, if the drapes weren't closed, you'd know it's raining out there. And I didn't bring an umbrella."

"As if you didn't already know I owned more than enough."

"What did you just say? Did I hear correctly? *More* than enough?"

"You've got me all twisted in my thinking. I can't do this anymore." He pushed on the arms of his chair and raised the footrest again. A benediction to the conversation.

She stood. "I'm going to call my team of organization experts, Chester."

"If that's what you want."

"It's what you need if you want to keep living here."

Crickets. She turned her head at the sound. Literal crickets. Somewhere in the bowels of the overflowing house.

Chester repositioned himself in his chair. "Go ahead and call."

"I'm not going to pretend it won't be hard. But I'll be here with you. We'll do it together."

A wild chorus of crickets and nothing more from Chester.

"I'll call you tomorrow with the arrangements and to answer any questions you might have. You'll like the team."

No response.

"You're brave enough for this. I know you are. Keep reminding yourself of that. Talk to you tomorrow."

"Dr. Brooks?" He looked up, almost making eye contact. "Grab yourself one of those umbrellas on your way out. Frail thing like you will catch her death of something if you get wet."

"Are you sure?" Who knew an umbrella offer could lead to an adrenaline rush of hope for managing her client's obsessions?

"Just one though." His gaze drifted to the floor again. "I . . . I might need the others."

Camille texted her contact at Rosies's Refuse Removal. What an unfortunate name and typo. The company logo looked like it was refusing to remove anyone named Rosie. Or that multiple Rosies were refusing. The presence of their trucks in a hoarder's driveway had always made her cringe. But the typo and logo remained.

The cleaning team was on board for starting in two days. But she needed the trucks and the haulers. Why wasn't someone from Rosie's—or Rosies's—responding?

Her phone dinged. *There we go.* No. A message from Shyla. Would Camille be okay postponing their appointment to record two more podcasts this week? Not only okay. It would relieve a little of the stress of pulling together the crew she needed and managing the anxieties of a man who was unlikely to let a little thing like eviction compel him to make a radical change.

Camille answered Shyla, then called the flower shop to have an arrangement sent to the grieving almost-mom and her husband. She should have thought of that yesterday. Tough break for them.

Maybe flowers was a dumb idea. A gift card to their favorite restaurant? How soon before Shyla would feel like getting out of the house? Camille should make them a meal.

But that would mess up her kitchen.

chapter four

WHERE HAD CHESTER GOTTEN A Vera Bradley umbrella? Resale shop? Online?

And that was the one he was willing to part with?
The curiosities might never end in this profession.

Possessions Obsession Profession—her life reduced to three
words. Their obsessions over their possessions had become her
career, and in turn her obsession.

Walking Chester through the next few days would call on
all her resources. She wouldn't have time to ease him into what
was ahead. Not ideal to have those kinds of decisions forced
upon someone who had let his life disintegrate into a puddle
of decision-less-ness. His emotional distress could soar off the
charts. She'd have to stay close through the whole process.
Close and alert. Chester could check out permanently if she
didn't . . .

Camille exhaled through fluted lips.

A client. She could care, but not too much. Maintain the
professional distance that would save her from— No. That was
textbook talk. Theoretically a great idea. Hard for Camille to

pull off, which was what kept her performance evaluations on the shaky side. Given the choice between the rule book and what her heart told her . . . and tried *not* to tell her . . .

She and Shyla could joke about Camille's lack of an empathy gene, but both knew better. Who in their right mind would choose this profession without an overactive capacity to empathize?

Her client Allison loved books. Why would she think about that now? Maybe she could get Allison to leave the house for an hour a week for a book club discussion. This time Camille didn't trust her memory but recorded the idea in the notes app. How long would it be before Cam could introduce an idea like that?

The Vera Bradley umbrella came in handy when Camille stopped at the grocery store for a small piece of salmon and a bunch of asparagus for dinner. It was too much asparagus for one meal, but she'd do her best to finish it. The shoots were still thin and tender this time of year. She asked the produce manager if she could purchase half a package of cherry tomatoes for blistering. They'd add a sweet yet acidic touch to the meal. He told her it was against policy. She'd have to share the rest with someone else in the building. Or . . .

She took an extra produce bag from the roll above the radishes and headed for the checkout. A few minutes later, she was holding Chester's umbrella over her head, extending half a container of cherry tomatoes toward the homeless man who camped out on the stoop of an abandoned storefront six blocks from her apartment. She'd had to go out of her way, but it would be worth it not to worry about leftovers.

As she pulled away from the curb, she glanced back at the homeless man, pleased that he apparently appreciated the hot coffee too.

Camille let herself into her apartment, grateful that she could do most of her work from home. The skies weren't lightening up. If anything, the rain was coming down harder now.

She slid the double-wrapped salmon and asparagus onto separate shelves in the echo-chamber fridge and flicked on the switch of her teapot.

She stared at her phone. "Rosie, come on. I need to know if you guys can help me out or not."

Instead, it was Shyla who called.

"Are you in the field, Cam?"

"No. Home. What's up?"

"Don't panic until you hear both halves of what I'm going to tell you."

Camille gripped the edge of the countertop. "Shyla, are you okay?"

"Me? I'm doing fine. I will be fine. It'll take a little time."

"What can I do for you?"

"Nothing. There's nothing anybody can do."

Such a brief pause held so much awkwardness.

"I thought of something," Shyla said.

"Good. What?"

"You could send me flowers."

Camille turned and leaned back against the counter, sighing. "I did already. Now when they arrive, you'll think you had to ask."

Shyla chuckled softly. "The delivery gal just left. They're beautiful, Camille. I love them. And not a hint of pink or blue anywhere. Thoughtful."

"I'm glad you like them. It's just . . . there's nothing . . ."

"We'll be okay. It's you that you should be worried about."

Camille dug a tea bag from the white canister. "That sounds ominous."

"You know that hauling service you use?"

The tea bag slipped from her hand onto the countertop. "What about them?"

"Out of business."

"What?"

"The hard way. The police shut them down this morning."

"How does a garbage-hauling service get in trouble with the law?"

Shyla drew in a noisy breath. "According to social media, they were dumping garbage in unlicensed places to avoid processing fees."

"Unlicensed places?"

"Like abandoned farmland. Remote woods. The river."

"Shyla! You're making this up."

"Multiple rivers, according to complaints."

Camille abandoned her tea brewing and sank onto the couch. She blocked out images of the kinds of things Rosie's people might have dumped onto other people's property. Or into the water. "Unbelievable. The people I worked with from Rosie's were a little gruff, but they did their jobs. I never had to worry about them criticizing my clients or goofing off when they should have been working."

"They had other vices, apparently."

"Innocent until proven— Oh no! Now what will I do about this week?"

"This week?"

The peach ginger tea bag called to her from the counter, but its voice was overridden by the crisis. "I need to find another outfit. Fast."

"You've abandoned your two-choice wardrobe, Cam?"

"Another refuse disposal outfit, Ms. Still-in-Comedy-Bootcamp."

No response.

"Shyla?"

"Don't make me laugh. I'm still cramping."

"This isn't your worry. I'll get on the case."

"That's the other half of the news I have for you." Shyla's voice perked up a notch. "You know how I put that sponsorship opportunity ad on the podcast website?"

"The one everyone has ignored?"

"Yeah, that one. We got a nibble today and . . ."

"And . . ."

"The guy listens to the *Let In the Light* podcast."

Camille crossed her legs and tucked her feet under her. "Is that a bad sign or a good one? I mean, does he listen because he's a hoarder?"

"You have something against compulsive hoarders, Cam?"

"Very funny. I was processing how curious it would be for someone currently fighting a hoarding disorder to be named as a sponsor. Although . . ."

"Just listen to the rest, please?"

"I'm listening."

"He owns a trucking company that specializes in—"

"No!" Cam sat bolt upright.

"Yes. Somebody's looking out for you. With a capital *S*."

"Do you think the guy heard about the Rosies's situation? Is he trying to capitalize on—"

"Camille, you are going to have to lose your suspicious attitude toward men. They're not all like the men in your past who have disappointed you."

"*Now* who's preaching?"

Shyla huffed. "His call came in before that news broke. So unless he has insider information or, so, okay, I stalked him online. He's legit."

"Shyla."

"Camille."

"Quit it."

"You."

"We're more mature than this."

"No, you are."

"Shyla, just tell me about this person. Was he asking for us to throw work his way?"

"Didn't mention it. He just said he'd seen the ad and wondered if he could snag a sponsorship spot if we had any openings left."

Cam lay on her back and stretched her legs the full length of the couch. "What exactly do you mean by 'legit'?"

"It's a commonly used expression meant to convey—"

"If you weren't my best friend . . ."

"He has an impressive résumé."

"A guy who drives a garbage truck?"

"Owns the company."

"Okay. Go on."

"He often works on hoarder cleanup projects and understands the nuances."

"Stop right there. He understands hoarder cleanup *nuances*."

"Says so in section three, bullet point two on his résumé."

"He didn't once work as a used-car salesman, did he?"

"Is that judgment I hear in your voice?" Shyla sounded like she was standing with a hand on her hip and a finger wagging Cam's direction. "I don't have to tell you how important it is that we're able to keep funding the podcast, do I?"

Camille rolled onto her side. She put the phone on speaker mode and propped it on the coffee table. "I suppose we can't be picky. But honestly, *nuances*? I mean, by all means, hoarder cleanup is far more nuanced than most people know, but he used that word in his résumé? And who writes a résumé to become a podcast sponsor?"

Shyla coughed. "He didn't exactly send it to me. I found it online."

"Ah. My clandestine producer."

"Just looking out for your best interests."

"I suppose I need to meet him. See if he's, like, breathing and can produce a legitimate form of ID and does know about how this process works."

"So it's yes to the sponsorship?"

"We'll see. First I need to know if he can work the Chester project in two days."

Coffee shop. Safe, nonthreatening, casual environment. No pressure for Camille to enlist Eli Rand's trucking company. Talking. That was all. Although if Eli wasn't her answer, then who was?

Camille had a visual picture from his website. Although despite the "Awe-Done Clean and Haul" (*really?*) slick, crisp, modern site, she knew better than to expect his professional headshot would match his actual looks and demeanor.

With a cheesy brand like that, she half expected him to walk in looking a little like Cousin Eddie from the classic movie *National Lampoon's Christmas Vacation*. She stopped her thoughts. "Don't judge a garbage truck by its cover." She stirred the foam on her cappuccino.

"I disagree." The voice, low and smooth, came from over her shoulder. "May I sit?"

Eli Rand. Almost exactly the image she'd seen on the screen, and wearing the same cranberry-colored shirt. Correction. Jumpsuit. Clean, maybe brand-new black work boots. A small triangle of a charcoal undershirt showed through the open collar. Garbage guy. Impeccably dressed, except for *jump* attached to the word *suit*. In public.

They exchanged "Nice to meet you" verbiage, and she invited him to take the chair across the table from her.

"It's been my long-held opinion," he said, as if only momentarily interrupted from his train of thought, "that you *can* judge a garbage truck by its cover. Or its paint job, logo, color branding . . ." With two pinched fingers, he tugged at the fabric in the middle of his chest. "Cranberry."

She'd guessed right on the shade.

"Not crimson, which would be a little too-too, if you know what I mean. Not fire-engine red—whole different service. Not burgundy—dull and lifeless. Not scarlet because, well, you know. Cranberry. Bright, but not overly so. Appealing. With a little sense of holiday, which is completely intentional, in case you wondered."

Camille took a sip of her cappuccino. Might need more caffeine for this conversation. "I hadn't wondered, but thanks for explaining."

"Your clients, I'm sure, have enough resistance to the idea of a fleet of garbage trucks parked in their driveways or in front of their houses."

A fleet?

"Which is why we never bring more than one truck at a time. The client's less overwhelmed and less embarrassed by what the neighborhood sees. And why we've chosen a cheery color like—"

"Cranberry?"

"Right. White exterior to the trucks, with the cranberry lettering. Cranberry interior that looks more like the inside of a . . ."

"Great white shark's mouth?"

His eyes widened, jaw slack.

Success. She'd stopped the ceaseless flow of only mildly interesting information. "Your breath mint is showing."

"What?" He moved the nearly dissolved breath mint around in his mouth and took a man-sized swig of coffee, apparently hot enough to make his face flush. "I—"

"I was going to ask you to tell me a little about yourself, Mr. Rand, but that may no longer be necessary." She pushed away from the table an inch.

"You're turning down my sponsorship application? Look, I might have come on a little strong. It's not that I haven't been accused of that in the past. But I'm working on it. You should have seen me before I started drinking Calm Me tea with breakfast."

"Seriously?"

"No. Come on. Do I look like a tea drinker?"

"That's too bad. I love tea."

He leaned back in his chair and crossed his arms. Head

46

nodding, eyebrows raised, smile growing, he said, "You're enjoying this more than you let on. Putting me in my place."

Camille mimicked his posture. "And you seem to derive an excessive amount of pleasure from decorating a garbage truck."

His smile disappeared. "Then I gave you the wrong impression. Thanks for your time." He pushed away from the table a full foot and stood.

"Wait." Jumpsuit or cashmere sweater, she needed someone to help with the Chester project. "Please sit down. I'm not trying to be difficult."

"It comes naturally?"

Is growling in public considered socially acceptable behavior? She drew a deep breath instead. "Mr. Rand . . ."

"Eli."

Somehow she'd known he'd insist on that. "Eli, we are exploring the sponsorship idea. But for now, if you wouldn't mind, I'd like to discuss hiring you and your crew for a major project Thursday and Friday."

"This week? Both of us?"

"Both? You have a crew of two? That's hardly a fleet."

"Yes, a fleet is technically four hundred and thirty, if we were navy ships. But our insurance company says that although they prefer a minimum of three trucks to qualify for fleet status, they were willing to give us the fleet rate with just two trucks. For now. They see the Awe-Done growth potential."

You don't need this guy, Cam, but Chester does. "So two trucks total?"

"For now, as I believe I said. Me and my dad."

His elderly father. Great.

"This Thursday, huh? Let me check my calendar." He pulled out a smartphone at least one upgrade from hers. "Thursday and Friday. Sorry. I can't help you with—Oh! Look at that. The week just opened up."

"Fired from another job?"

"No." He pocketed the phone. "Canceled the colonoscopy. So are you sure two days will be enough?"

"Wait. Your colonoscopy was going to take Thursday *and* Friday? Never mind. I don't want to know."

"Dad's colonoscopy. I'm just his driver. Mom has her book clubs every Thursday and Friday. So I told her I'd step in. But Mom canceled both book clubs this week since this cancer follow-up test is so important to Dad."

Camille shook her head to align the fragments of the man's conversation. She'd gotten distracted by the words *book club. Allison.* First Cam would have to check out the kind of woman who gave birth to someone like Eli Rand though. Who did the talking at a Mama Rand book club? He'd said *cancer*?

"Your dad is battling cancer?"

"Did battle. Won. Thursday's test is the five-year mark."

"Oh. Yes. Important. So you'll have a fleet of *one* truck for this job?"

He took another sip of coffee and *aah*ed. "Good point. You earned that PhD, didn't you?"

"Did you mean that to come out as unkindly as it sounded?"

"What? No! Admiration. I know what it—I can imagine what it takes to reach that level of accomplishment. It was supposed to be a compliment."

Garbage.

Camille reined in her ire. The look on his face seemed either genuine or a work of brilliant acting.

"My friend may be able to help out. He's good with people."

"But can he drive a truck?"

"No. Can you?"

"I mean, does he have a license to drive a rig like that? For that matter, I should probably ask you."

He held up one finger while draining the rest of his coffee. She waited.

"Now, let's see." He squinted. "Yes. My cordial and fun loving is back where it belongs. I'll get my friend, who is licensed and has had all his shots, to drive the other truck. But he only has one arm, so the hauling part is harder for him. Between the two of us, though, we can—"

"Stop." Camille drained her cold brew. "You're hired."

What? That was not what she meant to say.

"Great. Except not so."

"Excuse me?"

"Not hired. Let me do this first assignment for free. After that, you can pay full price for all our future projects together."

Oh, Eli Rand. You are delusional on so many levels.

chapter five

FOR FREE?"
Camille pictured Shyla swallowing her gum with those
words. "Yes, my friend. For free."

"Did he ask you to marry him too?"

"(A) No. And (B) No! You won't believe this guy, Shyla. I
don't know if he's off-the-charts arrogant or delusional or . . ."

"Or what?"

"Well, the other possibility is that he's completely sincere,
kind, thoughtful, and accommodating."

"No, that can't be it."

Camille switched to speakerphone to give her arm a break.
"Agreed. The least likely of the options. But he's able to work
Thursday and Friday, and Rosies's crew is on their way to jail."

"Innocent until proven—"

"I know. I know."

"Where are you now?"

"Sitting in the parking lot at your favorite fast-food poison."

Shyla's gasp traveled well through cyberspace. "No way!

My cravings didn't leave me when we lost the baby. Would you pick me up—"

"Do you think I'd be here for any reason other than to get something for you and your poison-proof husband? I'll be at your place to drop off your dinner in five minutes. Five and a half if traffic's bad."

"You're the best, Camille."

"Not even close. I lied to you."

"You did?"

"I ordered coleslaw for both of you."

"Love coleslaw."

"But it's technically a vegetable."

Shyla laughed. "Not the way they make it."

Camille woke four times in the night with an uneasy feeling. The kind accompanied by whispers of terror and stranger danger. Eli Rand could be the biggest mistake she'd made in her career. She was too young to die. Or suffer the humiliation of headline news—*Clinical Psychologist Raises Hands in the Air Over Awe-Done Clean and Haul's Lead Driver.* Owner. Whatever.

He made her laugh.

No. First thing in the morning, she'd search for other options. That was the thought that allowed her to fall asleep again. Until the next whisper.

And now it was morning and she'd found no other options. She widened her range, looking for another licensed disposal service experienced in hoarder cleanup.

One day's stressors at a time. She closed her laptop and slipped into her workout clothes. The reports waiting for her attention would have to keep waiting until she worked some kinks out of her muscles.

Worry made a bad pillow, which made a stiff neck, which made everything else harder than it had to be.

Sometimes the weight of other people's concerns made Camille feel like the depository to which the dump trucks backed to unload the haul from hoarder houses. Shovelfuls of debris, now on her pile. Rooms cleared at their houses, the refuse now hers to own.

She tied one shoelace and paused. She'd volunteered for it. *Give me your tired, your weary, your rotting, your expired, your useless and worn and excessive. I'll be the shoreline to which your garbage drifts.*

How many tragic stories had she heard? How much angst had been downloaded onto her?

And she'd volunteered.

Trained for it.

Chosen it.

Two images lingered in her mind—Allison's face and Camille's mother's. So similar in soft roundness, paleness, distress . . . It was too late to change the expression on her mother's face. But she might be able to change Allison's.

The odds were against her. Weren't they always? Nature of the beast.

She tied her other shoelace. It seemed to take twice as long as it should have.

Deep breath. Hamstring stretch. *I've gotten myself this far on my own. On to the next step.*

Ten thousand of them if she took the stairs instead of the elevator.

When did a phone call not interrupt something? This one had all the earmarks of more than a blip in Camille's morning routine. Caller ID: Allison.

"What is it, Allison? How can I help you?" Cam lowered the blinds on her apartment windows to keep the sun from fading the sofa.

"The police are here! Please help me! I'm being arrested!"

Camille breathed a sigh of relief that the red and blue lights weren't flashing when she pulled up in front of Allison's home. For whom was that sight not a panic trigger? Two officers stood in the yard, one taking a statement as he spoke with a woman Camille assumed was an irate neighbor. The irate part was obvious. The neighbor part, less obvious.

Another officer was at Allison's front door, talking through the slit Allison apparently refused to widen. A too-familiar scene.

"Excuse me, Officer. I'm Dr. Camille Brooks. Clinical psychologist. Mrs. Chase is one of my clients. What's going on?"

The officer eyed Camille's activewear. "You run all the way here?"

You skipped "first impressions" training at the academy, didn't you? "I drove. Allison called me. What's the issue?"

"Theft." He let the word hang, as if it were sufficient to stop the conversation.

"They're here to arrest me!" Allison cried out through the slit.

The officer turned to fully face Camille and leaned his ear toward his shoulder. "I keep telling her I just want to ask her a few questions. I'm not taking her to jail. But she won't let me in."

"What is she accused of stealing?"

"I can't tell you that." The officer sneered.

"Joey, lighten up," one of the two policemen called from the yard. He approached and laid a hand on his fellow officer's shoulder. "It's not as serious as it sounds, Dr. Brooks."

"Hi, Blake. Good to see you again. Not under these circumstances, but . . ." Camille kept her voice calm for everyone's sake.

"Joey's just trying to do his job, with a little extra enthusiasm. We got a complaint that your client here has been helping herself to other people's garbage in the middle of the night again."

One step forward with Allison. Two steps back. "Dare I ask if she took anything of value from the garbage bins?"

"The neighbors have a legitimate complaint," Joey piped in. "She's digging in their trash like a raccoon looking for a two-day-old ham sandwich."

"Joey. Why don't you interview the man standing under that tree? I'll take it from here."

"Guh-lad-ly."

Camille raised her eyebrows. She and Blake had been through this routine before. "Any way I can help de-escalate this problem?" she asked.

"We're not going to arrest Mrs. Chase. I've tried to discourage the complainant from filing trespassing charges, since her garbage cans were technically sitting at the curb. Public property."

"Good. Thank you."

"But"—he leaned in—"you don't want us coming out here time after time to warn your client it's in her best interest to keep her neighbors happy, do you?"

Camille glanced at the dark slit and the place where Allison was likely trembling in the darkness just beyond the door. "I'll talk to her again."

"Good. Wish that was all it would take." He adjusted his hat. "Can I ask? What did she take?"

"As far as I can gather, old magazines, which should have been in the recycling container, but that's beside the point. The neighbor said it was an invasion of privacy since her mailing address was on the cover of the magazines."

"Blake, she lives across the street. Allison already knows her address."

"Takes all kinds." He shrugged and turned to leave, but then turned back. "Dr. Brooks, I can't be here for every one of these calls. One day a neighbor's going to take it too far. I'd hate to see that happen."

"Me too."

The older gentleman standing under the tree had disappeared. Something about him . . .

She'd noticed a ring of grass stains on his deck shoes. The man must mow a lot of lawns. One of these days she'd ask Allison about him. Not today. The woman didn't need an inquisition. She needed a calming presence.

"Allison?" Camille tapped on the now closed door. "It's me. Can I come in? Allison?"

"Are they gone?"

"Yes."

"All of them?"

Camille heard tears in the woman's shaky voice. "Yes. All of them. It's just me. Please let me in."

"It's a mess in here."

I know.

An hour later, Camille was back in her well-past-aging car, heading toward even more paperwork. And an incident report. Computerized, but still . . .

The addictive nature of a hoarding disorder couldn't help but cause frustration. Allison was a bright woman. Educated. She knew the downsides of digging in her neighbor's garbage but couldn't stop herself for fear that somewhere in the depths of those massive wheeled receptacles might be something she couldn't live without, something that needed her to "rescue" it, something that could be useful someday.

It never was. But the inkling that it *could be* was irresistible to a person dealing with a hoarding disorder. Logic took a back seat to the pull, the draw, the possibility, no matter how remote or illogical. If Camille could change one thing about her job, it might be the ability to reintroduce logic into conversations with her clients. If only linear reasoning worked . . .

Hoarding is directly linked to health issues, relationship issues, financial issues . . . ISSUES!

But that line of reasoning usually remained in Camille's toolbox until well into her work with a client. Some of her colleagues and most of the neuropsychology resources claimed that it could be as long as two or three years into counseling before the concepts of action and reaction, choices and consequences, could be embraced.

She signaled to turn onto her street.

Layers. So many layers to this process. In some ways, finding the path to a hoarder's healing was like digging the way through layers of accumulation in order to uncover the floor.

Hmm. That could work as a podcast topic. How many mental notes could her brain hold?

As she parked and removed her keys from the ignition, her phone pinged. A text from Shyla. Camille read it, then reread.

"You have lunch plans. Fork & Spoon at 12:30."

Since when was Shyla her activities director? Or executive assistant? Or life coach?

She texted back: "I do?"

"Don't miss it. Eli Rand is bringing a check."

Manipulator? Stalker? Who was this guy?

Shyla's next text made her squint. "Check's enough to sustain the podcast for a year. Be there."

Camille saluted the phone, as if Shyla could see her action. *It may be the death of me, but I'll be there.*

The Fork & Spoon. One of the up-and-coming foodie spots in the city. She'd never eaten there but had heard enough about it to know Eli either had good taste or a gift certificate for a free meal. Or two.

Ten to one it was—

"Hey! Dr. Brooks! Thanks for coming." Eli took her elbow. "We have a table already. This way."

He guided her to a spot by the front window. Good. At least if things got weird, she'd have witnesses.

Camille, you are such a fraud! You pride yourself on refraining from judging your clients despite their addictions, their compulsions, their chaos, their habits, their resistance to change, their oddities . . .

But you've prejudged this business owner, tried, sentenced, and personally driven the jail van to lock him away from society. Your personal society. No wonder you have no friends. Except Shyla, who—the world knows—barely tolerates you.

"Is that okay with you?"

The guy was talking to her. "Excuse me? The noise level in here . . ." Yeah, even she saw straight through that flimsy excuse.

He moved the small vase of wildflowers in the middle of the table to the side, as if they'd been in the way of her hearing. "I wondered if we could talk for a bit and then order. It's a . . . vigorous menu."

"Sure. But I do have paperwork waiting for me at home."

Eli drew a breath as if to say something, then stopped, picked up the menu, and studied it.

"I mean, not right away," she said. "I will need to get back to work eventually, but I have time for lunch. And to hear what you have to say." Her doctoral dissertation was easier than this.

"First of all"—he stared for a moment at the tablecloth, then looked her in the eye—"the inside of a great white shark's mouth is, not surprisingly, white."

"What?"

"Your comment about my trucks. About the interior color."

"Cranberry."

"Yes."

He was wearing jeans and a marine-blue T-shirt today. Why hadn't she noticed that earlier? "Oh. Your truck. White on white. I apologize for the snarky shark comment."

"Trucks. Plural."

"Yes. Your *fleet*."

He picked up his menu again, then set it aside. "I recommend you order the chimichurri grilled chicken."

"Why?"

"It's highly acidic. You should find it charming."

"Where are you going?" Her chair scraped on the hardwood floor as she turned to watch him retreat.

He stepped back and leaned toward her. "To the restroom, if it's all the same to you. Would you mind ordering a basil lemonade for me while I'm gone? And an antacid?"

Was he insinuating she—He was, and she was. Acidic. Or was it acerbic? She hadn't been anything but skeptical and condescending—two of her pet peeves—since meeting him. She wasn't used to having such a hard time reading people.

The true test would be whether he would make her life easier or miserable at Chester's tomorrow. But—she glanced over her shoulder—he was probably thinking the same thought about her.

A Fork & Spoon employee stopped at the table for their drink order.

"A basil lemonade and . . . no, make that two."

"Good choice. Be right back with them."

What was wrong with her? She'd just ordered herself a glass of sugar because it also promised an herb. And because a man with a "fleet" of trucks favored artisan lemonade as if he knew what he was doing.

Might be time to make an appointment with one of her colleagues. Or pray. That wouldn't necessarily help, but it couldn't hurt.

Eli's head hung low when he returned to the table a few minutes later.

"What's that in your hair?" Camille reached to flick out what looked like a dust bunny—where'd he get that?—but retracted her hand.

He felt where she pointed and brushed the object onto the floor. "Lint from my pocket. I'm repenting in dust and ashes, and that was the closest I could get."

"You—"

"Do you happen to have any hand sanitizer in your purse? Yes, I washed my hands in the restroom, but—" He nudged his head toward the piece of lint now waiting for a broom.

"Eli." She dug in her purse and handed him a travel-sized sanitizer for him to remove whatever germs the lint was carrying. "Repenting for what?"

"For reverting to old passive-aggressive language."

"No, that was me."

"I beg to differ with you, miss. I was the one shooting darts of passive-aggressive. I believe I know it when I see it."

"And our lemonade's here. Perfect timing. My throat's a little *dusty*."

He smiled. Orthodontic work in middle school, no doubt. Had he thanked his parents sufficiently?

She ran her tongue over her one protruding canine tooth that sometimes caught her lip. One of these days, she'd invest in getting that fixed.

chapter six

"NOW THAT YOUR CONFESSIONAL IS complete," Camille said, "what did you want to discuss?" She sipped her lemonade. Tart, refreshing, not too sweet, and the basil added an unexpected kick of flavor. Good choice.

"I'd like to partner with you."

Lemonade went everywhere but down her throat.

"Are you okay?" He shot out of his chair and pounded her back, as if trying to restart her heart.

"Stop! I'm okay. Just swallowed wrong." She coughed, wiped her lips and her shirt with her napkin, and straightened her posture to prove how perfectly okay she was. "Partner?"

"If you insist."

She growled.

"Go ahead," he said. "Take your time to clear your throat. That can be nasty, snorting lemonade up your nose."

"Mr. Rand, I'm not looking for a partner."

"Doesn't that make it all the more wonderful when one comes along?"

He smiled in a way that made her think of the word *imp*.

And of the Calm Now app on her phone. Where was that thing?

"Eli, you score high points in enthusiasm. I'm sure that's taken you far already in life."

"You have no idea." His expression sobered for some reason.

"But the podcast sponsorships we're searching for, the sponsorships we've advertised, are simply to help fund the production and marketing costs of the podcast. No partnerships."

"Shyla explained that to me. But I believe I can make a strong case."

Camille's stomach rumbled. It rarely rumbled, except when she was fasting, which she was seriously considering. "We're happy to create an ad for you that we can use on the *Let In the Light* podcast and on our website. Or you're welcome to submit one of your own, although we do reserve the right to edit and make sure it's in compliance with our vision statement and values."

Eli yawned. He yawned, right there in public.

"Narcolepsy? Or are you just rude?" she asked.

"A touch of both, some would say. Late night last night."

Oh. One of those.

"But we finally got Nana settled down so she could sleep about three this morning. It's been tough on her since Papaw died. I tell you, if I keep getting all this practice singing to her at night, I might be ready to audition for *The Voice*."

Oh. One of *those*.

"All that talk about ads and stuff, it's good. Necessary. But I don't just want Awe-Done to be a jingle or cartoon version of what we do."

She couldn't help it. In her mind, she envisioned a great white shark on wheels with a cranberry Awe-Done logo near its pectoral fin. Camille might regret it, but she had to ask. "What do you do, Mr. Rand? Other than the obvious."

"Yeah, my modeling career history is just unavoidable. Recognized everywhere I go. 'Aren't you the lumberjack from the pancake commercials?' 'Didn't I just see you on TV?'" He leaned closer. "I get that all the time."

Stomach roaring. Throat growling. She sounded like a race car revving up for the green light.

"You still fighting a touch of that lemonade snort? Here." He handed her a crisp white handkerchief. "Blow your nose. It'll help. Don't worry. I haven't used it."

Shyla, this is all your fault.

"Mr. Rand, what I do is serious business. Sometimes it is literally a life-or-death matter for my clients. It's heartbreaking. Hard. These are not simple cases, and I don't appreciate your making light of them or our conversation."

The man—oh yes he did—bent over and picked the bit of lint off the floor and repositioned it on his head.

"Dust and ashes?"

He nodded. The lint fell forward into his lap. "My nana warned me from the time I was a toddler that people might not find my sense of humor amusing. I believe she used the word 'intolerable.' Third word I ever learned how to say. Da-da. Ma-ma. Intolerable."

"Eli—"

"I'll get to the point." He laced his fingers and wiggled the connection back and forth as if trying to fit a puzzle piece into a misshaped spot. "My papaw died of shame and regret. He made my nana's life miserable, even though he loved her deeply. He was a hoarder. Collector, he said. But it went way beyond that."

"I'm so sorry for what that must have done to your family." Was it her imagination, or had his facial expression softened?

"I could tell you stories, but I want what I do with my career—this one—to mean something. I want steady work. Who wouldn't? But I want to make a difference for people like my grandparents."

Familiar theme. She hummed it in her sleep.

"I don't have a psychology degree like you do. But I know

63

how to be kind and patient. Don't look at me like that. I do. And I understand a little bit about what can happen if a hoarder is pushed to his limits during the declutter phase."

He did know more than he let on.

"I have a fleet of trucks."

"We've established that."

"And I want to learn how to partner with—"

She cringed.

"Okay, you hate that word. Pair up with—"

"Not winning me over with that phrase either."

"Look, Dr. Brooks. I think having a consistent hauling team you can count on, especially one sensitive to that delicate dance when trying to help hoarders find their freedom, could be a genuine benefit to what you do. Don't you?"

She waited for the comedic line sure to follow. None did.

What choice did she have? "I can't commit to more than this first project, Eli. Yes, you're helping me out of a bind tomorrow and the next day. But it is way, and I mean way too soon to start talking about any kind of more permanent contract."

"Don't like the word *contract* so much." He grinned.

"Arrangement."

"You're not winning me over with that phrase either, Dr. Brooks."

Confirmed. Thousands of dollars of orthodontic work to get a smile that straight and white.

"Could we eat? Then get through the next two days? *Then* talk about this?" *Shyla, you owe me big time.*

He leaned back as if considering, then nodded. "Sounds like a plan."

The guy better have a real live Nana and Papaw or he was going to be in so much trouble.

The Fork & Spoon did not disappoint. How did the chef cram that much flavor into a simple grilled shrimp salad? Eli's prime rib sandwich looked equally delicious, though calorie dense.

And the table company turned out to make for enjoyable conversation, as long as Eli steered clear of subjects related to business partnerships. She updated him on Chester's situation and how she expected to proceed. But beyond that, all discussions hovered around safer subjects—salad dressing versus vinaigrette, shredded versus shaved Parmesan, and philosophies of suffering.

Yes. Eli Rand entertained interesting ideas about suffering and its role in reshaping the human heart, growing empathy, and solidifying maturity. Who was this guy? A deep thinker in a cranberry jumpsuit. Well, not today. But he would no doubt be wearing it in the morning at Chester's.

Speaking of which, she needed to get back to work. In an uncharacteristic lull in the conversation, Camille said, "Eli, I do need to—"

"Right. Back to work. Me too. Garbage doesn't just happen, you know. Well, garbage does just happen, but managing it doesn't."

"Can I pay for your lunch?" It seemed like the right thing to say.

"I invited you, remember?"

Ah, yes.

"But if you insist . . ."

She hadn't. Not even close.

He nudged the tab folder toward her.

Okay then.

"Trying to be all sensitive to equality issues and everything," he said.

"You're broke, aren't you," she stated. "That's it. You didn't bring your wallet. Your cash accidentally went through the washing machine. Your dog ate your credit card. Pick one."

He was taking a little too much joy in watching her ramble. From his back pocket, he drew an envelope. "Don't want to forget this."

She took the envelope and peeked inside. Shyla was right. The sponsorship money would cover a year's worth of their expenses. "I don't know how to respond. Thank you. We appreciate your interest in what we're doing."

"I've been listening to the podcasts for quite a while. Like what you have to say and how you say it. This is just a start."

Tiptoeing too close, Eli.

Eli, the conundrum.

"Hey," he said, "can I leave the tip?"

Tab folder in hand, she considered. *Let him tip? Don't let him tip?* "If you'd like."

"Oh. Uh, then . . ."

"You need to borrow a few dollars?" She already had her purse open.

"If you don't mind." His smile was a clear invitation to punch him in the teeth. She resisted.

He reached into his other back pocket. "You do know I'm kidding, don't you?" He slapped a ten-dollar bill in the center of the table. "See you tomorrow. Seven o'clock sharp." He reached his hand out, palm down.

"What?"

He picked up her hand and set it on top of his. "Go, team!" Hands in the air.

We are not a team!

⌐

"Knock harder," Eli said over her shoulder. "Maybe he's sleeping in."

"He's not sleeping in. It's an avoidance tactic. Chester," she called through the locked door. "It's me. Dr. Brooks. I know you know what day this is and why we're here."

"Who's 'we'?" The voice wiggled its way from inside the house.

"I'm here with . . . a gentleman who is going to assist with taking care of the items that you decide have outlived their usefulness."

"My things. *My* things."

"Those that interfere with your quality of life, Chester. I explained earlier that we're not removing anything from your home without your permission."

"Then you might as well turn around and go back where you came from. Because I'm not giving my permission."

Too many of these cleanup moments started like this. No matter how convinced her clients had been days earlier, when the time came, reluctance, resistance, and refusal spoke louder than reason.

"Chester, please open the door. We only have one option. We have to stay and tackle this project or you lose your home. And I don't want that to happen. The organizer specialists will be here in a few minutes. I want you to be ready for them. No surprises. We'll make it as easy for you as we comfortably can, but—"

"Tell him," Eli whispered in her ear, "that we'll mitigate his pain."

"What?" she whispered back.

"*Mitigate.* It's a great word."

"I am not going to tell him that we'll—"

Click. The door opened the width of an envelope. "Who's the clown?" Chester asked.

"Eli Rand, sir." Eli stuck his hand through the slit.

Oh, for the love of—

The door opened wider. "Good, strong handshake, young man." Chester eyed Eli head to toe. "You prepared to get those fancy duds of yours dirty today?"

"Whatever it takes to help you keep your home."

Huh. Good answer, Eli.

"I guess you'll have to come in then. We're not going to have hordes of people traipsing through here today, are we, Dr. Brooks?"

Camille swallowed the sigh that so badly wanted to express itself. "Chester, you know this is going to take a team of people. We have to move faster than either you or I would want. It's been put off for so long now that you're up against a tight deadline. I know you understand that. But we'll have to remind each other often these next two days. There's no going back. It's time."

Eli leaned near her ear. "I like that soft-voice thing you did there. Nice touch."

She clenched her fists, then released them and addressed Chester. "Mr. Rand will be practically invisible during this process." She enunciated every word so none could be mistaken.

"Should'a brought my cloak of invisibility," Eli said.

Chester laughed. Camille had never heard him laugh before. "Good one," Chester said. "I suppose the cape would have clashed with your bloodred onesie."

"They're coveralls," Eli countered. "And the color is actually cran—"

"Boys." If Camille didn't interrupt now, the sun would be setting while the men were talking fashion. "We need to get down to business. Here's how this is going to work. We'll start here in the living room, since this room is very important to you. Right, Chester?"

"It's all important to me."

"I know. You spend a lot of time in this room."

"I do."

"One of our first goals," she said, "is to clear a wide enough path for the organizers to have room to work and for you to have some elbow room for sorting."

"Sorting." Chester said the word as if it stung coming out.

Camille glanced Eli's way. He mouthed the words *cloak of invisibility* while raising his fist above his nose, forearm parallel to the ground.

"Do you know what I believe, Chester?" She addressed the compulsive but sane man in the room. "I believe you can do this. And I believe that when we've conquered this task, you will be amazed at how good you'll feel about yourself. And about your future."

"You keep saying that as if I have one."

"I heard on this fascinating podcast the other day," Eli said, stepping over a limp cardboard box, "that hope for our future is often hiding under a pile of unnecessary things. It's there. It just needs to be uncovered."

"Mr. Rand."

He turned his apologetic, dust-and-ashes face toward Camille. "I apologize. My invisibility cloak slipped off my shoulders temporarily. Chester, do you have a safety pin I could borrow?"

"Would you *please* wait outside?" Cam made her face communicate what her words couldn't.

"I like him," Chester said. "Can he stay?"

Isn't that what people say when taking in a stray dog? But if Eli Rand could somehow serve as a security connection for her client, so be it. "Why don't you and I begin with the area right around your chair. We'll start small and ease our way into the larger decisions, okay?"

"Okay," Chester and Eli answered in unison.

Camille's smartwatch alerted her it was time to breathe. Too late for that.

Half an hour later, when the professional organizers—hoarding disorder specialists—showed up, Chester had made one decision. One. He was willing to part with the broken television on which his working television had been propped. Eli hauled it out before he could change his mind.

Camille conferred with the organizers. They confirmed their game plan and laid out a staging area in the yard to delineate what would stay, what could be given away, and what needed Eli's services.

She shouldn't have taken so long with the organizers. When she returned to the living room, Eli was sitting in a chair next to Chester, with a badly chipped coffee carafe in his hands.

"Tell me the story behind this item," Eli said.

"Eli!" Her head throbbed.

"I don't mind," Chester said to her, then directed his attention toward Eli. "Every day of our marriage, Marlene made me coffee in that coffeemaker. Nothing finer than waking up in the morning to the smell of coffee brewed by someone who loves you."

"That's a sweet memory, Chester, but—" She stepped closer, working up her courage to ask him to hand it over.

"So even though it is cracked beyond repair, it has value to you because . . ." Eli didn't rush to fill in the blank.

"Well, because if I get rid of it, I might lose that memory. I can't afford to lose—" His voice dissolved into tears.

Great. We'll get a lot done with the client crying. Way to go, Mr. Rand.

"Wouldn't want you to lose a memory like that." Eli ran his finger around what was left of the rim. "Ouch. Ooh. That's dangerous." Eli took out his folded white handkerchief to wrap around the pad of his finger."

"You okay?" Chester asked.

"I'll get a bandage from my truck glove compartment." He stood. "But you might want to consider finding something else, something not chipped and dangerous, to remind you of your morning coffee with Marlene."

"Like what?"

"Did she have a favorite coffee mug?"

Camille pressed her fingertips to her forehead.

"Every morning she'd drink her coffee out of a pottery mug we got on our honeymoon."

"Do you still have that?"

Chester chuckled. "Young man, I still have everything— you might have noticed."

"What's it look like?" Eli leapfrogged over stacks of refuse on his way to the kitchen.

"Kind of blue green with the impression of the White Gull Inn on one side."

"Is this it?" Eli emerged with a surprisingly intact mug.

"That's the one."

"So," Eli said, bending to Chester's eye level, "every morning when Marlene made you coffee, she drank hers from this very mug."

"Yes, sir."

"Between the two things—that cracked carafe or this mug your wife's lips touched every morning—which one would hold those memories best without their leaking out?"

Could Camille file a restraining order against a guy for interfering with her counseling techniques?

"It's pretty obvious, I guess," Chester said. "The carafe can go. I don't want it hurting anybody. But I'm keeping that mug."

"I think that's a wise decision." Eli set the mug on a rare blank spot on the end table near Chester's chair. "I'd be happy to remove the broken glass for you."

"I'd appreciate that, son."

What just happened?

"Eli? A word with you?" She followed him to his truck, steaming until out of earshot, then spewing. "May I ask what you think you're doing? We have clearly defined roles here. I am the psychologist, and you are the hauler."

"Which," he said, brandishing the broken carafe, "is what I'm doing."

"This is never going to work."

"And yet it is working."

Camille clenched her fists and let them stay that way this time. "I am very good at what I do."

"What a coincidence! So am I."

chapter seven

NEIGHBORS COULD BE WATCHING. HOARDER cleanup often
drew a crowd. She tempered both her voice and her
facial expression. "Eli, people with hoarding disorders
pose a very complex challenge. We have protocols to follow.
Clinically proven techniques."

"And then we have those ideas that just pop into our heads,
and one can't help but stand back and say, 'That was amazing!'
I don't know what you call it, but I call it a gift from God."

Her jaw tightened. Heels of her palms to her eyelids this
time. "Eli, you are the most—"

"Dr. Brooks. I just helped that man let go of something that
had him bound. One thing. One . . . broken . . . thing. And
right now I'm feeling pretty good about myself"—his voice
shook—"because it's possible it might work again. That I or
you or somebody else who cares could convince him to let go
of the broken and hang on to something that really matters
and still keep his tether to his memories."

Her repressed argument lost steam.

"I couldn't do it for my papaw. It felt downright glorious to

73

have that tortured man in there respond just because I listened to his story. Everything he owns has a story behind it. We just have to find out which stories hold more meaning for him than the others. I didn't think of that in time to save my papaw."

His words rocked her. She couldn't let him see that. This was her turf, not his.

"I'm fired, aren't I?" Eli set the carafe in the back of his white-with-cranberry-trim two-ton truck and turned toward her with both hands extended, wrists together and higher than his fingers. One finger still sported the handkerchief he'd tucked around his wound.

One of his wounds. Some weren't visible, she guessed.

"Arrest me if you must."

Ah. The caught-in-the-act stance—wrists ready for hand-cuffs. "For what?"

"Excessive intentional caring."

She crossed her arms. "You know I can't afford to fire you—or have you arrested either, for that matter—for at least the next forty-eight hours."

He dropped his arms to his sides. "True."

"But will you please let me do my job and you stick to yours? We can't afford to have taken the time for this conversation. It's that critical."

"You can put your pointer finger back in its holster. I got the message."

Had he? Not likely. But she had a hurting client whose anxiety level was probably on the verge of meltdown. And so far they'd succeeded in removing two—count 'em, two—items from Chester's overcrowded home.

"Thank you. Let's get back to work. And by that, I mean you stay here until we have something for you to haul."

As she marched back to the house, she heard his voice call, "I'm going to assume you didn't mean that to sound as condescending as it did."

He'd let himself get poked with a sharp edge of that broken, filthy glass? To reach Chester?

She turned back. Hands on hips. That should convince him. "I'm going to assume you're all caught up on your shots, including tetanus? And . . . distemper?" She didn't wait for an answer.

The check he'd written wasn't sponsorship money. It was bribery. If he thought for a minute he could buy his way into hauling garbage for her these next two days . . . Wait. That didn't seem right. But then, few things about Eli Rand *did* seem right.

Back to business. Chester needed her, and the organizing crew was probably ready to stage a walkout for abandoning them before they'd gotten started.

The house was the same when she walked back in. Of the thousands of inappropriately saved items, only two had been thrown away. Two. Massive cleanup, too little time, and Eli was making it harder than it already was.

"There you are," Chester said.

"I apologize for the delay. We'll have to stay super-focused now. Can we step up the pace of decision-making, Chester? It's going to take that. I don't want you to feel rushed. I want you to be decisive. We'll need you to assess the true value of each of these possessions, but it's going to have to be a quick assessment."

He was pacing now, in what little space he had. "It's so overwhelming. I don't know where to start."

"That's what we're here for, to help you make those decisions that don't have to be yours—like where do we start—so you can be free to direct which things you want to donate, or sell, or have—"

"Removed? Thrown in the trash?"

"As we go through the day, I expect you'll be getting into a rhythm of just that. You'll see things you once had a hard time letting go of, and today it will feel right to say, 'It's time.' It's worn out, no longer useful, hazardous, or keeping you from living the life you want to live."

"So overwhelming." He shook his head from side to side in an escalating tempo.

"Chester, look at me. Being overwhelmed by the accumulation, not knowing how to stay on top of what you were acquiring, not being willing to throw anything away, is what got you here."

"I know. You don't have to tell me that."

Camille touched him lightly on one shoulder. "I'm going to be here for you long after these two days are over. You know that, don't you?"

"Yes."

"But we need to accomplish a lot in the next few hours so you can see it is possible for you to stay here in this home."

"Maybe I just need to light a match to it all and—"

Smoke. A strong whiff of smoke. The room grew darker, more claustrophobic than before. Why hadn't they turned on any lights?

"You can't sit there, Dr. Brooks." A woman's voice. One of the organizers?

"What?" She choked the word out through the smoke filling her lungs.

"You can't sit there. The whole pile will topple."

An arm around her shoulders. "Dr. Brooks?"

A deep gasp. No smoke. The odor of a long-neglected home. Chester's home.

"I'm . . . I'm sorry. I should have had more for breakfast. I have a protein bar in my purse."

"Had me worried," Chester said.

"You had *me* worried. Don't even joke about torching the place. For one thing, you don't own this home. You're renting."

"I guess that would be a glitch in the burn-it-to-the-ground plan." He sounded like a recalcitrant eight-year-old caught smoking cigars behind the barn. "I won't talk like that anymore. I know you're trying to help."

"Why don't you and I and"—she looked at the organizer team—"and Kimberly spend time in the kitchen. We should be able to make some quick progress"—she was back to her true self—"if we start simply, with more obvious items. Expired food, for instance. Will you give us permission to get rid of the food in your fridge that is rancid, moldy, or long expired?"

"Most of those dates on things are just a government conspiracy to get you to throw away perfectly good—" He stopped his speech and nodded. "I can't tolerate wasting things. Seems a *criminal* waste. Might be okay for human consumption yet."

"Might."

"I'm willing to take the risk."

"I'm not willing for you to risk your life over the faint possibility it might not kill you, Chester. Will you keep that in mind?"

He followed her to the kitchen, Kimberly not far behind. His foot slipped on something, but he caught himself. "Plastic bag," he said. "I probably have more than enough of those things."

Camille smiled. "I'm proud of you. Good call."

"Are you going to make me use one of those white paper masks like the rest of your team?"

"Not going to force you, Chester. But it would be a good idea. Mold spores could be contributing to the lung issues you've been dealing with. And there will be plenty in here." She yanked open the handle on the refrigerator. She might never need Lamaze breathing to give birth, but she needed it for refrigerator reveals. And bathrooms.

Chester's fridge was like so many others she'd seen. Did those with hoarding disorders really believe keeping food at forty degrees would preserve it eternally? Most of the containers and zipped plastic bags held unrecognizable food items. Some that had been liquid were now in chunk or powder form. How did meat turn from solid to liquid? She didn't really want to know the answer, but the question always raised its ugly head during refrigerator cleanup.

Reticent as he was, Chester eventually gave Kimberly permission to use her best judgment for that task. Other items in his dwelling held far more interest to him.

Camille pulled out her laminated card detailing the biohazards of plastic food containers that hadn't been washed soon after use. She hoped the chemical reactions described in the articles she'd found would appeal to his hobby-science interests. She held an old whipped-topping container with gloved hands and pointed to the pitting along the interior edge and the Mojave Desert landscape of the brown substance caked at the bottom. "This pitting means the plastic is breaking down. We can clean up and put back into service these ceramic and porcelain bowls and plates. But not the plastic ones that look like this. And not the porous surfaces, like those wooden salad bowls that have been on the counter for how long?"

"They were a wedding gift."

"How long have they been tossed aside on this pile?"

"You know I couldn't . . . couldn't say."

Such a delicate balance of when to push and when to back off. "Tell you what. If you'll allow us to dispose of these toxic plastic items, I will find someone to take a look at the salad bowls and see if they can be restored."

"You'd do that?"

"They might be able to be sanded, then tested for toxins and resealed. They must have been beautiful at one time. I can see why they're important to you."

His eyes pooled with tears. "Thank you. Yes, you can get rid of those others."

"Are you starting to feel differently about what holds intrinsic value, what holds sentimental value no matter its worth in other people's eyes, and a separate category for the things that hold no intrinsic or emotional value but have a grip on you anyway?"

"The plastic grocery bags?"

"That's a great example." Hope rose. "And perhaps this collection of—what are these? Blueberry containers? Or raspberry? There must be a stack of a hundred of them."

"They have an interesting shape."

Camille could feel the jostle as the train began to slip off the tracks. "It is an interesting shape. And I can understand that interesting shapes intrigue you. Is there something particularly meaningful about having this many of that shape? Are they serving a purpose?"

"Do things always have to serve a purpose? Can't they just be curious or beautiful or fascinating to look at?"

Nothing in Camille's apartment was without purpose. It didn't stay if it didn't have a purpose. She appreciated beauty. No one would question that. The answer she wanted to give was no. But not only would that slice at her client's values, it would undermine his trust in her. She'd determined not to resort to lying to her clients, but she could pick her way through piles of words like they picked their way through piles of rubbish.

"Can you tell me how many of these interesting clear plastic berry containers you would consider enough to satisfy you as a complete collection?"

"Collections aren't like that. You can't put a number on them. And 'complete' isn't the goal. It's acquiring." His countenance fell at that final word.

The urge to glance at her watch was strong. She resisted. "Remember the flood in Houston?"

"We all do. Tragic. Just tragic."

Camille caught Kimberly in her peripheral vision. The woman had gathered the plastic plates and bowls that had been eaten away by neglect and was sliding them into a cloth grocery bag just beyond Chester's line of sight. The sound of a crinkly garbage bag often triggered panic attacks in a person with a hoarding disorder. Smart woman.

"So many lost all their belongings in that flood, Chester."

"Why are we talking about this now?"

"If your place flooded, you could lose everything."

Chester removed his baseball cap and repositioned it on his head. "Can't imagine."

"What would you replace first?"

"Don't confuse me."

"I'm trying to help you *unconfuse* the situation. What do you think you'd need to run out and replace right away, after the waters receded?"

"I'd need clothes."

"Yes."

"And towels. Toiletries."

"Uh-huh."

"Pots and pans and silverware. More mugs. I would've taken Marlene's with me when I escaped in the hovercraft."

He hadn't completely lost his sense of humor. Good. "Of course. And how far down the line would this stack of disposable berry boxes be on your list of 'must replace' items? Would you go out that first day, week, month and make sure you found more?"

Silence stretched for a long moment. "I'd miss them. But no."

"So . . ."

"At a time like this, I should let them go. They're . . . part of the flood."

"I'm proud of you. Proud of the way you're thinking. You're making good choices. Let's keep up that track record, okay?"

A long red—correction—cranberry arm reached around the corner from the living room.

"Eli?"

"I was told to stay out of the way until I was needed. I'm needed."

Still only the arm showed in the kitchen doorway. Camille couldn't afford a scene right now. Victories had a way of sneaking out the back door if you didn't keep your eye on them.

"Chester, would you like to do the honors?" She handed one stack of berry boxes after another to her client, who handed them off to the man with the long cranberry arms. Judging from what little she could see, Eli bowed to Chester before turning and heading through the maze.

Chester turned toward Camille. "That man's not all there, if you know what I mean."

"Oh, I do."

"But I like him."

"Me too."

Had she broken a promise to herself not to lie? Or was she simply dodging piles of emotions she wasn't yet ready to deal with?

chapter eight

B Y THE END OF THE workday, the table in Chester's kitchen was cleared, the refrigerator was as clean as it was ever going to get, and the sink was accessible. Who knew Eli had plumbing skills and could replace the trap that hadn't worked in months or years?

Kimberly and her team had power cleaned the dishes and utensils that were salvageable, emptied and scoured one bank of cupboards, and revealed that Chester did indeed have countertops underneath it all.

But they had so much more work to do before the deadline. And Camille's client was visibly shaken. He'd taken to his recliner in the living room, pretending to sort through a shoebox full of paper clips.

"I always meant to sort these by color."

"Chester, you know we don't have time for that."

"Well, I'm not getting rid of them. You have to admit that these are useful. They have your all-important *purpose*." He hadn't even tried to hide his irritation. He had reached his limit.

So had Camille. Sometimes a chicken egg emerges without

a shell. With only a thin membrane to protect it, the yolk or chick inside doesn't have much of a chance of survival. Camille's job was to protect shell-less eggs and keep them from splattering on the floor. Exhausting work. And not always successful. Chester had seemed genuinely pleased with the progress in the kitchen, but now he was reverting to old habits, old ways of thinking. To press any more would risk all they'd gained.

"We can keep your entire paper clip collection if you'll do me two favors."

"What are they?"

"Let's put them in a sturdier storage container so you don't lose any and they're easier to fit on a shelf. And make me a promise that you won't spend tonight sorting them by color. You can do that *after* you've saved yourself from eviction. Some cold day this winter. Agreed?"

"You're not the boss of me."

She recoiled.

"I always wanted to say that to someone. Especially my stepdad." He dragged his finger through the color riot of paperclips. "Couldn't, of course."

Something they needed to talk about at one of his next sessions. Not now.

"You didn't mean to offend me, Chester?"

"I would never want to do that. I'm not very good at jokes. I'm very good at shopping though."

"You're very . . . experienced at it. That's true."

"You're all coming back tomorrow?"

"Yes, we are. Keep this momentum going. I wish I could say we were more than halfway done, but as you can see, we have a long way to go. And it's going to take all of us, cooperatively, to get this place in shape enough that your landlord will give you a reprieve. He's not obligated to do so, you know."

"I know. I've gone back on my word with him and his wife

too many times. Did you know this was her family home as a child?"

Oh my. Offense upon offense for those long-suffering landlords.

"How does that make you feel?" she asked.

"Like you say, once you have a pile already, it's easier to make the pile bigger than it is to get rid of it. It's like with me and guilt."

"Imagine how grateful she'll be to step into that kitchen after we've done some work, considering the way it is right now. Just imagine how grateful she'll be."

"I see you took the cardboard out of the kitchen window."

"Let in some light."

"I didn't want people snooping around."

"I understand. Looks pretty nice with it so bright in there now though, doesn't it?"

Chester set the shoebox at his feet. "You probably can't understand how scary it is to shake off darkness if you've been living with it so long it seems normal."

I understand more about that topic than you know.

Eli emerged from around the tower of boxes making a tunnel out of the hallway. "Bathroom sink is fixed," he said, brushing his hands together. "That one took some doing. Do you remember stuffing a washcloth down the drain, Chester?"

"Is that what it was?"

"Eli," Camille said, "it's time for the crew to depart. We'll be back early in the morning again."

"Are you leaving your truck in my driveway, Eli?"

"Did you want me to?" Eli looked at Camille as if searching for the right answer to Chester's question.

She shrugged.

"I thought if it was sitting there, it might mean something to the landlord's wife, should she happen to drive by. Show her I'm trying."

Camille nodded to Eli.

"Then I can leave it if I can bum a ride off your friend Dr. Brooks."

"Is that a problem, Dr. Brooks?"

This was not how the day was supposed to end. "I can do that."

They said their goodbyes, and she headed toward her tidy but showing-its-age car parked at the curb.

As if reading Cam's mind, Shyla sent a text just as Cam pulled her seat belt across her chest and settled in to wait for Eli to retrieve his personal belongings from the Great White. Shyla sent three simple words: "His check cleared."

What did it say about Cam that she was more than a little surprised?

Eli approached wearing street clothes. He must have left his coveralls in the truck. He smelled like hand sanitizer trying hard to cover up other odors.

"Where to?" she said, begging the heavens for a short, uneventful commute to drop the man off at his place so she could get home before she collapsed.

"Elm Grove."

"I'm not familiar with Elm Grove Avenue."

"Not the street. The town."

"How far away is your house, apartment . . ."

"House. It's about twenty feet from my folks' house. Nice area."

Camille started the engine. "How far from here?"

"An hour and a half."

"What?"

"I assume we'll stop somewhere for a meal on the way. The trip's only a half hour, but then another hour to eat. I don't imagine that you feel like cooking tonight, do you? I sure don't."

A cold thought slapped her across the face. "I suppose you need me to pick you up in the morning too?"

"No. I wouldn't impose on you for that."

Really?

"I can have my friend bring me back."

"I thought he was going to tag-team with you today."

"We kept in touch by phone. He wasn't needed. We didn't fill any more than about a quarter of that truck. I know we were both hoping for more. We didn't need the second in my fleet."

We. He threw that word around like he was comfortable with it. "Tell me which direction I'm headed."

"I can do better than that." He punched something into his phone and set it on the dash. "Kermit will get you there."

"Kermit? The Muppet?"

"I programmed my navigation system to sound like Kermit the Frog. Keeps me from taking myself too seriously."

I doubt that is an issue with you, Eli Rand.

⌒

It doesn't take an hour to eat fish tacos, Eli. But it may take me the full hour to lay out the parameters of your role tomorrow, all of which you ignored today.

"It's going to be a beautiful sunset," he said.

Another window table. Coincidence or obsession? After the day they'd had, he was consumed with thoughts of the sunset?

Talk about oblivious.

"Eli, we're both dead on our feet, but we have a few things to discuss."

"Oh yeah," he said. "About the money you owe me for those plumbing parts? Don't worry about it. My contribution to Chester's cause."

The latest superhero—Exasperation Man.

"I . . . appreciate your doing that. But by contract, we're required to use licensed contractors for any significant repairs needed."

"Oh. So, like, that lightbulb I replaced?"

"No. A lightbulb is fine."

"What if I—"

"No. Let's assume that just about anything you decide you want to do, other than the specific role for which you were hired, is off-limits."

He finished chewing another salsa-dipped tortilla chip before responding. "A little harsh, isn't it? I'm there to help. So let me help."

"Most people," she began, weighing her words, "who are untrained in working with people who suffer from hoarding disorders have a tendency to exacerbate the problem. A family member or friend will step in and think they're helping by shaming the client into action, which makes the client retreat even further, refuse to make any decisions."

"I never shamed Chester."

"Let me finish please. Others will coddle their loved one or step in and take over the cleanup operation or otherwise hinder the incredibly difficult challenge of persuading a hoarder to un-hoard. The stress often makes the hoarder physically ill or compounds their anxiety."

"Is that what I did today? Shame Chester? Coddle him? Increase his stress level?"

She sighed. "You're missing the point."

"Did I?" His voice wasn't accusatory. He looked mortified at the possibility.

She had to keep the upper hand. Two years' worth of investment in Chester's healing could disappear in an instant if Eli made a wrong move. Or if she did. And with Chester's history of suicidal thoughts . . .

But that was information to which Eli was not privileged.

"Eli, what I observed is that you befriended him."

He laid his last taco to the side of his plate. "I hope he saw it that way too."

"You have a connection with him. I won't deny that. You were able to reach him with story, a powerful counseling tool. He responds to you."

"I liked your Houston flood analogy. Easy for him to picture, I imagine."

She clasped her hands together and pressed her pointer fingers against each other until her joints ached. "May I finish?"

"Yes, please. I was just going to take this last taco in a to-go bag, but you can have it."

"I don't want to finish your dinner. I want to finish my—"

"Speech? Lecture? Rant?"

"How can I get you to understand what's at stake here? It's not just Chester's residence. It may well be his life."

"Why would you think I couldn't understand that?"

She crossed her arms and leaned on the table. The fish, intoxicatingly good—grilled and seasoned to perfection—had left flakes of itself among the shreds of vinegary cabbage and carrots and remnants of mango salsa.

"Did you get enough to eat, Dr. Brooks? The way you're staring at your plate—"

"See, Eli? That's the thing. The letters behind my name don't give me bragging rights. But they do give me a great deal of responsibility. And I earned, through lots of hard work, the privilege to be entrusted with these very unique cases."

"People. They're people, not cases."

"Yes, of course."

"And I earned my insights by living with it and then living without my papaw. And now, every day I watch my grandmother try to breathe through her regrets. For her it's almost like an endless death rattle. Do I take it seriously? Yes, I do. Do I want to usurp your professional expertise?"

She waited for the yes.

"No. I admire and respect what you do." He reached for his wallet. She let him.

But he didn't pull out cash or a credit card. He used two fingers to extract a small bit of—No, not seriously.

"I've gone to carrying a little batch of dryer lint with me.

Comes in handy with you around." He set the piece of lint on his head like a miniature hat. Or poor imitation of a toupee.

What was she going to do with him?

Nothing! She was going to have nothing to do with him as of the end of the day tomorrow. But . . . Shyla had already cashed his check. That didn't mean Cam couldn't keep her distance. Shyla could handle all the specs for the website ad and an audio clip, if he wanted one.

Oh. Cam would hear his voice in the sponsorship slot on her own program. Maybe Shyla would consent to muting his ads when they played.

And that didn't sound at all middle school-ish.

The man had bled to try to reach Chester. *Who does that?*

chapter nine

READ AN INTERESTING QUOTE LAST night on social media," Eli said the next morning before Camille had fully exited her car. Great. He'd arrived early.

"What was it?"

"Max Lucado, I think. He said, 'Do not meditate on the mess.' Good one, isn't it?"

"Not familiar with his work."

"You're kidding, right? Oh. I bet you read all textbookie kinds of things."

She shut the car door with great restraint, considering Eli was already fraying her nerves. "I don't have much margin for recreational reading."

He stopped her stride toward Chester's house with a hand on her arm. The look in his eyes was half cocker spaniel, half himself. "I am so sorry."

"About what?"

"That you don't have time to read for the joy of it." He stood that way, locked into that expression for way longer than was comfortable. She waited for him to break character and laugh, but he didn't.

"'Don't meditate on the mess'? I'll have to remember that one, Eli. Thanks. Now, we have work to do."

"I can stay out of your way," he said, "by reading to you through the window while you work."

She was three steps ahead of him and intended to keep it that way. "I have other things to occupy my focus."

"I'll be here outside if you need me."

"Won't. But thank you." She tapped on the door.

Chester opened immediately this time. "Come on in. I think you'll be pleasantly surprised at what I've done. Is Eli here? I'd like him to see too." He paused. "You okay, Dr. Brooks? It looks like your neck hinge is loose."

She lifted her chin from where it had landed on her chest. "Yes. Yes, I'm doing great." Pivoting, she found Eli wiping dew off the taillights of his truck with the sleeve of his coveralls. "Eli?"

His head jerked up.

She gestured for him to join them, already regretting it. In a way.

He didn't hesitate. A cocker spaniel let off his leash.

"What do you have to show us, Chester?" She picked her way carefully through the tunnel that seemed no wider than the day before.

"I thought it would go quicker if I put a sticker on everything I'd like to keep. Then the cleanup team won't have to ask me so many questions. It's the questions that bogged me down yesterday, I think."

Camille scanned the room that was probably supposed to be a living room, once it was cleared. A couch likely groaned under the weight of what hid and threatened to break it. All she saw was sticker after sticker on the bins and boxes and piles. He must have had a collection of fluorescent orange stickers. Until he used them.

"It's an intriguing concept, Chester. But can you point out to me what doesn't have a sticker? My eyes haven't adjusted to the dim light in here. I can't seem to locate anything at first glance."

"I put throwaways in that box by my chair." He pointed to an economy-sized cereal box.

"What's in here?" She opened the top gingerly. "Chester, this looks like dozens of cereal box liners stuffed into the box."

"And cracker liners. Those liners are made of waxed paper. I figured I could reuse them for something someday. That's why they're folded so neatly. Plus, then I could fit a lot more in. But"—he breathed deep—"I am willing to part with them."

"Oh, Chester."

"And I did that on my own. I worked hard on the sticker system. It got tricky in the bedroom with all the clothes."

She could feel Eli's presence behind her before he whispered, "Did you bring yourself some coffee today?"

"I left it in the car," she whispered back.

"I'll just go get it for you." She heard his footsteps crunching paper and plastic grocery bags in his retreat.

"Thanks."

And she meant it.

Before her, holding his hard-won accomplishment, stood a prime example of the complexities of hoarding disorders. Camille guessed they were looking at a literal ton of items in his home that needed to be discarded within the next several hours, and her client was beaming over a cereal box full of used, disposable waxed paper liners. Her role was to encourage his progress while urging him to consider the ton.

If it weren't for her intense training that alerted her and equipped her for moments like this, she would on the spot consider a career change. In her line of work, job satisfaction couldn't be linked to steady forward progress. Few of her clients had or ever would fit that mold.

"It's certainly a start, Chester. Now, let's amplify that by quite a lot as we take a careful look at your sticker system."

It was going to be a very long day.

They all were.

―

By 10 a.m. Camille knew the situation called for drastic measures. Chester was in meltdown mode, as was the early summer midwestern humidity level, which caused his stickers to give way and float to the floor or wherever they hit first before they could reach it.

Kimberly and her team were doing what they could, but they hadn't been allowed much elbow room in which to work. Chester's phrase of the day was, "I can't decide. Let's just put that over here for now."

But that habit had gotten him to this crisis point. Eviction seemed inevitable. He'd regressed when his sticker system failed him and when faced with the reality that he was out of options.

"Chester, I don't like to do this. I rarely recommend it. But it's crunch time."

"Don't push me. I can't go any faster." His voice shook, edged with a brewing tantrum.

She asked the workers to stop where they were and take a five-minute fresh-air break while she talked to him.

"I'm going to recommend a temporary—and I emphasize that word—solution to today's deadline and our obvious inability to come even close to that at this rate."

"I'm doing my best. These are my . . . things, you have to understand. They belong to me. They need me. Who else will take care of them?"

This was Chester's description of taking care of his items?

"We can rent you a storage unit," she said. "Several units."

"I can't afford that."

"That's actually a good thing. It will buy us only a little

time. Your possessions will all be there, in storage. We will have to move our base of operations to the storage units next week sometime and do the kind of purging that needs to happen. It needs to happen, Chester. But we'll be able to get this house in good enough shape to satisfy your landlord."

Chester sank into his chair. "That's like sending my children away to boarding school. Don't you see? I want my things here with me."

"I know you do. But that's not possible."

"There's no storage unit, is there? You're going to trash it all and pretend I have lost everything."

"Chester, have I ever been dishonest with you?"

"No. But we all have our breaking points."

"I can take him there."

Eli. Eli, Eli, Eli . . . Wait a minute. "What did you have in mind?"

He stepped farther into the room. "If you want, Chester, you could ride in the truck with me so you can supervise our putting your things safely in storage. Temporarily."

"I haven't been out in a while."

"We'd have to make several trips, so you'd get more than a little fresh air traipsing back and forth with me. I'll do the heavy lifting. But you'll see exactly where your things are being kept for now. Isn't that right, Dr. Brooks?"

How long could they afford to explain a plan that still might not be finished before the deadline? "Would you give us permission to do that, please?"

His bottom lip quivered. Eyes darting from listing pile to listing pile around him, he wept softly. "Maybe it's . . . easier . . . if *I* just disappear."

Of all her nightmares, this was the worst. The theme of all of them—someone died because she couldn't reach them in time. *Chester, you can't—you won't—be in my nightmares.* But it wasn't encouraging that he'd hinted at such a thing twice in recent days.

"You may feel that way, Chester, that it would be easier on everybody if you disappeared. But it isn't the truth. The truth is that you are a loving, intelligent, important man who is facing an especially difficult aspect of your disorder right now."

"Important? To who? *You're* only here because the courts assigned you to me."

Camille groaned internally. Yes, she'd been assigned to Chester. But that didn't mean she didn't genuinely care. If his pattern followed that of most, the words would ring hollow to him at a time like this. They were what she was expected to say.

Everything was on the line. His life. Her reputation. Her job. His home.

An electric pulse raced up the outside of her arms. Her job and reputation shouldn't be a consideration at all. Not with her client in such a fragile emotional state. But they did matter. Eventually, she could help no one if she couldn't continue to help some.

"I know for sure that Dr. Brooks cares about you, Chester." Eli laid one arm casually over her shoulder. "She talks a lot nicer to you than she does to me."

Chester turned his head to the side. Hiding tears? When he turned back, his eyes were bright, but his shoulders shook with reserved laughter. "That is true," he said.

"Courts or no courts, I wouldn't be here if you didn't matter to me." She shrugged off Eli's arm and drew closer to her client.

"And when this is over?" He seemed consumed with the hoard approaching nearer rather than receding.

"I'll still be available to you. We can talk by phone or in the office, or I can stop in for a visit."

"For how many of your past clients do you 'stop by for a visit'?"

She needed a truthful answer but one that would keep him talking about the future and keep him moving toward it. "As many as will let me in."

He sniffed. Chewed the inside of his cheek. Then he looked at Eli. "I ride shotgun."

Eli chuckled. "There is *only* shotgun, Chester. No back seat on this truck."

"I guess I meant that it's time I started riding in the front seat where I can see out the windshield instead of sitting in the middle of the stuff in back, if you know what I mean. How soon can we get us one or two of them storage units rented?"

Camille turned toward Eli, who was already searching on his phone. "I'd suggest a minimum of four," she said under her breath.

He nodded.

She signaled to the cleanup crew to huddle for their new strategy. "We'll need half of your team, Kimberly, to focus on removal to the truck, starting with obvious storage items—solid bins, enclosed boxes, clothing items which you'll either box or hang on racks."

"That would be convenient, if you don't mind," Chester interjected. "I think if they were on racks, I could tell better which ones I need to save when we go through them . . . next week."

The needles prickled the backs of her arms again. He'd crossed a line into thinking proactively. Some of her clients never reached that point. It was curious but not entirely comforting that he so quickly throttled back on the "easier on everyone if I disappear" threat.

"Good thinking. Then the other half of the team will work on the physical cleaning process while you and I do some speed dating with items you believe are not worth transferring to the storage bins and not in good repair for donating to others."

"I hope you'll leave me something to sit on."

Fear always hovered so close to the surface. "We will leave

you with all you need to not only survive but enjoy the end product. Trust me. Please."

"No offense to you, Dr. Brooks, but you'll remember that is one of my key issues—trust."

"I haven't forgotten."

Eli had walked away to talk privately on the phone. He came back now, four fingers raised, then a thumbs-up.

She grabbed a bright-green heavy-duty garbage bag from the supply basket. "When I was a very little girl"—she choked on the word but regained her composure—"my mom would ask me to put away my toys before dinner. It looked impossible to me, bits and pieces of all the games and puzzles and odds and ends I'd taken out during the day."

"I'll bet you money it didn't look anything like this," Chester said.

"No." *Not then. That came later.* "It might have felt that way to a toddler though. My mother made a game of it. I knew it was a ploy, but it had to be done, and the game made it more interesting."

"Can't see anything fun in this," Chester said.

She'd lose him fast if she didn't finish. "She told me to only pick up the blue things I saw out of place and return them where they belonged. I raced to get the blue items taken care of. Then she chose red. By the time we'd gone through all the primary colors and a few lesser known— She liked to throw in a color I'd never heard of at the time, like puce or aubergine so I could grow my vocabulary. By the time we neared the end, the chore was no longer overwhelming. At each level, I felt a sense of accomplishment."

"Smart mom."

Until . . .

"You want me to try that?" he asked.

"Let's see how fast you and I can make decisions on the throwaways by applying that concept. Red things first. What can we determine truly needs to be thrown away?"

Chester surveyed the room too long, activity buzzing all around him. Finally he bent to the floor to retrieve something. "This price tag. I don't even know what it's from. I guess I didn't want to throw it away because it said 'Clearance' on it. And that seemed worth something."

Camille took it from him as if he were giving her a gift. "Good work. Wise decision. What's next? Something red . . ."

It took less time for him to find a second item. "These envelopes. I kept them because I liked the font that company uses for their logo. Isn't that interesting?"

"Yes, but . . ."

"I know. Not interesting enough to have to pay to store."

"Right. How do you feel about tossing them?"

"I feel okay. I've seen that font on other things. And online." He tossed them into the garbage bag himself and dusted his hands of their memory.

The attachments for some hoarders stuck more firmly than barnacles on a ship's hull. The ship wasn't aware of their presence. The ship's owner could ignore them only so long before they became an issue. Those who dealt with the problem saved their vessel. Those who refused lost their ability to launch out into the sea. A font. For Chester, a font had latched on to him and had been eating away at his hull.

Cam's mother's penmanship had changed toward the end. It had been the one tidy element to which her mother had clung, no matter how deep the chaos that swirled about her. Then in the final months, the smooth, flowing lines had turned to a mix of flowing and choppy, as if her mind couldn't decide what it wanted to be.

Camille could understand the pull of ink.

chapter ten

WITH ELI'S TIRELESS—AND TIRELESSLY optimistic—help, Chester's excess had been safely ensconced in storage units about half a mile away that afternoon. Even with such a short distance separating them, Eli reported that Chester's anxiety ramped up with every rotation of the truck's tires carrying his belongings farther from home.

Cam asked later that evening how Eli had dealt with it. "Told a few stories," he'd said. "Got him to tell me a few."

She was torn between wishing she'd been there and glad she hadn't been.

By the end of the workday, Chester's home was livable. Still more cluttered than most people would appreciate, but no longer dysfunctional. The cleanup crew had done a masterful job dealing with stubborn carpet stains and "staging" the remaining furniture. Their nontoxic odor neutralizers performed their magic. And Chester had been granted a six-month reprieve from the threatened eviction.

Still euphoric from the grace Chester's landlord showed him, though it was all a temporary fix, at her Monday morning client visit, Camille drew new courage to ask Allison, "You've heard of the term self-sabotage, haven't you?"

"Of course. And I know that describes me." She kicked through the papers on the floor of her home as if they were no more than leaves on a woodland path in autumn. The sound they made was distinctly similar.

"It wouldn't be uncommon to see new purchases stuffed in corners while ridding your home of what already consumes it, if self-sabotage is an issue."

"You know it is. Did you know my husband used to drink? A lot?"

Was Allison determined to lead Cam on a rabbit trail? Or was this exactly the journey she intended to take with a statement like that? "No. You hadn't mentioned it."

"He'd probably tell you that too was my fault. He drank to escape . . . all this. He headed for the bar because coming home meant facing what I'd become."

"Your husband—"

"Ex-husband. I should have clarified."

"The divorce wasn't a trigger for your hoarding?"

Allison leaned against the back of a three-legged chair piled high with new debris. "Well, it didn't help. But it wasn't the start of it all."

"What was?"

"That's a conversation for another day. Don't get me off track. I was talking about his excessive drinking."

"Do you have a picture of him in the house?"

Allison turned to face her. "Thank you for that. You've reminded me that I am capable of throwing some things away. I'm sure the kids have pictures. But I have purged." She seemed pleased with herself, but the look dissolved faster than a snowflake on a warm mitten. Or a flake of hope on hot resentment.

"I didn't mean to interrupt. Please go on."

"The man had several DUIs. Lost his license more than once. And like clockwork, the weekend before he earned the right to apply for a new one, he'd mess up and throw himself into another waiting period. Throw us all into that waiting period."

"Sad."

"We paid the price too. The whole family did. For a while, he was the only driver in the family." She grew pensive. "Maybe that's why he did it. To show me how inconvenient and costly my habits were to the whole family."

"Maybe."

Allison let go of her grip on the chair. "At any rate, I am well aware of the concept of self-sabotage. And . . . self-awareness."

But somehow radically unaware of or unable to conquer the cause and effect of her ongoing disorder on the children she cherished but never saw.

Camille followed Allison, her steps cautious, avoiding what she could. "I brought us both coffee from that new shop a couple of blocks from here. Have you been there yet?" She handed one cup to her client.

"You know I haven't."

"Why don't we sit on your front porch today to talk?"

"The sunlight is hard on my eyes. I guess I'm more sensitive now."

"Since living in relative darkness, you mean?" Camille pointed to a pulled-shut, pinned-shut drapery on the front window.

Allison's expression changed—startled. "I attributed most of my vision issues to age."

"You're not that old, Allison."

"Old enough to be your mother."

The words pierced like a barbed arrow. *Your mother, your mother, your mother.* As if puncturing her weren't enough, the words tore at her flesh on either side of the wound.

"If you wore my sunglasses, could we please sit outside for our appointment today? A few minutes?"

"You've had enough of this house? Of me?"

"That's not it. I'm hoping we'll both benefit from a different view and perhaps a different *point* of view."

"I'd rather not."

Camille waited to let Allison's answer have room to breathe. "I'd like you to trust me that something you don't want to do might have actual benefit. A few minutes? Five minutes on the front porch with me? It's a beautiful day. I know from some of these book titles that deep inside you is an appreciation for the beauty of nature."

Allison huffed at the comment. "Neighbors might look."

"And what would they see? Two friends talking."

"With fancy coffee-shop coffee."

Camille smiled. "Maybe I'll get a discount next time for helping advertise the place."

"Why the front porch? We could sit in my kitchen."

"Allison?"

"One of us could sit."

"I chose the front porch because you have very carefully— and I assume intentionally—kept the front of your house from becoming a receptacle of your collections. The lawn is always neatly trimmed. Nothing clutters your front yard. Though the house could use fresh paint."

"I know. Everybody tells me that."

Cam wondered who the "everybodies" were for a woman who had withdrawn from normal social practices like leaving her house, shopping in stores, meeting with or hosting friends. Her family? Someone from the city council? Camille couldn't pursue that train of thought right now and risk distracting both of them from the conversation task at hand. "And the window boxes were empty that first day I arrived, but since then there have always been bright flowers in the boxes."

"Ivan puts them there, without even asking."

"Who's Ivan?"

They shuffled through the layer of fallen "leaves" of debris until they reached the front door. Allison put her hand on the interior doorknob and froze in place. "He's a . . . neighbor. We went to the same church a long time ago. That's all."

She opened the door a little wider than normal. The action crushed the stack of lidded cardboard boxes that lived behind the door. Allison's shoulders crept upward.

"It'll be okay," Camille said. "They're still standing."

No newborn fawn stepped more gingerly than Allison did when walking the few feet to one of the two patio chairs on her narrow cement-floor porch. The overhang kept the sun from hitting them directly, but Allison squinted anyway.

Camille handed Allison her sunglasses. "I'd like to hear more about Ivan." Sometimes the greatest insights came from a client's relationships with the "others" in their lives—postal workers, neighbors, a cousin who maintained contact when siblings or children refused.

"He's an old fool."

"You haven't said that to his face, have you, Allison?"

"Not to his face. Or behind his back either. But he is. He comes every week to mow my lawn. I told him not to."

The older gentleman with grass-stained shoes she'd seen the day of Allison's latest encounter with the police. "How did he respond to that? To your refusing his offer?"

"The first year, he listened. Then one day he just did it. It was like clearing brush by then. Took him weeks to get it looking healthy again."

"Hmm. Tenacious."

"Stubborn." Allison swiveled to face Camille. "The two are a lot alike. After a while I quit hollering at him to stop. It looked like he was enjoying himself, whistling, sometimes dancing a little behind the mower . . ."

"I'd like to see that."

"Hang around long enough and you might."

"And he fills the window boxes?"

"The first time he did that, I was so mad that I snuck out in the night and pulled all the flowers."

"Allison."

"I didn't say I was proud of myself. Just mad. But the old fool showed up again the next day with a new batch. I felt so guilty about the money he was spending that I quit griping."

"How far away does he live?"

"Around the block. He asks me to go walking with him. I always tell him no. He asks me out for coffee or ice cream."

"You always tell him no."

"Yes. He brings fresh strawberries or raspberries from his garden or the farmer's market. Just leaves them on the doorstep and rings the doorbell, like he's in grade school."

"He has a crush on you, Allison?"

"Goodness no! I think I'm his charity project. His good-deed outlet."

"Do you see him at church?"

"I don't go anymore. I suspect he does."

Camille shifted in her aged patio chair. Still uncomfortable. "When did you stop attending?"

Allison's squint had relaxed. Now it tightened again. "If you're trying to get me back across the threshold of that church—"

"That's not my intention. It's been a while since I've seen the inside of a church too."

"Why'd you ask then?"

"The more I understand about what's important to you, the more I'll be able to help you discover what will work best and allow you to live free of or at least manage your hoarding disorder."

Allison flinched visibly.

"And . . . I genuinely enjoy talking with you."

Allison waved off the compliment. Her knees bounced. She was spiraling.

"Allison, how do you feel sitting out here in the fresh air, freshly mowed lawn, beautiful flowers, the quiet neighborhood?"

"Exposed. Naked."

"Fearful?"

"I'm always fearful."

"How do you think other people would feel about a scene like this?"

"How would I know?"

"Imagine it. If you were any other person sitting in your spot right now, what would you see?"

"Is this one of your psychobabble games meant to trick me into saying or doing something I don't want to?"

Camille's phone thrummed. Shyla had texted. Now what? Shyla would have to wait.

"I paid good money to gain my extensive vocabulary of psychobabble."

The woman with Camille's mother's soft eyes and self-sabotaging house allowed herself a brief giggle. "Well, you must have started young to get such a good grasp of it."

"Seventeen. Done with undergrad work in three years. Started grad school at twenty."

"Impressive."

Why had she shared that personal information? She knew better. Too many moments of weakness strung together lately.

"That's young to hit the college campus."

"I needed to."

"Why?"

Long answer to that one. My fault for not stopping this thread a while ago. Camille turned her attention to the houses across the street. An average neighborhood. How many of the residents knew about the secret behind Allison's front door? How much did Ivan know? Would he still be so kind if he knew?

Maybe in part because of the sensationalized examples on TV, people with hoarding disorders often became society's outcasts, she knew. Few could see past the disorder, the addiction, to connect with the wounded human being. It galled and frustrated Camille. If the podcast could change people's perceptions, all the hard work would be worth it.

Camille looked at every addiction differently these days.

She used to think the person and their chaos were inseparable, welded together. It had taken her a while, but she was beginning to see the person and the addiction as separate entities. Both needed attention. Although society often lumped them together, treatment protocols and compassion knew they were not fused.

"You're not talking to me now?" Allison popped off the lid of her coffee cup.

"I apologize. My mind wandered for a minute. Where were we?"

"I asked why you started college so young, other than your genius status."

Camille's leg itched. Sitting outside during bug season had its downside. "Started kindergarten when I'd just turned five. I took every college prep class I could in high school. An accelerated learning program. It allowed me to start college early."

"With a full scholarship, I imagine."

"That helped with tuition. I worked a lot, sometimes two jobs, in addition to school."

"Not surprised."

Allison's facial expression seemed more relaxed than it had been. If it took Camille talking about herself more to set her client at ease, she'd have to put guardrails on her words. "I suppose people would have called me driven." *Driven by desperation to escape.*

Speaking of desperation, Shyla's text message had that air to it. Camille had ignored two "Call me ASAP" messages. This one was all caps.

"Excuse me, Allison. I have a work-related call I have to make."

"I'll go back inside."

"No, please. Stay right there. I'll walk out to the curb so I don't disturb you. But you'll still see me. I won't leave you out here alone."

"Dr. Brooks—"

"Two minutes. You can do two minutes." She jumped off the porch and jogged toward the street, backward, so Allison could still maintain eye contact. She dialed Shyla's number, then waved at her client. "I'm right here. See?"

Shyla picked up immediately. "Where are you?"

"Allison's. What's up?"

"I'm in bad shape, Camille. Here at the hospital. They're talking possible hysterectomy." Shyla dissolved in tears. "You . . . know what that would . . . mean. And Jenx doesn't even know about my little adventure in the ambulance. I can't reach him."

"I'll be right there." She glanced back at Allison. Crises didn't abide by schedules and gave little concern to what they interrupted. Both women needed a listening ear. But right now Shyla's was a higher-priority need.

"What's wrong?" Allison asked as Cam neared. "Bad news?"

"A friend of mine was taken to the hospital and is facing a tough surgery. I'm afraid I need to cut our conversation short today."

"I understand." Allison was already on her feet, rising in that achy way Allison's mom had always gotten out of a chair. She headed for the front door without preamble. "See you next time." The door was closed and barred before Camille could utter another word.

All for the better. The hospital was across town and . . . Her keys were in her purse, which was in Allison's house. Somewhere. She knocked. The woman couldn't have gone far. *Please answer.*

Camille danced from foot to foot waiting for Allison to come to the door. She didn't. Camille knocked again and called out, "Allison! Please let me in! My keys."

Nothing.

What now? The back door is inaccessible. Ah. Our next project. Must have access.

She tapped on the window. Then harder. With every window covered, there was no point in trying to peek in and catch Allison's attention.

Her phone. She dialed Allison's number. *Pick up. Pick up. Pick up.*

"Hello?"

"It's me. Dr. Brooks. Please open the door. I left my purse and keys inside."

"Oh dear. I'm sorry. I didn't know it was you." She still had her phone to her ear when she slid the locks to the side and opened her front door. "So sorry."

"I need to get my purse and get on my way to the hospital for my friend." Such dim light in here. Where had she left it? She made it a point to take little with her when she visited her clients. But today she'd taken her purse inside. Who knew why? Now it lay somewhere in the melee. Her signature purse—brightly flowered. And washable. Its distinct pattern became a saving grace at a time like this. There it was. On a stack of storage totes. Never again. She'd have a new system created before her feet hit the hospital tiles.

"Got it. Thanks, Allison. I'll call you soon."

"Tell your friend I'm praying for her."

Camille nodded her gratitude and flew out the door as fast as she could without colliding with chaos.

Shyla might actually appreciate those prayers. Or maybe Allison was the one who needed to pray them. Another breakthrough. Putting someone else's needs above her own.

Hope propelled her the entire length of the trip to the hospital where, ironically, hope was losing its battle.

If Shyla hadn't lost so much blood, they might have sent her home that day, the medical staff said. But her hemoglobin had dropped so low, along with her blood volume, that she became an overnight guest of Slade Memorial Hospital and sported IVs in both arms. One replaced her blood volume; the other kept her hydrated and as pain-free as possible.

No medication could ease the emotional pain written all over Shyla's otherwise beautiful face.

"I wish Jenx could have been here. Maybe he would have thought of some other option, something other than such a drastic surgical move."

"Shyla, you know these doctors had your best interests at heart. They wouldn't have advised you in this direction if they didn't think it was absolutely necessary. It may not seem so right now."

Tears trickled down both sides of her face. "I hadn't finished grieving the loss of the baby. This seems too cruel."

"Does one ever finish grieving the loss of a child?"

"No."

Those words. Those awful words. *No one can finish grieving the loss of a child.* The loss was ongoing, endless. The immediacy of the pain, the intensity might lessen or be overridden by other concerns, but grief remained. She hadn't believed it when the grieving woman had been her mother. And it cost them their entire relationship.

She wouldn't make that mistake with another person as long as she lived.

"I'll stay until Jenx gets here, hon. Then I'll let you get some rest."

"Are you going back to Allison's?"

"Maybe tomorrow. We'll see. Oh, Allison said to tell you she's praying for you."

Shyla closed her eyes. More tears fell. "Please tell her how much that means to me."

"I will."

Allison hadn't met Eli yet. But Camille had a feeling they might find common ground.

What was that man doing invading her thoughts at a time like this?

chapter eleven

SHYLA'S LOSS HAD FOLLOWED CAMILLE home to her apartment. The living room seemed enveloped in darkness that had less to do with the lateness of the hour and more to do with atmosphere. She kept the air conditioner setting especially cool in the summer in the Midwest. Heat rose to her eighth-floor apartment and the windows remained closed to block traffic noise, so a breeze wasn't an option. But cold air rushed at her when she opened the door this time. Cold and empty.

She uncustomarily dropped her purse on the end of the sofa. Hot tea. Yes. Even with June advancing into July. She turned on every light in the room, as if they could lend heat as well as illumination.

The finality of Shyla's surgery hit her hard. Every comforting thought—*no more miscarriages*—dissipated in the swirl of foreverness. There was no undoing what the scalpel had done to Shyla and Jenx and their plans. They'd survive. She was confident they would. The familiar shiver climbed the back of her arms. But they couldn't escape their dream's death cries.

Nor could Cam.

She'd attended too many funerals for dreams.

She'd left her phone on in case Shyla needed her. The plan backfired. Eli was calling. *Answer? Don't answer? Make a decision.*

"Eli. What's up?"

"And a gracious good evening to you too. Let's skip the formalities. Who has time for courtesy, right?"

Not what she needed. "Is this an emergency?" *A garbage emergency?* "If not, can I call you tomorrow? It's been a rough day."

"It may be about to improve. I'm here."

"What do you mean?"

"Look out your window. I'm on the street in front of your apartment building."

She did. And he was. "Eli, how did you find out where I live?"

"You told me."

"I certainly did not."

"Sure you did." He waved up at her.

"I do not give out that information. For a hundred reasons."

"Can I come up? It'll be easier to explain without the traffic noise behind me."

Her apartment was her domain. Few people crossed the threshold. And today of all days . . .

Today of all days, maybe what she needed was another voice in this apartment other than her own and those that whispered in the corners of her memories. "I'll buzz you in."

"What floor?"

"I thought you knew where I lived."

"Building only. I couldn't guess which floor or apartment number. Gups is good but—"

"Gups?"

"Long for GPS. Get it? It's not short for GPS, because frankly, GPS is pretty short as it is."

She could change her mind. Should change her mind.

"Watch the light board in the entry when it buzzes. That will tell you."

"See you in a few."

"Uh-huh." *Uh-huh.*

Her domain no longer felt empty. It felt . . . sacred. Still. Quiet. Hers. For the next "few."

Too few. An exuberant knock sounded at her door. It echoed through the open-concept room as if the walls were mountain ranges.

When she opened the door to him, he had to ask if she'd please open it wider for him to enter without having to lose weight first. Not her best moment.

"I like your apartment," he said, nodding slowly. "Nicely done. It's . . . spare."

"Spare?"

"Sparse? Is that the word?"

"Trim."

"Minimalist. That's the word I was looking for."

"I suppose you could call it that. Can I make you a cup of tea, or aren't you staying long enough?" Wait. He'd said, "Do I look like a tea drinker?"

He deposited two boxes—one a grimy cardboard box of metal parts—on her glass coffee table. "Oh, I have time. I dropped Mom and Dad off at the Cheesecake Factory to celebrate five years cancer-free."

"You didn't want to eat with them?" *Why* didn't he want to eat with them?

"I could tell they needed some alone time."

"I know the feeling."

"Having Nana around all the time wears on them. Not her presence. Her sadness. It wears them down." He washed his hands at her kitchen sink. And left droplets on the faucet.

"I know that feeling too."

"Paper towel?" he asked, hands dripping.

"There's a bamboo towel hanging inside the lower cupboard, under the sink."

"No paper towels?"

"No desire to create trash."

He dried his hands with the towel without taking his eyes off her. "I've known some minimalists in my day, but— No, I guess I haven't."

"Did you have a reason for stopping by, Eli?" She set the timer for his tea to steep and cheated it by thirty seconds.

He brightened, as he always did. "I brought some parts that might work for your car. Brand-new set of windshield wipers"—he pulled them from the box—"never used, and a set of brake pads. I can't install them in a hurry, of course, but someday. Did you hear how the engine is knocking when it idles? Could be low on oil. Could be the air filter. Or the carburetor. If it's the air filter, I may have just the thing to fix that."

"Where did you get all this?"

"Around. I've got a little supply of scavenged car parts. They come in handy."

The room was suddenly oppressively warm. The grandson of a hoarder. Despite his unusual wealth of understanding when dealing with her clients, was Eli hiding his own disorder?"

"Dr. Brooks?"

"What?"

"Did I embarrass you with my offer?"

"Your offer—" What had she missed?

"To do a few minor repairs on your car? Your face is flushed. Ears too. I didn't mean to offend. I just thought with how much you need dependable transportation for your job . . ."

"Shyla had emergency surgery today," she blurted. No filter. She'd lost her filter—air and otherwise.

"Oh no. How's she doing? Anything serious? Appendix?"

She should have known better than to mention Shyla's surgery to a guy who actually cared about people. Bad move. Now he'd ask more questions.

"She'll heal quickly." Physically. Emotionally could be an-other story. "I spent most of the day at the hospital with her, and I'm not much for conversation tonight, much less thinking about car repairs."

"You're a good friend to her."

No, I'm not. "Your tea's ready."

"I should go," he said, "unless you need someone to talk to."

Nope.

"But on the other hand, I understand more than ever"—he glanced around the room—"how opposed you are to wastefulness."

Oh dear.

"I'll have my tea first before I go. We can't waste good tea."

She had to give him that. And all of a sudden he *did* look like a tea guy.

———

Slowest tea drinker in the history of tea drinking. Would he never get to the end of that cup?

"Have you been in this apartment long?" he asked between micro sips.

"Three years this fall. Found it the day I got the job with the social services agency."

"You don't work independently?"

Endless questions. "Not yet. Someday, I hope. As much as I appreciate what they're doing and the workload pressures they're under, I'm not a fan of their rules and restrictions. All necessary, I'm sure, but—"

"That comes as a surprise," Eli said. "I thought you were Queen of the Rules."

Only when it comes to you, Eli. Only when it comes to you. "Mixed blessing. Some are of course necessary. Some rules get in the way of new methods I'd like to investigate with my clients."

"I hear you." Another micro sip.

She had to be proactive. "Eli, tell me more about your family." As soon as the words were out of her mouth, she realized her faux pas. The story would no doubt delay his departure. But she also had to admit she was curious.

"I can swing by here after I pick them up at the restaurant if you'd like to meet them."

Her dismay must have been written all over her face. She reined it in.

But he said, "On second thought, not tonight. Shyla's heavy on your heart. For good reason. We'll do that another time. Maybe I could haul you out to the farm so you could meet my grandmother too."

Haul. Such a smooth talker.

"Can I take your cup for you?"

He paused a moment, then drained what was left in it. "Yeah, I have to get moving. Mom and Dad aren't the lingering kind. When their meal's over, they're ready to get on the road again." He glanced at his watch. "Maybe I can make it in time for the dessert course."

"Mmm. Cheesecake Factory." She could be pleasant when she wanted to.

"Hey, that reminds me." He tapped the lid of the non-grimy box on the coffee table. "A little something from there for you. You need to eat, Dr. Brooks."

The look in his eyes didn't say, "You're too skinny." It said, "I'm concerned."

Who in their right mind would refuse cheesecake on those grounds?

—

Camille had fallen asleep to the sound of her own podcast. The "Baby Steps to the Elevator" episode encouraged both hoarding disorder sufferers and family members to celebrate small victories while awaiting the larger ones.

Like five-year all-clear anniversaries.

And not engaging the extra locks on her door until Eli had left the hallway.

And . . . actual hoarder victories, like Chester's coffee carafe and Allison's five minutes of sunshine.

"Throwing things away seems like such a waste."

The words could have been Camille's. But they came from Allison, who clutched a handleless pancake flipper to her chest. "I don't want this to end up in a landfill." She drew in a sharp breath, as if punched in the stomach, and groaned.

"What is it? What's wrong?"

She sank onto the arm of her couch, the only surface not piled high. "I remember saying those very words to my daughter, Lia, the day she moved out."

"Did she have a response?" Camille tossed the sentence lightly. It needed to feel casual, curious, not probing.

Allison's shoulders rounded. "She wondered why I was worried about that when I was creating my own . . . my own . . . *landfill* right here."

"I imagine that must have hurt."

"It did. But it wasn't untrue, I guess. It almost seems comical to think about my diligent efforts to keep all this from the trash heap when I'm creating one. Living in it."

"Did Lia's reaction change anything?"

"Everything," Allison said, her eyes misting. "In her. And between us. It was the revelation she needed to finally make the decision to walk out."

"How old was she at the time?" Camille braced herself for the answer.

"Twenty. She'd delayed college to help me out. I know she regrets that. Always will."

A pushy ray of sunlight gained entrance through a pinhole

in a window shade and sent a troupe of dust mites into motion. Mesmerizing. Distracting. Camille had not delayed college to help her mother. She'd sped the process. Regrets? She recognized their odor.

"Let's keep working while we talk, Allison." Camille nudged a storage bin with her foot until it rested in front of Allison.

"I'm tired."

Typical reaction to an emotional touchpoint. "Let's press past that weariness for a few more minutes before we stop. Then you can rest."

Allison rubbed her palms up and down her face. "My heart's just not in it right now."

The heart rarely was the first to get with the program. "We can't wait for your heart to catch up with your goals. You want your kids back. Tell me about Ryan."

The story was like so many others Camille had heard. Too much common ground. The disappointment, attempts to regain control, failure, more disappointment, enabling followed by anger followed by guilt-ridden enabling followed by guilt-ridden anger.

Somehow, she had to make a difference for families like Allison's. Or her own losses might permanently cripple her.

"Did you ever consider dating again after your . . . after the divorce?"

"I'm keeping this." Allison laid the deformed pancake flipper in a pile too far away for Camille to reach.

"We can discuss that later."

"No, I'm keeping it."

"I meant, your ex-husband and relationships and those topics."

Allison eyed the flipper, assuring herself it was still there, and said, "I'll tell you what you want to know. The divorce threw me. It's not that I didn't expect it. I'd been anticipating it for a long time. But when it got real, yeah, it rattled me."

"Did your compulsions ramp up after that?"

"Not right after." Allison's lips disappeared into her mouth for a moment. She swiped at her nose with the back of her hand. "I can tell you the exact moment."

"I'm listening."

"I know you are, and I appreciate that. Most would have given up on me by now."

They hadn't discussed other counselors Allison might have had, private practice counselors not on the social services books. Had Allison experienced rejection reactions from past counselors? Did that contribute to her hesitance to work on cognitive-behavioral therapy exercises?

"The exact moment," the woman said, lifting her chin. "I'd fallen and was hospitalized overnight."

"Was it serious?"

"I tripped in there." She nodded toward her bedroom. "It would have been worse if that pile of clothes hadn't cushioned the fall. Broken ankle. Could have been worse."

"Oh, Allison."

"And yes, I know it was also the piles of clothes that caused the fall. Anyway, I ended up in the hospital, eventually."

"Eventually?"

"The swelling and pain got so bad, I kept passing out. So Lia called the EMTs. But—"

Camille braced herself for the next words.

"But they couldn't get in with the flat board or their gurney. They . . ."

Camille cleared her throat in an effort to stem the rising tide of tears.

"They had to call in reinforcements and form a bucket line to transfer me from one EMT to another. A bucket brigade! And I was the bucket. And everybody saw. They all saw"—she waved her hand—"this. All this."

I wish I could have spared you that. I wish I could have kept it from happening. Right now I'm not sure I can keep it from happening again.

"And, the hospital. Loneliest I've ever been, I think, even though the medical staff kept bugging me for this and that. I saw it in their eyes. They knew what the EMTs had seen. The story probably got to the hospital before I did."

What comfort could she offer? Privacy laws were not infallible at preventing gossip.

"But the moment, that one, the one when my hoarding 'ramped up,' as you said, was when I had to call my ex to pick me up at the hospital after my release."

"Allison. How hard that must have been."

"He'd stopped drinking by then. That was good. Because I'd been his reason."

"I don't believe that's the only thing that drove him to . . ."

Or was it? His home, their home, had been invaded by hoards that destroyed normal life and threatened his sanity. And his wife was unable to resist the compulsion to keep making it worse. But Camille's first class in grad school made it clear hoarding is rarely a solo issue. Obsessive disorders, anxieties, panic issues . . .

"You still listening?" Allison asked.

Her eyes, Camille's mother's eyes. What if she had listened this intently when her mother needed her attention?

"I am."

"He was the only person I could think of to call for a ride home. The kids weren't driving yet. He didn't see much of them, but he'd let them hang out at his place once in a while if they asked. So I took the risk of calling him."

"What happened?"

"The moment you're talking about. In the car on the way home, he said, 'Whatever you do, Allison, don't remarry.'"

"Oh?" Camille leaned forward.

"Wipe that hope off your face. It's not what you think."

"Oh."

"He told me, 'Don't remarry.' Then he lowered his voice to a snarl that still rings in my ears. 'Don't ever do to another human being what you did to me and to our kids.'"

Camille leaned back and covered her mouth with her hand.

"I wasn't just not worth loving. He was warning me to stay away from other people so I didn't ruin them too. So I did."

Words. Where are the words to make this okay? There are none.

"Did I scare you, Dr. Brooks? Are you worried now that you're next?"

"No." She attempted a smile faint enough to look like sympathy and not so large that it made light of what she'd heard.

"If you don't come back next time, I'll understand."

Torn between decades, Cam ached over the words that had so deeply wounded her client and ached for confronting her father because he chose to stay with her mother.

chapter twelve

MAYBE ALLISON WASN'T QUITE READY to be introduced to Eli's mom's book club. Camille wasn't ready to be introduced to Eli's mom. That was a given.

In the ongoing saga of *Chester and the Storage Units*, protagonist Camille Brooks and antagonist Chester Paulson fought an ongoing battle against the bulging containers while antihero Eli Rand (not possessing traditional qualities of a hero, in fact an irritant, but still necessary for victory) hovered nearby in his sharkmobile.

In episode one, Chester refused to leave the house.

Episode two saw Chester agreeing to go to the storage unit but having a significant meltdown before the garage door of the first unit was raised. His memorable line: "It's like knowing you threw the man in prison and can't bring yourself to visit him."

Episode three ended in tears. Eli's. He was so moved by Chester's pain during the sorting process that he cried all the way back to the house, according to Chester, who was so moved by Eli's tears that he cried the rest of the night.

Episode four. Will the young psychologist find a portal

through which to reach the troubled Chester and rewire his brain to process the truth about the objects that hold him captive?

Camille finished brushing her teeth, cleaned the sink, and pushed Pause on her rambling thoughts. She'd known it was a risk to skirt around the landlord's eviction deadline by hauling Chester's belongings to yet another space, and a space that didn't feel at all like home to him. Out of his element. Way out of his comfort zone. Decision-making? Even more difficult.

Today was the day. Something had to happen to unclog the process.

And her car wouldn't start.

Who you gonna call? Antihero.

Eli picked up before it occurred to Camille that she could have called an Uber. Quick thinking wasn't always the best thinking.

"Good morning, Dr. Brooks. Are you on your way?"

"Not exactly. My car isn't cooperating."

"Dead battery?"

"Checked that."

"Hmm. Might be the starter. That model and year is notorious for starters going bad. At this age, it's going to start nickel and diming you to death. Are you sure you want to keep messing with it?"

"Not a discussion for this morning. Episode four."

"What?"

"Never mind."

"Want me to come and see what I can do with it?"

"No. That would delay us even longer. And something breakthrough-like has to happen today. Today."

"Agreed."

"Can you . . . would you mind coming to get me?"

"I have Chester in the truck. We'll be there in twenty minutes, give or take."

"Wait. I—"

Her phone politely told her the call had ended.

She closed her car door, locked it—as if someone could or would want to steal it in its current condition, or anything in it—and made her way through the parking garage to the lobby of the building. It would be a long fifteen minutes anticipating all that could go wrong with this plan. But she was grateful that Eli hadn't balked at having to go out of his way.

He never did, interestingly enough.

She did not, however, relish a road trip, no matter how short, with two crying men.

Eli had sounded upbeat. *Let's hope it stays that way through the whole process from here on out.*

"Keep the car? Of course I'm keeping the car."

A young mom in workout clothes, pushing a baby stroller, stepped up her pace when she passed the woman sporting a freshly washed quilted purse talking to herself.

"Thinking out loud," Camille called after the mom. *That* would explain everything.

She decided to wait outside on the sidewalk, as close to the curb as possible. He'd probably come from the west, so she'd need to cross the street. Should she wait near the crosswalk? This park-the-garbage-truck-so-I-can-hop-in procedure had to be swift and seamless, no hitches. Nothing to draw attention to an Awe-Done Clean and Something Else truck and a driver in a skinny Santa costume without the hat. Or beard. Or white fur trim.

And Eli was more sturdy than skinny.

Cooking classes! What if she could convince Allison to attend a cooking class? No, there'd be at least as much human interaction as in a book club.

Random thought number 314 for the day. Was this how people acted right before their psychologists prescribed a nice long vacation?

The day was a little cooler than the past several. A good day to spread out storage-unit contents in the driveway to give

Chester room to navigate. If they could get through one of the four units today, it might provide Chester the momentum he so desperately needed.

As she trained her eyes to the west, a sound startled her from the east. It grew closer. And louder. Until it was right in front of her. A white garbage truck with red trim. Honking all the way. Classy.

Chester opened his passenger door and hopped out with surprising agility for his age. He held out his hand to help Camille climb in. "I prefer the window seat," he said.

Wonderful. She'd be sandwiched between them. At least they were both smiling.

"I thought you'd be coming from the other direction," she said as she buckled in.

"Eli drove how many blocks out of the way? He wanted you not to have to cross the street. Nice of him, huh?"

Both men were smiling. For now. Chester handed her a cup from one of her favorite coffee shops.

"We went through the drive-through with this rig," Chester said, his voice bearing a hint of pride. "Ought to have seen the look on the kid in the drive-through window."

"Sounds like you two have had a good morning already."

Eli nudged her ribs and shook his head almost imperceptibly.

Chester filled in the blanks. "Didn't start that way."

"Oh?"

"Eli kind of startled me when he showed up so early. He must have come in through the kitchen. Thought I'd locked that door."

"I found him in his bedroom, fully clothed, with a bottle of pills in his hand and a note on his chest."

Camille's heart sank. She hadn't been there. She would have if her car had started. No, Eli had come early. Why? And why would he have entered without knocking? Not protocol.

Chester leaned on the truck's armrest. "I had a bad night. Thought I was at the end. Don't know why I remembered where I'd put that prescription after my knee surgery, but there it was inside the pocket of my funeral suit. Seemed fitting. But I couldn't get the cap off. Ready to end it and I couldn't get the stinkin' cap off the pill bottle. That's my life for you. I just laid there, pretending that it was all over."

"Chester! Eli, why didn't you call me?"

"I wouldn't let him," Chester said. "And he wouldn't let me out of his sight. Don't blame him. I finally figured out, too late, that I could have cut into the bottle with a knife or something. But by then, Eli was standing over me, hollering like I was his own father and he had a right to be that mad. Actually, he started—"

"Don't tell that part," Eli said.

"It's one of the best parts of the story, Eli. You'll get a kick out of this, Dr. Brooks. Eli started chest compressions on me until I blinked my eyes and told him to cut it out."

"I know. I know. Call 911 first, *then* check for a pulse, *then* start chest compressions."

"Good thing my mattress is so saggy, or you could have broken my ribs," Chester said.

Heart racing, anger mixed with relief rising, Camille asked, "Where are the pills now, Chester?"

"*That's* the best part. You can tell it, Eli."

She swiveled her head toward the antihero.

"Well, I grabbed them from him and ran to the toilet to flush them. But . . ."

Chester put his arm across Camille's middle when Eli slowed abruptly for a yellow light on its last blink. "I'd followed him into the bathroom, not sure what he was aiming to do. But when I saw him open the bottle and start pouring those pills into the toilet bowl, it was all I could do not to bust out laughing."

"You did," Eli said.

"No louder than you."

"I didn't know your water had been turned off, so the toilet wouldn't flush."

"Funniest thing I've ever seen."

"There is nothing funny about any of this, men! And that's not the proper way to dispose of—" Camille squeezed her hands together so tight her knuckles turned whiter than the truck. "You could have died, Chester."

"That was the original plan."

"How can you take this so lightly? It's not a laughing matter. You were supposed to call me if thoughts like that came at you again. Call me. And you!" She turned toward Eli. "I don't know what to say to you."

"We wrote a list on the way over here," Chester said.

"What?"

"A list of things you could say to him. I'll just read a few." He cleared his throat. "Thank you, Eli, for disposing of the snake sunning himself on the front steps. I can completely understand why you wouldn't want to use the front door today." Chester glanced her way out of the corner of his eye. "Or this one. Eli, I'm so grateful you showed up so early. And that was mighty nice of you to sit up all night with your grandma since she couldn't sleep."

Chester looked her straight in the eye then. "I added that."

"Read the one I wrote," Eli said, signaling for a left-hand turn.

"Nah, I . . ."

"Please? I think she'll like that one the best."

Chester waited another moment, then read, "Thank you, Eli, for listening to that nudge in your gut telling you to show up early when you didn't have a clue why. We might have . . ."

"Read the rest of it." Eli negotiated the turn.

"We might have lost a good man."

Camille's breath caught in her throat.

"Can't remember anyone ever calling me that—a good man—except Marlene. It's been a long while, anyway."

They rode in silence the rest of the way to the collection of storage units.

⌐

"You do know prescription drugs aren't supposed to be flushed, right?" Camille's anger and relief still battled for dominance.

Eli raised the accordion door on the first of Chester's storage units. "I remembered about two seconds after I tossed them into the bowl."

"And the chest compressions?"

"I've been trained. Honest. And not just from TV. Certified. But it was dark in there, and he sure looked dead to me."

"Forgiven."

"Really?"

"What can I say? You probably saved his life by showing up when you did."

"I promise we can talk about this later. He's on his way back from the porta potty. So . . ."

"Hey, Eli!" Chester called. He thumbed over his shoulder toward the bright-blue porta potty. "I found us another disposal location."

"No more jokes," Camille said. Then more softly, "My heart can't take it, Chester."

"I apologize. You're right. And I'm blessed that you care. You have to know I wasn't trying a grandstand play. I wasn't looking for sympathy. At the time, I just wanted out."

"I know. I do understand that. Which is why my advice to you has always been to ride out those feelings until they pass, no matter how painful."

"It's like with a kidney stone," Eli said.

"It is not like a—" Camille bit her tongue and reframed her next words. "Chester, look me in the eye. Never again. Promise me never again. And keep your word to me."

"It might not hurt," Eli said, "if you promised me too. And even better than either of us, make your promise to God."

"Sounds like something Marlene would say."

"Chester, Eli, I'm not sure this is a good day to tackle sorting. It's natural to feel rattled after a thing like this."

The men traded glances. "I was rattled," Eli said. "I think I passed the stone."

"Good one," Chester said. "I'm not as rattled as I probably ought to be. I'm still here. I guess it's a good day."

Camille turned her back to them. "I was talking about me."

chapter thirteen

ELI WOULD NOT MAKE HER feel like a failure. By rights, he shouldn't have been side by side with Chester all day during the sorting. He should have been . . . idling the engine of his truck or something. She was the hoarding disorder expert of record. The fact that Chester turned to Eli for every decision, and that Eli's nod was enough to get Chester to free himself from half the contents of the first storage unit, was a fluke, afterglow from Chester's near-death experience.

Not that he tried to make her feel like a failure. He was everything Chester needed. A good listener. Firm but kind. Decisive when Chester couldn't be. An antihero without the *anti* part.

Today.

But this could not go on. What did he think he was going to do, hang a shingle and start his own practice?

If she were a better person, she should suggest he consider going back to school. He had a natural knack. If she were a better person, she wouldn't wish this kind of daily distress on him.

Including office days. Tough call—show up for the

mandatory monthly social services staff meeting and allow Chester a breather from the intensity of the last few days, or skip the meeting, risk yet another raised eyebrow from her supervisor, and maintain the momentum Chester was riding.

Momentum—a priceless commodity in the hoarding world. Mandatory meeting in the morning. All the *M* words collided.

Music. She couldn't tolerate music with lyrics or a recognizable melody when destressing or faced with an impossible decision. Too easy to get distracted by the music itself. She turned to the playlist she called *Soothing*. Smooth, random notes with no repeated melody line.

It would either lull her to sleep or propel her to finish filling out her client updates and Chester's incident report. Another one.

How hard would she have to fight to keep Chester as her client? Multiple incidents usually demanded a counselor change, for the sake of the client. Or further psychiatric evaluation, for his protection and hers. Camille's distaste for the default methods and regulations under which she was forced to operate, even as a contracted team member rather than a social services employee, had set her up for deeper scrutiny than other colleagues. But she couldn't imagine seeing Chester reassigned. Not now.

Her fingers paused over her laptop keyboard. How was she supposed to explain Eli and his role? Or the liberties he'd taken with protocol? Or her seeming inability—*or was it unwillingness?*—to stop him?

The administrative changes at the office in the past six months made her job security all the more tenuous. If the podcast would just take off . . .

Did she have the energy to create more podcast content tonight? Something she could use to fortify her standing in the morning's meeting? She and Shyla had only one more prerecorded podcast ready to air. They'd have to work a recording session into next week's schedule if possible. Right now

Camille had a collection of random thoughts no tidier than the amorphous music that floated around her.

She hadn't heard from Shyla recently. Cam googled *recuperation time for hysterectomy*. She skimmed a few articles, then keyed in "emotional recuperation time for child-bearing years hysterectomy." Not as encouraging.

Back to business. She'd leapfrogged over piles of debris before. Almost daily. She could leapfrog over the messy spots in her reports. That done, she scheduled an Uber pick up for 7:30 in the morning to take her to the county government building for Mandatory. She texted Eli to fill him in on the noonish, if that, start to their workday and called Chester.

His voice held a calm she usually recognized as a sign he'd been self-soothing with purchases, acquisitions. But he insisted the peace he felt wasn't rooted in late-day spending. He described it as contentment, a word she'd never heard cross his lips.

All the more reason to keep that forward movement going in the morning. All the more reason for her to resent the meeting that would prevent it.

Sometime while she and The Boys were discussing porta potties and their connection to suicide attempts, her car had left the parking garage, hitching a ride on a tow truck. It would be at least a few days before it returned from the repair shop with which she'd become all too familiar over the past year. Was Eli right? Had she crossed into the nickel-and-dime-you-to-death season with the thing?

He'd balked—just shy of sulked—when she'd insisted on sending her car to the shop rather than have him tear into it for her. What the repair would cost her was worth keeping a safe distance from Eli Rand. *Business partners.* He thought those words appealed to her?

She turned off the music. It wasn't helping.

With those odds and ends taken care of, she focused on the podcast schedule for the coming weeks. They had a sponsor now, which meant they'd have to stay consistent. The sponsorship money came with a catch. Their sponsor would expect a regular pattern of podcasts in order to get his money's worth out of his marketing investment. Cam and Shyla could no longer afford the luxury of a week off here and there. Every good gift came with a hitch. Eli's gift came packaged with increased pressure to make the podcast viable for readers and profitable for him.

Cam mapped out a strategy that would meet listener needs and—she hoped—make a positive impression during the team meeting. The least it could do was erase a few negative impressions with which she'd been saddled. "You can't mass counsel, Camille. No two hoarder disorders are alike. You're grandstanding. Making a name for yourself rather than offering genuine help. This is not a side show. You can't capitalize on your clients' disorders."

No matter how much she'd protested and debunked each point, the negatives kept swirling.

First episode of the new *Let In the Light* series: "It's No Laughing Matter."

A third-grade teacher surveys her classroom of students, watching them diligently work on the assignment she's given them. Some work with heads bent over their paper, scribbling as fast as they can, filling their pages, erasing and rewording as necessary. Others—the ponderers—stare out the window, at the ceiling tiles, or floor tiles, or somewhere beyond the walls, as if they are hawks waiting in the tips of trees for any movement that would feed their idea stomachs. A few—God bless them—sit with crossed arms or frowns that barely fit on their young faces, convinced the assignment is "lame, impossible, stupid."

Eventually they all write something on the page and march, stroll, or skulk to her desk to turn in their paper.

It is as she suspected it would be. Dreams of becoming teachers, firefighters, superheroes (always a few of those), video game creators, veterinarians (as long as they never have to put an animal down), doctors, lawyers, chefs (more of those showing up these days since kids have started taking to the cooking channels), and a few whose career goals include a focus on art, music, business, travel, the theater . . .

Not one this year, not one in all the years she'd taught, turns in a career-goals page listing "I'd like to be a professional hoarder." "I'm working toward recognition as a compulsive acquirer." "I hope to attain level 5 as a hoarding disorder addict."

It's no laughing matter. No one sets out to accumulate more than their house, their mind, and their family can tolerate. No one intends to create a health hazard for themselves or their families. No one intentionally decides to pursue a life crippled by fear, anxiety, and regret.

But we often view any addict as having chosen to become one. They may choose to taste the poison. But none choose the prison attached to the poison. They may make decisions that put them in dangerous territory, but they don't do so to intentionally wreck relationships, sabotage careers, and render them—many of them— penniless and hope deprived.

It's no laughing matter. It's no accident, but the consequences aren't intentional choices either, after addiction and other disorders have rewired the brain, disabled built-in guardrails, unplugged warning systems, and left them vulnerable.

What does that mean for you, listener, if you're fighting an addiction and losing ground? Your addiction, your disorder doesn't define you. You are a person of worth and value, and worth saving. It also means that you may feel reduced to one option only—reach out for help. That is a choice you still have the ability to make. Among your most valuable assets in your path to freedom are people trained in helping you reframe your thought processes, reattach the broken connections between action and consequences, and strengthen your ability to reclaim your right to choose other than what until now the addiction has been deciding for you.

What does it mean if you love someone fighting an addiction?

You reacted to the word love, *didn't you? It is the most effective treatment option we know. You've probably already discovered that you can't change the hoarder. You can't make them stop. You can threaten and warn and beg and plead. And the situation grows worse. It's in addiction's DNA to behave badly when warned and threatened.*

Addiction also raises its fists against love. But this we know. Love is the stronger opponent.

And that's no laughing matter.

The last number she remembered seeing on her digital alarm was 1:37. It had silently blared its announcement that she still hadn't slept. The most she could hope for was five hours if she fell asleep right . . . now. Right now. Now.

But when the alarm found its voice at 6:30, it woke her from troubled dreams she didn't have time to replay. A quick shower, quick hair and makeup session with an extra moment for a double layer of under-eye concealer, quick trip to the closet, and she was in the lobby by 7:22, waiting for her Uber app to announce the arrival of her driver.

The commute to the county building was a study in small talk—her least favorite kind of talk. But the driver was pleasant enough and kept her mind off the thoughts that consumed her in the night and the panel of naysayers waiting for her inside the building.

Group meeting first, then each had one-on-ones with the supervisor. She could probably fade into the woodwork during the group meeting if she resisted her desire to object like an overachieving defense attorney. Contrarian. Someone had once dubbed her a contrarian. Oh, that was right. It was her supervisor, the one with all the clout.

Ack! She'd been reduced to snarkiness. *This is not who I am!*

"Who are you?" her mother had asked during a

fiery—during a heated debate shortly before Camille left for good.

"I'm your daughter!"

"I don't recognize you. The hardness on your soul. The harsh edge. You used to at least attempt to keep your anger from showing." Her mother was in tears by then.

"You did this to me, Mom. You. The question is, who are you? You can't be my mother. A mom would choose her daughter over things. Things."

Seventeen, and she thought she knew it all.

Five minutes into the group confab and she felt the impact of how little she knew spilling over like a science volcano experiment. Her confidence rode waves of sticky, molten emotional lava as it poured from her soul onto the floor. Was she the only one who saw it? The glowing red goo?

New regulations—yes, more—would be implemented on the first of the new quarter. More paperwork. Less freedom to innovate. More procedural steps. Less instinct.

Eli would storm the fortress if he were listening to this.

But she'd promised herself she would not be contrary today.

Wasn't this a no-smoking facility? They all were now, weren't they? That acrid smell. Gagging. Breath stealing. She needed fresh air, but she couldn't bring herself to raise her hand and ask permission to leave the room.

By furiously taking notes, longhand, she kept her head down and mouth shut. The regulations and protocol conversation threw shadows on all that was right with the department. They cared about the people they served. In some ways, it was like medics on a battlefield watching their patients die because they hadn't yet received an answer to their requisition request for more units of blood. And the blood was right there, at their elbows.

Eli had bled for Chester. And brought him back from the dead.

Seemed like a smarter approach.

"Rough week for you, huh, Camille?"

"In this line of work," Camille answered Clout Woman, "most are." She tamed stray strands of hair with one hand and her tongue with what was left of her brain after the group meeting had nearly drained it.

"Anything to report, other than what's here in your official documents?" Greta Brunwald asked, her eyebrows hiding under impossibly short bangs.

"What do you mean?"

"I didn't see a notation about an uptick in podcast followers like last month's report. Has that initial flurry of interest waned, as I predicted?"

"It's not a downward trend, if that's what you're asking."

"Oh? Quite an undertaking though. One has to wonder how it's either pulling you away from other job responsibilities or potentially compromising confidentiality issues."

Ah. Cut to the chase. Chase. "My newest client, Allison Chase, is a direct reflection of the podcast's potential." *And "one" does not have to wonder.*

"Yes." She flipped through the report. "She was a 'fan.'"

"We connected through the podcast. It developed a level of trust we wouldn't have had if she'd merely been assigned to me by the agency."

"Any others? Any other direct reflections?"

"Not yet. But we now have funding to expand our marketing, and that should—"

"Wait a minute. Funding? That didn't funnel through the department?"

"Greta, the podcast is an independent endeavor. It doesn't fall under the auspices of this office or its regulatory umbrella. I'm doing this on my own, with help from my technical assistant. I'm not required to report its activity. I do so because I hope to see a"—how far dare she step into this pile of steaming refuse?—"greater openness to original thinking regarding our reaching those with hoarding disorders and their families."

"So you've said." Greta's office chair creaked, as if weary of the conversation. "But how can that 'experiment' of yours not cost you time and emotional energy that should be devoted to the clients entrusted to your care?"

"They're people. Can we just call them people? And frankly, it's meetings like these that cost me time and emotional energy I should be devoting to them."

"Dr. Brooks!"

"Give me six more months. Will you do that please? Give me until the end of the year to prove the validity of this additional level of resources for our clients, this layer of connection."

"And when you can't?"

"If I can't, I'll . . . step away from this position so you can replace me with a rule follower." She meant what she said, but the consequences of losing the income and venturing completely on her own tightened her throat, stomach, and every working muscle in her body. Her nerve endings vibrated with the negative impact on her current and future clients.

"Now, Dr. Brooks, nobody wants that . . . necessarily."

One extra word. That one extra word sealed the decision. "Six months. Please."

Greta tapped an uneven beat on her desk with the tip of her pen. The wood didn't deserve the abuse. She dropped her eyelids to half-mast. "Granted. Six months. The end of the year. I hope you're prepared for the fallout."

chapter fourteen

CAMILLE BURIED HER HEAD IN her phone as she sat on one of the concrete benches outside the government building. Could she compose herself enough to call for an Uber? Yes. But it might take a minute.

Where were her sunglasses? Ah, she'd loaned them to Allison. The likelihood of finding them again were slim. Small price to pay for the joy of seeing her step into the light for a few moments.

If Chester and Eli weren't waiting for her call, she would have asked Allison if she were up for another visit. She had to find Allison's entry wound. Where had it all started? Allison had already battled the disorder when her husband told her she should never consider remarrying. If Cam could retrace to the first wave of hoarding or other events when it escalated, maybe they could untangle its stranglehold.

She punched Eli's number, now on speed dial. He took longer than usual to pick up. Not a good sign.

"Yeah?"

"Eli?"

"Dr. Brooks. You're done early."

Six months from now, I might be done for good. "Yes. Grateful. What's that noise in the background?"

"Did you know that a female elephant is only fertile for three to five days a year?"

"What? Where are you?"

"We're at the zoo. It's a little loud here right now. Can I call you back?"

"Who's we?"

"Chester and me. Talk to you as soon as I get to a quieter spot."

He took Chester to the zoo? How did he pull that off? Why? She glanced over her shoulder. If Greta Brunwald over-heard their conversation . . .

So much for getting an earlier-than-expected start on the storage unit. But maybe speed wasn't the priority. She hated to lose the momentum, but with Chester's eviction deadline no longer pressing them, her easing up on the accelerator might be what he needed. They couldn't back off on making forward progress, but she'd seen others disintegrate when pushed to tackle cleanup at a pace that intensified their anxiety. The zoo, huh?

Her phone thrummed. "Eli, what are you doing watching elephants mate?"

"Excuse me?"

"Shyla? I was expecting a call from Eli." And she was sor-rier than sorry for the subject matter and for not checking the caller ID.

"Eli's watching elephants mate?"

"At the zoo. He took Chester to the zoo."

"Still not following. That's a legitimate field trip?"

"Shyla, I don't know the whole story yet. He's calling me back when they're . . . out of . . . range. And I don't know what to say after that."

"I need to talk to you sometime. It doesn't have to be now."

"Sure. In person, you mean?"

"Preferably."

Camille swatted at a pigeon that found her purse intriguing. Or the power bar in its depths. She'd had every intention of eating that thing—the power bar—during the Uber ride. "When are you thinking? How soon?"

"It had better be soon. Within the next couple of days."

"We're recording on Saturday morning, right? Is that too late?"

"About that . . ."

Something in her voice spelled trouble. "Are you doing okay physically? Your recuperation is—"

"I'm healing fine. Camille, I didn't want to do this over the phone."

"Do what, hon?"

"Jenx and I are moving back to South Carolina."

"What? When?"

"This weekend. We'll stay with his parents until we find an apartment."

"Shyla!"

"He's had his résumé out at a dozen places back home. One of them came through. Too good to pass up. And we . . . we need a fresh start."

Camille had them—all the *feels*. Sadness, regret, loss, excitement for the couple, gratitude that they'd have family close by . . . Mostly loss. She was losing the closest thing she had to a true friend.

And the podcast! She might as well crawl her way back to Greta's office and admit defeat right now rather than prolonging it an impossible six months without her technical director and audio editor. And business assistant. And fundraiser. And—

"I know what this will do to you, Cam, but Jenx and I have to take this."

"Of course you do. I'm happy for you. Fresh starts are good

things. And family close? That's all good. I'll miss you like crazy, you know." *Gather up all the blue thoughts and put them where they belong, Camille.*

"There's more. Jenx has a niece who's still in high school and is . . . pregnant."

"Oh, Shyla."

"The girl's parents are devastated. Paralyzed. Not exactly what you'd call supportive. We're going to invite her to live with us and help her out so she can finish school next year and go to college, we hope. It's important to us to help her."

"That's brave of you."

"Not sure it's brave. But it feels like something we're supposed to do."

"Shyla, this weekend already? How can I help?"

"The company is sending a moving outfit to pack up and haul everything for us. I should ask you if you want my armoire, the one you bump your hip on every time you come here."

"No." She didn't need furniture clogging up her—"Yes. Can I change my mind? Yes, I do. I'd love that memory of you."

"I'll let you use the sound equipment for as long as you need it. Hope you can find another technician so you can keep *Let In the Light* going. It's important."

"Shyla, I can't hide that I'm just so sad to be losing you."

"That's the down side of this. I'll miss you too. Is that hum I hear Eli calling you back?"

Camille glanced at the phone screen. "Yes, it's him."

"Say goodbye to him for me, will you? I enjoyed our conversations. Wish I could have met him face-to-face. I'll let you get that. We'll talk soon."

Frozen in place, Camille missed Eli's call. He'd hung up. Must have assumed she was unavailable at the moment. She'd call him back as soon as she could jump-start her heart.

"Everything okay?" Eli asked.

She changed the phone to her other ear and paced in front of the concrete bench. "I should ask *you* that question." *And I'm not ready to let you know how not okay I am.*

"How did your meetings go?"

"Next subject?"

"That bad, huh? It sounds like you need a good dose of baby giraffes."

"What?"

"Come join us at the zoo."

Cam could hear Chester in the background. "Yeah. Tell her to do that."

Baby anything sounded like a cry-fest at the moment. "How much longer do you plan to be there?"

"We'll hang around longer if you're coming. Otherwise, we were heading out to the storage units. Chester thought up a great idea for where some of his clothing . . . uh . . . collection could go and do something good for people in need."

"I'll meet you at the storage facility. When will you get there?"

"We have corn dogs and deep-fried cheese curds enough for all three of us, so we won't have to stop for lunch."

"Great. I'll pick up root beer floats and some Ding Dongs."

"You'd do that?"

"No! I'm bringing kale smoothies and a big dose of 'You've got to be kidding.'"

"I see what you did there. Suit yourself. All the more for us. We'll catch up on the news when you get there. Is your car fixed yet?"

"It hasn't even been at the shop twenty-four hours, Eli."

"That long? You'd think they could have figured out—"

"See you in a few."

No car. No podcast. No friend/producer/director/technician. No guarantee of a job by the end of the year. But more than enough corn dogs and cheese curds.

Could life get any sweeter?

She looked up. "Don't answer that, God."

His name was coming up more often in conversation. Sometimes in her conversations. She probably needed to either stop mentioning him or take her for-all-intents-and-purposes dormant, singed, sooty faith a little more seriously.

⌐

Chester couldn't wait to tell her the story about the church group of kids making all the noise in the background while Eli was reading the pachyderm trivia sign in front of the exhibit. No as-it-happened elephant mating. Words on a sign.

He'd been on an adventure, thanks to Eli. A new thought ate the crusty goodness off her gratitude. She had to talk to Eli.

Chester kept rambling. "Eli mentioned this place down-town that provides clothing and training and help with résumés so homeless people can get job interviews."

"I know the place," she said.

"I came up with the idea that maybe that would be a good thing to do with some of the clothes that are hanging in the storage units. Not all of it, you understand."

She smiled.

"But if what I have *extra* could help some folks out, that would make good use of it. Maybe help them get jobs."

"It would, Chester. Great idea." *Do you have anything in my size? I might be job hunting soon.*

"I have a home, such as it is. Seems like I ought to show that I'm grateful somehow. Eli said he'd see to the delivery for me."

"Where is he?"

"Right here." Eli popped up from behind a stack of card-board boxes near the back of the unit.

"What are you doing?" She almost hated to ask.

"It's not so much *what* as *where*," he said. "I can see the back wall from here! I can touch it! This is glorious."

Chester leaned toward Camille's ear. "The man can sometimes get a little overexuberant, but I find it charming. You?"

"Yes. Charming. That's the word I was looking for. Eli, can I talk to you? Chester, would you mind working on your own for a few minutes while Eli and I discuss business?"

"Not at all." He walked toward the nearest stack in the storage unit. "You'll be right back though?"

Never without the need of reassurance. "Yes, sir."

"I'll go through these—Oh. Look at that."

Again, she was afraid to ask.

"What's up, Boss?" Eli asked.

"I'm not the boss of you. Wait. I am. But not. Eli?"

"Spit it out."

He smelled a little of deep-fryer grease, but she forgave him. Chester was happy. "We didn't discuss financial arrangements for this stage of the process. You agreed to two days."

"This? This is just friendship at work. I can't charge you anything for that."

"You can't be serious. How do you make a living?"

"How do you?"

He was a mind reader too? "Not very well at the moment."

"What do you mean?"

"It's a story for another day."

"Time to get back to work then?" He headed toward Chester, then retreated toward her. "Dr. Brooks, we'll talk about finances one of these days. I'm not ready yet."

"*You're* not ready?"

"Story for another day."

She couldn't let her imagination run wild over what his story entailed. It was time to focus on helping Chester learn to fly.

I may be banned from writing for Psychology Today *for life. Or have my license revoked. This afternoon I asked a hoarder to keep something.*

Chester's draft notice for the Vietnam War. It was postmarked the day after the draft was abolished in 1973. He and Marlene had been married only six months. The snafu, he said—that the notice was mailed at all—was apparently due to a clerical error. So he received the notice but was not required to serve. It probably saved him from a lifetime of bad memories. Maybe saved his life.

I made him keep it as evidence that way back then God had been looking out for him and still was.

And I used God's name again. For the first time with a client. How am I going to explain that in my next report?

I would blame my parents for the death of my faith. Or its comatose state. But faith isn't something you can blame on others. It was my doing. My responsibility. If it hadn't been my parents' dysfunctions, it would have been any number of college experiences that shredded it. If I'd nurtured it, protected it, my belief system could have survived all that. Maybe even thrived.

I couldn't blame anyone but me. And even I know that self-blame is self-sabotage.

So I decided to let it be. Let it see the sun once in a while and watch what happens. Will it shrivel in the harsh light? Or grow legs?

"No." Camille moved the words she'd typed from her podcast ideas folder to her journal folder. "I can't share details of a current client's case, even though it's a great story. And I will never be allowed to share anything about God or faith or Jesus if I hope to keep my job."

That was her goal, wasn't it? Keep her job?

chapter fifteen

ROM THE LOOK ON ALLISON'S face, Camille needed to do a better job balancing her time between clients. The woman wore a mask of regression framed in resentment.

"Are you going to let me in?"

The door remained at its customary two inches open. The interior of the home seemed darker than ever.

"Allison? I came as soon as I could. I've missed you. We have so much to talk about. May I please come in?"

"You didn't write me back."

"What do you mean?"

"I commented on your website after the last podcast aired. You didn't respond."

Camille leaned one hand against the doorframe. Another failure. "I apologize."

"You don't owe me that. You don't owe me anything, Dr. Brooks. I just thought you'd forgotten about me."

"I'm here. That means I didn't forget. I haven't looked at

any of the comments yet this week. But I will before the day's over. Can I come in so we can talk about it?"

The door eased open.

Something was different. It no longer smelled of lily of the valley in Allison's home. Something more like death warmed over permeated the environment.

What's that smell? hovered on Camille's lips. She stifled the question. Allison was too fragile at the moment.

"Anything new to report since I saw you last week?"

"Was it just last week? Seems longer."

"Anything especially good or particularly hard?" Was the smell coming from the kitchen?

Allison drew a deep breath, then covered her nose and mouth with her hand and talked through the muffle. "I think my refrigerator breathed its last. Everything in there, the freezer part too, is leaking onto the kitchen floor. It's making an awful stink." She dropped her hand to her lap. "Can't you smell it?"

"Oh, Allison. Why didn't you call me?"

She rolled her eyes.

"Or call *someone*. This is not a healthy environment for you. We may have to move you to a motel until the cleanup team can—"

"I'm not leaving this house."

"Well, we may have reached the inevitable then. We'll find a way to replace your refrigerator, but we have to tackle the entire kitchen. It can't be put off any longer."

Allison drew her cardigan tighter around her, despite the summer heat and lack of air conditioning. "I want to tell you to leave me alone. But that stink is about to make me—"

"I know. Me too. Let me call in the team. Why don't you and I retreat to your bedroom while we wait for them. Or better yet, we could wait on your front porch."

Allison didn't answer but climbed over refuse like a goat on a Swiss mountain to get to the front door.

Same two porch chairs. Same uncomfortable atmosphere, despite the weather's opinion that it was an ideal day. Allison kept her gaze at ground level. Camille was the one who noticed Allison had nothing to fear. Most of the neighborhood was otherwise engaged, not focused on the two women on the porch of the faded-blue house set back from the street.

"Allison, let me get your mail for you. The box is overflowing."

"No!" She huffed. "Oh, I shouldn't take this out on you. You're the one person who's ever been kind to me."

"I doubt I'm the only one."

The woman chanced a glance at where her mailbox stood at the end of her peanut brittle–cracked driveway. "I know what's in there."

"If it's junk mail, I can dispose of that for you before you even have to—"

Allison's look hardened.

"Bills? We need to attend to those bills, Allison. They have to be a priority."

"It's nasty notes from the neighbors. They say I have a responsibility to the neighborhood to get my house painted, that I'm 'ruining' the 'ambiance.'"

Camille's mind raced. If she suggested a solution, would it push her client deeper into the whorl of anxiety that had both of their heads spinning? If she passed off the neighbors' complaints as groundless, would she feed the ongoing problem?

"I know a guy . . ."

"I used to know one or two."

So she hadn't tipped over the edge where all humor slid into the darkness. Good sign. Hope.

"Allison, I know a guy who may be able to help with that."

"He can remove my mailbox? Isn't that a federal offense or something?"

Hang in there, Allison. There's a spark in you. Let it out, girl.
"I think he might be willing to paint your house."

"Then they win." She indicated the expanse of the faceless homes around hers.

"Then *you* win. As much as you fuss about it, you appreciate that Ivan mows your front lawn and keeps the window boxes filled. You may not want to admit it to yourself, but deep down it's a blessing, isn't it?"

"The fool man. Why doesn't he give up?"

"Would you really want to prevent him from those tasks that obviously mean something to him, even if you pretend they don't mean anything to you? Would you do that to him?"

Allison tugged at a pill of cloth on her rapidly aging cardigan. "I haven't . . . run him off. But I'm not going to ask him to paint my house."

"That's not the guy I had in mind." *Eli, forgive me if I'm— Forgive me for volunteering you for something by virtue of your character alone.*

Her thoughts pressed her into the back of the metal patio chair. His character. She'd known he'd say yes to the painting project if she asked. That kind of trust had cost her before. But she'd committed to Allison. If Eli wasn't "the guy," she'd have to find some generous handyman who would agree to help out. Maybe a Habitat for Humanity volunteer with nothing to do for a couple of Saturdays. Maybe *she'd* be the one getting up on a ladder with a paint brush and a new set of ignored regulations and one more black mark on her performance evaluation— helping too much.

"What if I don't want my house painted?"

"What if we chose the same color but freshened it up, removed the chips and peeling paint that isn't protecting anything anymore? Isn't that what we're attempting to do inside your house and inside your heart, Allison? Remove what isn't protecting you anymore and replace it with what will?"

Jaw jutted forward, Allison considered.

Camille watched another piece of mail flutter to the ground and join what had accumulated at the foot of the post, addresses washed away by past rains, messages smeared, unreadable but symbolic of all that was killing her client.

"It's not just the paint," Allison said, rubbing the thighs of her polyester pants. "They think I'm the reason we have a pest problem on this street. Like they wouldn't see a mouse or a rat or a cockroach if I weren't here." She huffed again.

Not a complaint Camille hadn't heard before. And not beyond reason either.

What had driven Allison so far backward? Why had the small steps of progress she'd witnessed after the initial visit disappeared, replaced by even more resistance, a more astringent attitude, Allison's defenses reinforced and more heavily armed than ever?

"Are those people coming for the refrigerator or not?" Allison asked, now slapping her thighs in a steady rhythm.

God, she's tanking. Help me help her!

Camille pointed to her phone. "I'm waiting to hear back. I left messages at a couple of my top choices for a project like this."

"Rescue operation?"

"It . . . it's more complicated than just asking an appliance dealer to send out a new refrigerator and remove this one."

Allison nodded. "I didn't say new refrigerator."

"I misspoke. New to you."

"What if no one can come? No. I know the answer to that. It's my fault. I'll have to learn to live with it. I'll get used to it, like I've gotten used to everything else."

"I can't let you back into that house the way it is right now, Allison."

Her client stood. "You can't stop me. It's my own house."

"Please sit. That's not what I meant. I'm not going to physically stop you."

"I'd like to see you try."

"You do realize I'm at least six inches taller than you, two decades younger—at least—and I work out every day?"

Allison clearly fought back a smile. "You do realize how feisty I am?"

"I'd say we're evenly matched on that front. Please sit down. It's my heart that can't let you go back in there with all that toxic ooze. We'll find a solution."

Polyester pants resumed their post in the metal porch chair. "What would make you care? You can walk away and go back to your—wherever you live. You could say, 'I'm done with you, lady.' Why don't you?"

Was someone barbequing? At this hour of the morning? Burning leaves? Not in July. Ah, memory smoke. Camille's nostrils itched. Her lungs ached.

"I've lived through it, Allison. I told my mother, 'I'm done with you, lady.' And I never saw her again."

Birds sang from a tree in someone else's yard. And a truck rumbled in the distance. The rumble grew nearer until it stopped ten feet beyond Allison's overflowing mailbox. From the passenger side, a one-armed man leaped to the ground, wearing an elbow-length rubber glove on the hand and arm that existed. The driver, in startling cranberry coveralls and similar gloves, two of them, pulled a portable ramp from the back of the truck and rolled a heavy-duty appliance dolly out and up the sidewalk.

Tears flowed down Allison's face. "Dr. Brooks?"

"What is it?"

"Can you ask them to park that thing in the alley behind the house?"

Why hadn't she thought of that?

She left Allison on the porch and ran to greet the men before they reached the house. "Thank you for coming."

"Sure thing," Eli said. "This is my friend Peg, short for Peg-Leg."

"Eli!"

The one-armed man waved off the concern. "Been known by that name since the water-skiing accident. I suggested it. Preemptive strike. I didn't want to be known as Lefty."

"Nice to meet you, Peg. Eli, I know you're set to get to work, but can I ask you to move the truck to the alley behind the house? Less noticeable?"

Eli looked lightning struck. "Should have thought of that. Yeah, sure. Right away. Here, hold this." He passed the appliance dolly to his friend.

Camille reached out a hand to help, but Peg had it under control. Camille glanced back at Allison, who was somehow making a stationary chair rock back and forth.

"Peg, pardon me if it takes a while to get used to calling you that."

"I find it a little too amusing how uncomfortable people are around me at first. And FYI, it wasn't a water-skiing accident. It was Eli's fault."

"Eli's?" *What did he do?*

"And I should mention, too, that we're both certified in hazmat protocol."

The man who intentionally let his finger be sliced open to get through to Chester?

"Part of our role in Afghanistan. We decided to work toward actual certification once our tours of duty were over and we reconnected locally."

Who are these people? "I'm grateful. We may need it. And by *may*, I mean *will*."

"Can I meet your client?" Peg asked.

"I need to clear it with her first. I hope you understand. This isn't your typical getting-to-know-you experience for her."

"Understood. I'll let you take the lead here. Punch me in the arm—this one—if I overstep my bounds."

Camille called off the other teams and services she'd contacted. Eli's and Peg's personalities more than filled the small debris-crowded kitchen.

Allison insisted on watching, tears flowing, which meant Camille was obligated to observe the process too. The curtain separating the kitchen from the rest of the house had been pulled aside, which released the stench even deeper into the fabric of the home.

Minutes into the assessment, Eli called a halt.

"Mrs. Chase, Dr. Brooks, I think it's in everyone's best interests if we approach this as a hazmat situation. I don't like what I'm seeing."

"And I see what you're stepping in," Peg added.

"Clever, Peg."

"No, seriously, man. I see what you're stepping in."

Eli looked at his boots. He addressed the homeowner, leaning against the doorjamb of her hoarder war-zone kitchen. "You can't be here for this. It's a health issue. We'll mask up, suit up, and take care of it for you, Mrs. Chase."

"Do you think any of my things are ruined? I mean, I know we can't save the contents of the refrigerator, but—" Her words died on the way out of her mouth.

"We'll save absolutely everything we can. I'll take pictures to document it all so you can rest assured we haven't disposed of anything salvageable."

"And who decides that?" Allison prickled.

"That's when we'll rely on our hazmat training, Mrs. Chase," Peg said. "We do want to respect what's important to you."

Allison looked into Camille's eyes with perhaps the most defeated expression Camille had seen from her yet.

"Can I take you to a motel, Allison? Get you a room just for today, maybe tomorrow?" She already knew the answer but had to ask.

"I'm not going to a motel."

"Let's see if there's a movie playing that you might want to watch. That will eat up a couple of hours."

"Will there be people there?"

"Maybe."

"Then no. I don't want to be around people any day. But especially today."

Think, Camille. Was it time to force a plan on her? She ached for the day when wisdom would win Allison's battles for her, when hope spoke louder than the chaos and her mind could welcome light rather than shrink from it.

"Let's go for a ride in my car."

"I don't want to do that."

"I didn't ask if you wanted to. Let's go."

Wonder of wonders, Allison followed her to the front door. They both drew in a deep breath of fresh air when they exited the house. Allison's breath ended in a shudder.

"I don't want to get your car dirty," she said.

"It's a loaner," Camille answered. "My real car's still in the shop. Let's see how many miles we can log on this thing before the men are done."

"I don't like car rides."

Camille watched her client settle into the passenger seat as if she were afraid to let her feet rest on the mat or her back against the leather. "Buckle up, Allison. We won't go far. No agenda. Let's get out in the country and drink in a little midwestern summer."

Slow as a tortoise emerging from a coma, Allison drew her seat belt across her lap and chest and snapped the buckle into place. "Do you have air conditioning in this loaner?"

"Absolutely."

"Could we use it? That would be a nice treat. Dr. Brooks?"

"Yes?" She adjusted the rearview and side mirrors. Where was the air conditioner button? Ah, there.

"Can we trust those men in my kitchen?"

Camille stopped fiddling with car features and angled toward her client. "I'm confident we can."

"How confident?"

Good question. "They're trustworthy men."

Allison nodded. Then, "You don't think they'd go snooping around and try to steal any of my things from other rooms, do you? I'm not . . . insured."

chapter sixteen

IT'S BEAUTIFUL HERE." ALLISON UNLATCHED her seat belt and
leaned forward, hands on the dash.

"I agree. So glad we found this place."

"You haven't been here before, Dr. Brooks?"

Camille unbuckled her own belt. "No. I didn't even know
this little park was here. I've driven past the entrance before
over the years, I'm sure. Never stopped to investigate. Would
you like to get out so we can take a better look?"

They were alone in the parking lot of the small tree-studded
park with a walking bridge over a meandering creek. It wasn't
surprising, though, that Allison would hesitate getting out of
the car. How long had it been since she'd been off her property,
out of her yard?

The last time might have been her miserable extraction for
her broken ankle. The hospital stay that wrecked her.

But that still wasn't Allison's entry wound. Camille had yet
to discover the true catalyst for her client's disorder. Few hoarders didn't have one. Abandonment, loss, unspeakable abuse,
or disappointment or rejection or betrayal. Camille had no

delusions of being able to erase a wound like that. But seeing it in a new light or helping Allison redirect her thinking so it no longer threw shadows on all of life might be key to helping her find ways of reframing the pain into something manageable.

She waited for Allison's answer about getting out of the car. Everything about the day had upset Allison's equilibrium. Cam felt her client's stressors resonating in her own body. She'd wait as long as it took.

Her mom used to sit like that in the passenger seat on road trips their family took before—

She'd grip the dashboard like a child, noticing everything. The rising water of the Mississippi or the Wisconsin River. The lone kayaker navigating around rocks. The tree that stood as a lone sentinel on the edge of a field, its branches hooked to the trunk high up, as if it were longer in legs than torso, its arms draped elegantly out and down, like a willow tree, but without the willow's frailty.

Camille's mother had often doodled images of one tree in particular. Its position at the near end of a field probably meant that when the original owner had cleared the land for planting, he'd left that tree as a rest stop, a spot to sit in the shade for lunch or take a moment to wipe his brow while picking rocks or harvesting.

How many owners had later blessed that farmer for his foresight?

Whatever happened to her mother's sketches?

Ah. Ashes. Reduced to ashes.

She leaned her head against the driver's-side window. She might have her mother's sketches now if she'd treated her as she treated her clients. If she'd been mature enough to see past the piles. If she'd known . . .

And if she allowed herself to save things. Or feel things.

"I'm ready now." Allison's quiet words filled the vehicle.

"Ready?"

"To maybe go for a little walk. Not far."

"We won't go far."

"And if a bunch of people show up?"

"We'll come back."

"Okay then." Allison opened her door, swung her feet out, then used the handhold above the door to bring herself to standing.

Camille tucked her purse under the front seat, grabbing only her phone and the loaner keys. She locked the door and followed Allison to the head of an asphalt path that wound through the park and over the small footbridge.

The path was more than wide enough for two, so they walked side by side. Camille matched her pace to her m— to Allison's.

"I can smell the cottonwoods," Allison said.

"You have an especially astute sense of smell, Allison."

"For a hoarder? Yes. Not always a good thing."

"On my first visit, I noticed a lily-of-the-valley candle burning."

"You're a noticer. You pick up on things like that. You don't always say something, but I can tell you're processing information faster than most of us can think it."

"As you said, not always a good thing."

They took a few more steps before Allison suddenly stopped. "You going to answer that?"

"What?"

"Your phone has been dinging since we left the car."

"Just a text message. It can wait. I'll put my phone on silent." She retrieved it from her pocket and reached to tap the Off switch but hesitated.

"What is it?"

"A text from the . . . hazmat team."

"You'd better get that. Maybe they're done already."

"It will take a lot longer to do what they need to—I'll just see what they want."

"Good idea."

"Well, here's something you'll appreciate, Allison."

"I don't want to see a picture of it."

"They sent a screenshot of their hazmat certification." Camille shook her head.

"How'd they know I was wondering about that?"

Or me? She pocketed her phone. "Somehow"—she looked through the tree canopy to the sky above—"Eli just knows."

"I'll race you across the bridge," Allison said. She lifted one foot, then put it down again. "On second thought, the best walks aren't always the fastest ones."

"Right."

Allison leaned on the railing of the bridge longer than Camille had ever seen her sit still. She seemed mesmerized by the water flowing under the bridge. Shallow and clear, the creek didn't even try to hide its pebbled floor. The water kept coming, often propelling a leaf or twig on a wild ride to parts unknown.

"Are you watching that?" Allison said, her voice only a decibel above a whisper.

"Watching what?"

"That tangle of leaves and twigs stuck between those two rocks. Don't know how long it's been there, but as the water rushes over it, it takes a bit of the tangle with it. The mess looked too large to dislodge a few minutes ago. *Now* look at it. There goes another chunk."

They stood together, noticing, until the final bit of the clog unraveled and the water flowed freely between the rocks.

Allison stood back and clapped her hands. The sound rang like laughter.

"Well done," she said to the water. "Well done."

The expression on her face changed. She stumbled backward until she bumped into the far railing and slid down until she was sitting on the planks of the bridge.

Camille sat beside her.

"My tangle's far worse than that," Allison said.

"Same principle."

"A little at a time?"

"Letting go a little at a time until the water flows freely between the rocks."

"The mess looked permanent when we first stood there. Could hardly see anything happening."

"Isn't that how most life changes go? We can't see much happening at first. The picture still seems hopeless. But one piece pulls free. Then another."

"I'm going to tell you something that you can't put on your podcast."

Oh, the podcast. About that . . .

"Or in your reports."

"Okay."

"You promise me?"

"If it's about self-harming or it's dangerous to your health or others, you know I can't promise."

"I'm glad my refrigerator died."

"You are?"

Allison's legs had been bent at the knee, but she now stretched them out onto the sun-dappled surface of the bridge. "I needed to see this."

"I did too."

"Yeah, I know you're hurting."

Allison said it so casually, Camille almost missed its impact. Hurting? Cam was careful to keep people from seeing that side of her. Where had she slipped up? "This is about you, Allison. Not me."

"If that's what you think. Fine." She rose to her feet awkwardly. "I know better."

Camille followed her across the bridge to the rock garden on the far side.

＝

"Does that phone of yours take good pictures, Dr. Brooks?"

"It does." Camille looked up from her screen and the photo she'd taken of the light dancing on the clusters of Queen Anne's lace flowers. She'd zoomed in to catch the fine hairs on its stem.

"Would you take a picture of me?"

She'd never, ever heard that question from one of her clients. It took considerable determination to keep the shock from showing in her facial expression.

"Don't look so shocked."

Unsuccessful.

"I'd like to have you take a picture of me wading in that creek," Allison said.

"Is that safe?"

Allison planted her hands on her hips. "I have a feeling it's more dangerous if I don't. I need a record of this moment. And by the way, did you know those flowers are also called wild carrots? You wouldn't think so, would you?"

"I did not know that. Thanks. I was fascinated by what the light did to them." She showed Allison the image.

"Yes, fine. Now, will you help me or not?"

Allison's spunk was far more becoming than her despair. "Show me what you'd like."

They headed toward the water's edge at a spot where the bank offered smooth entry, a gentle slope to the creek.

"I only want my feet and the water, that's all. None of this." Allison indicated her midsection to her face and hair.

"Do you know how beautiful you are?"

She waved off the comment. "I just need my feet and the water in the picture. Got it?"

"Got it."

Allison kicked off her shoes and no-show socks. Her pink

toenail polish caught the light as she dipped the toes of one foot into the water, then the other.

"Be careful," Camille called, phone at the ready.

"Dr. Brooks, you've seen me crawl over far bigger obstacles than this to get from one room of my house to the next. I think I can handle a creek bed."

She liked this side of Allison. Her personality had room to express itself. "Is that far enough?"

"To my ankles. I want to wade in to my ankles. Cover a scar or two."

Camille waited. When Allison turned to face her, the unexpected smile almost toppled Camille. Her mother's smile, crinkled eyes and high cheekbones and a little gap between her front teeth.

"Please," Camille choked out. "May I take one picture of the whole you? For me? Only me?"

"Oh, if you must. Then quick, get the shot of my feet in this water. It's colder than I expected for midsummer."

"Must be spring fed," Camille said as she clicked, zoomed in on the pulse of the creek washing over Allison's sixty-year-old feet, then clicked again. And again. "Can you turn just a little toward the bridge? If I crouch, I think I can get the bridge in the background."

Allison pressed her hands together. "All the better. Wish I'd thought of that." She moved cautiously but followed directions.

"Is the sun in your eyes now? I'll hurry."

"Don't worry. It feels good on my face."

Within minutes the two women were sitting on the bank, perusing the collection of images.

"I like that one," Allison said.

"Interesting angle, isn't it? It almost looks like you're walking on water."

"It almost felt like it too."

"I'll send the picture to you later."

"Can you have it printed for me? I'd like to frame it and hang it where I can see it every day. Two copies?"

"Did you want to share it with someone else?"

Allison breathed heavily while Cam waited.

"Yes. My kids. Someday I want to send them this and let them know it was a mile marker for me."

"Milestone?"

"Milestone. That's it. A turning point."

Cam had witnessed a thousand turning points in her clients. Most of them disappeared in a black hole of broken promises and the vortex of the hoarding compulsion. But she pressed on, because *most* wasn't the same thing as *all*.

"A watershed moment, Allison?"

"Yes." She picked at the ever-present flakes of pink polish on her fingernails.

"Are you getting hungry?"

Allison pulled on her socks and shoes. "I think I've had enough adventure for one day. Don't know that I'm up to a restaurant."

"My app says there's a summer-kitchen kind of restaurant zero point six miles from here. Salads and sandwiches. They do takeout. You can stay in the car, and I'll go in to pick up our order, if you'd like."

"You'd do that for me?"

"Allison, I've been your foot photographer. Running in for takeout will not be a strain on our relationship."

Allison's laughter refreshed the scene more completely than the spring-fed creek and the nodding Queen Anne's lace. "I suppose you have a point. But I'm not sure I'm ready to leave yet."

"Take your time." Cam scrolled through her pictures. She made it a point that for every new picture she saved on her phone, an older picture had to be deleted. Unlimited memory didn't mean hers was.

She flipped back a year, then two. A friend from college

had met Camille at an alumni event. She and Sarah had kept in touch but hadn't been in contact for a while leading up to the event.

By then Sarah was already divorced. Her husband's infidelity had left her with newborn twins and more heartache than any young woman should have to shoulder.

Camille hadn't expected her to show up at the event, given her circumstances. But she'd made it a point to seek out Cam and reconnect. She handed Cam her phone and let her scroll through pictures of her then two-year-old twin girls. They were dressed like expensive designer dolls. Posed like miniature models. Playthings for a brokenhearted mama.

Camille scrolled one picture too far.

Sarah reached for the phone but didn't attempt to snatch it from her hands. "That. That's what I'm dealing with right now."

The image showed an overflowing kitchen. Dishes and pans covered every inch of what must have been counter space. Cam didn't see a stove top, although there had to be one. The island was stacked so high with toddler paraphernalia that it almost reached the bottoms of the pendant lights hanging overhead.

"My sister's helping me get a handle on it," Sarah said, reclaiming the phone.

How long would it take Sarah to reclaim her life? She had to have known what waited one image beyond the photos of her little girls. It hadn't been an accident that Cam saw it. Was it the only way Sarah knew to ask for help without losing face?

Cam hadn't acted on it. It seemed intrusive. She had to risk stepping into the water with Sarah. If the friendship collapsed because of it, those regrets wouldn't weigh as heavily on her heart as the remorse of not answering a two-years-old call for help.

chapter seventeen

ELI TEXTED AGAIN WHILE CAM and Allison finished their taco salads, a decisively messy meal to eat in a rental car, they discovered. The good news was that Cam had complete control over the disposal of their plastic utensils and the plastic clamshell in which their salads came. As soon as Allison took her last bite, Cam was prepped to collect anything that didn't belong in the car and leave it in the waste receptacle in the parking lot of the restaurant.

She paused, though, to answer Eli's text. It would spell either trouble or progress or a mix. Those men. What courage. She had to give them credit. And a paycheck!

"What's he say?" Allison asked, pulling a piece of stray lettuce from the front of the faded and pilled pink tank top she wore under her cardigan.

"They're going to send a photo of a replacement refrigerator they found at a resale shop. It's a fairly recent model, he says, but it's missing the handle for the freezer part. Says he could create one for you. Oh, and it's dented on the left side near the bottom, but that doesn't affect the function. It passed an appliance inspection, he says."

"I don't mind a dent or two." She pointed to her ankle. Then her head. "How much?"

"Let's take a look at the picture attached before we ask. Oh."

"Too fancy for me."

"It looks like a decent refrigerator, Allison. Not too large, but that's okay."

"Hard to picture it in my kitchen."

"Take a closer look. That *is* your kitchen. Apparently they took it for a test drive. It looks like it's yours now."

"That's my kitchen? What have they done? Where are all my things?"

Oh dear. Meltdown alert. Eli, you might have thought this was helping, but—

"Allison, he sent another picture. A wider shot." Cam swallowed hard. They'd done just as Allison asked. They'd cleared only what was damaged beyond repair and enough to allow them access to the back door but had left everything else as it was. Exactly as it was before.

It was the right thing. A sudden ta-da reveal of an immaculate kitchen couldn't come without Allison's approval, or she'd regress, perhaps beyond reach. Yes, they'd done the right thing. But that meant Allison would return to a home in no better shape than it had been, except for a layer of the odor and fumes removed and a four-foot-by-four-foot clear spot between her back door and a temporarily pristine refrigerator sporting a handle that looked as if it once had a life as a golf club.

He'd made the repair already. With Peg's help, no doubt.

"It's going to take some getting used to," Allison said, still staring at the image.

"Eli said he and Peg went together on its purchase. They had some 'disposable income' that needed to find a home." If it took a sit-down conversation with him, Cam was going to get to the bottom of Eli's secrets.

"They said that?"

"In the first text. Your new-to-you fridge is free."

"It has its charms."

"I'm proud of you, Allison. Do you want to go home and see it?"

She crumpled the leftover napkins and stuffed them into the restaurant's takeout bag, then handed the bag to Cam. "Dr. Brooks, is it wrong if there's a little part of me that doesn't want to step back into my own house?"

"Not wrong. It's a sign of hope."

"Like ankles in the water."

"Right."

Eli and Peg had left the premises by the time Camille and Allison returned to the house. Cam was grateful sunset was still hours away. The thought of walking back into that house in the dark . . .

The curtain to the kitchen had been taken down, probably to aid in odor removal. The men had done an admirable job of that. It no longer smelled of death, merely illness.

"What do you think?" she asked Allison as they ventured into the kitchen.

Allison pressed her fists to her mouth. What did that mean? Holding back tears? Laughter? Anger?

Allison crossed a layer of debris before reaching the clean square, then opened the refrigerator door. "It's cool in there."

"Kind of the main idea of a refrigerator."

"Mine must have been dying slowly. I just didn't notice."

"You're a noticer, Allison. I have a feeling you'll notice even more now than you did before."

"I observed one thing. There's food in here."

"What?" Cam joined her in front of the fridge. The bluish-white light from the interior illuminated a carton of eggs, a small block of cheddar cheese, a quart of milk, and a bowl of blueberries. The blueberries came with a note. Eli's architect-like penmanship.

> *Found these in this dish on the front porch, along with a jar of local honey. Plum honey, the label says. We shoved a few things to make room for it on the counter. Sounds delicious. Don't know who left them, but we hope you enjoy them.*

"Allison?"

"I'm not even going to pretend I'm not crying. Someday I'm going to conquer all this and start doing kind things for people. Someday."

"You're closer to that goal than you were this morning."

She turned to face Cam. "Will you keep telling me that? Even if I don't want to hear it?"

⌐

Cam's apartment welcomed her with a refrigerator-like blast of cool air and an almost endless expanse of nothingness. Nothing to trip over. Nothing to step on or shove out of the way. As empty as Allison's house was full.

Camille's to-do list had mushroomed during the day. It crowded the tunnels in her gray matter. Time to purge.

She texted Eli to thank him for what he and Peg and done and insisted they send her an invoice for their time and expenses. Peg. He had to have a real name. She'd ask the next time she saw Eli. Tomorrow. At Chester's.

So little breathing room.

Everything else would have to wait until after her shower and at least one cup of tea. What a day. What wasn't physically or mentally exhausting was always emotionally exhausting in this profession. But once in a while she was privileged to witness an ankles-in-the-water moment.

She spent the tea's steeping time praying Allison would stay strong in her commitment. Then armed with tea and resolve, she searched the internet until she found the number she needed.

"Hello?"

"Is this Lia?"

"Yes. Who's this?"

"My name is Dr. Camille Brooks. I'm a clinical psychologist. I work with your mother."

"What do you want?"

"A few moments of your time, if that's possible."

"I guess so."

"Is that a little one I hear in the background?"

"I have a newborn."

"How wonderful. How old?" How heart wrenching. Allison's daughter had completely distanced herself from her mother, even during a life-changing event like this.

"Six weeks. Mom . . . Mom doesn't know. I wanted to tell her she has a grandson, but I . . . I can't. I know you won't understand that. Maybe I'm as crazy as she is."

"I understand more than you'd guess, Lia. I'm not calling to do anything but ask how much you know about your mother's condition."

"More than enough." The sentence was tinged with weariness and that all-too-familiar air of hopelessness Cam had heard often from family members of a compulsive hoarder.

"Are you willing to sit down and talk to me about it sometime? I have a few insights that might be beneficial, but I really would like to hear yours. Do you have any idea what might have set this all in motion?"

A newborn's cry formed a backdrop to the palpable silence.

"Selfishness," Lia said. "Pure, utter, boundless selfishness."

The call's disconnect exploded like gunfire in Cam's ear.

She laid the phone on the coffee table and rubbed her temples with her fingertips. That had not gone as planned. Or hoped. And Lia was a better bet than Allison's son, Ryan. He'd left without a forwarding address.

That didn't mean he couldn't be found. It meant he didn't want to be found. Family cooperation usually didn't succeed without family-wide counseling. But addiction was skilled at burning bridges to such fine ash that even the ash disappears with the slightest breeze.

Eli texted. "Sent invoice by Pony Express. U didn't receive it yet?"

She dialed his number. Not that she wanted to talk to him. She had to.

"Awe-Done." A singsong greeting.

"Eli?"

"It's me."

"I've never heard you answer like that before."

"Testing out a new theory."

"Which is?

"I suspect that my brand might still need a little tweaking. What I thought was clever may be perceived as childish."

"No," she said. "Really?"

"You're mocking me. I meant Awe-Done, as in done with excellence and done with the help of an awe-inspiring God."

"Way to be up front there."

"I never intended to hide my faith."

I didn't either. It got buried under piles of debris. "I'm just saying that you may have a legitimate point in rethinking the brand." She'd kept her voice as even as possible, but he probably saw right through her intention.

"Did you have a purpose for calling?"

Enough advice, huh? "I did. More than one reason. First, I can't tell you what it meant to Allison that you didn't violate her wishes regarding the kitchen cleanup."

"It almost killed us to leave that mess when two or three passes with an end loader would have scraped all the rest of the . . . piles out of there. We could have had that whole room sparkling like a new tooth. You have the patience of a saint," he said.

"I don't. But that's a good goal. Anyway, thank you for honoring her wishes. I think she had a breakthrough today. And you were part of it. Can I get Peg's address or cell phone number? I'd like to express my gratitude for his efforts."

"I'll send it. He's in my contacts. I gave up memorizing numbers a couple of years ago for Lent and never picked up the habit again."

Who could not laugh at that? "Okay, Eli. Yes, send it to me when you can."

"ASAP." He yawned.

"Am I boring you?"

"Never."

"You must be exhausted. I'll let you go. The rest can wait." It couldn't, but it might have to.

"No. Nope. I'm good. We meet at Chester's in the morning, right?" Another yawn.

"Eli, I can talk to you then."

"What you don't understand about me is that as tired as I am, my imagination will keep me awake all night if you don't just tell me what you have to say. What is it? You're trading in your beater car for a horse? You're going to—gasp—hang a picture on your wall? You wanted to tell me about Shyla and her husband moving?"

"How did you know about that?"

"I called her for some info. It wasn't a secret, was it?"

"No." She leaned sideways on the couch until her head fell into the perfect *V* in the throw pillow. "I haven't had much time to process the news yet. It could change a lot of things." Like her whole career path.

"What did you say? Your voice is muffled."

She sat up again. "I said that Shyla's leaving could change a lot of things."

"Not the podcast."

"Well, that would be the main thing."

"What do you need?" He sounded oddly energized.

"Too much to list."

"My favorite kind of problem. Where do we start?"

"Eli. Go to sleep. There's no solving this. I just needed to let you know sooner rather than later that the podcast is all but lights out, so to speak."

"Can't happen."

Stubborn man. "Listen to me please. I think it already has. Shyla was my—"

"I know. She was great. And she'll be great in her new role in South Carolina. But she's not the only person with mad tech skills."

Can't listen to this. Shouldn't have called. This won't end well. "Not you, Eli."

"No. No, not me."

For once.

"Peg. He was kind of the 'Goooood morning, Vietnam!' guy for Afghanistan. That's what he did in the war."

"'Good morning, Afghanistan'?"

"Yeah, didn't have the same ring. Actually, it was not what you'd call 'broadcasting.'"

"Ah."

"All underground. But it was working with radio communications, and that's close."

In whose world was that scenario close to what she needed to keep *Let In the Light* going? In whose world was it smart to not at least investigate what it would take to get someone like Peg up to speed? Her six-month reprieve was disappearing fast.

And a world of Allisons and Chesters and Sarahs were suffocating in the dark.

Of all the regrets she'd known . . . "What's Peg's real name, Eli? I can't keep calling him that."

"I don't know if he even remembers."

"Does he have a mama? She'd know."

178

"We share a mom. He's my brother. I can ask her for you though."

She dropped the phone in her lap so she could raise her arms in surrender. Of course he was. Eli's brother.

From a muted distance she heard her name being called. She picked up the phone. "I'm still here."

"I didn't lie about Peg being my best friend. He is."

"It's the 'brother' detail you left out."

"To be fair, are there any details you've left out in your life story to date?"

"We've only known each . . . been working togeth . . . We haven't known each other long."

"So that means you're ready to tell me what you're hoarding?"

What does angina feel like? And why didn't the building manager put a stop to the guy smoking on his balcony. It was drifting in through closed windows. "Mr. Rand, that was out of line."

"We all hoard something, Dr. Brooks. We may not have a compulsive disorder, but we all hoard something. I did. I'll see you at Chester's in the morning."

chapter eighteen

THREE A.M.

The light from her laptop made her squint after four hours of closed eyes that led to no sleep. She punched the key to dim the light and sat with her fingers over the keyboard. It was probably pointless to create more material for her podcast. Maybe these thoughts, too, would have to live in a never-seen journal and help no one. No one but her.

Watershed moments are as much upheaval as they are breakthrough. We see our situations or ourselves in a new light, but the light isn't always flattering. But when those watershed moments come, nothing changes unless we respond.

Camille stopped typing and ran her fingers over a page in the Bible she'd long kept on her nightstand. A Bible she'd dusted more times than she'd opened. Did the biblical writers know how many people over the centuries would open it looking for a soul sedative in the middle of the night?

An ancient philosopher wrote that when we know the right thing to do and don't do it, that's a major, high-consequence disconnect. Families of those with a hoarding addiction believe their loved one won't *change. The person with a hoarding disorder believes he or she* can't *change. Both know the right thing to do. Both assume what's asked of them is impossible.*

But water, even in a slow-moving creek, is powerful. Over time it can polish rough stones until they're smooth, reduce rock to sand, break through tangles of debris and pull them downstream. A watershed moment holds the same potential.

The critical response lies in the space between the watershed moment and our next decision. Will we resist the change? Fall back into old patterns of resentment and hurt? View our impossible situation without the advantage of the new perspective we've gained? Continue to see it as completely overwhelming, impossible, beyond hope?

Or will we step into the light and into the watershed and let it do its thing—change us?

Allison's early morning call set Camille's nerves on edge. This stomach-roiling thing was getting old. Maybe she should take the sage—although scientifically debunked years ago—advice and not go into the "water" until at least an hour after eating.

"Good morning, Allison. How did you sleep?"

"Not great."

"I'm sorry to hear that." *Now what?*

"I didn't mind. I was more excited than anything."

Music to my ears. "And you'd like to talk about it? I'm heading out in a minute to meet with another client, but—"

"I have a story I thought you might enjoy. Guess what happened yesterday after you left."

"What?" Camille braced for the answer.

"I answered the phone without looking at the caller ID. I never do that."

Had Lia reconsidered and called her mom?

"It was a carpet-cleaning service." Allison's laughter bubbled and sputtered. "Can you imagine? Their computer randomly called a *hoarder* to offer 'four free rooms of carpet cleaning without obligation' if I would listen to their demonstration. I haven't stopped laughing. Don't you find that funny?"

I'm so glad you do, *Allison.* "That's a great story. It came on the perfect day."

"I thanked them for the offer and suggested they call back in six months."

"Six months?" At least she realized it wasn't an overnight process to get her home, her thinking, and her perceptions in a healthier place.

"I thought that was one of the funniest phone calls I ever got. And it tickled me so much, I had to share it with you. Sorry to bother you this early in the morning."

"Allison, it's no bother." *It's the kind of thing you'd normally call your daughter to report. Wish you could.*

"When are you coming back? When's our next appointment?"

Could she manage half days with her two key clients right now, or should she still keep the as-needed schedule? "Can I call you later today about that? I really do need to get out the door."

"Sure. That's fine. I've been thinking I might work on my kitchen a little today. I'm inspired."

"And you're inspiring, Allison. Sounds like a great idea. I'll talk to you later."

A little light. A tiny flame. Fan it too vigorously, and it would die out. Not feed it enough oxygen, and it would die out. The never-ending balancing act.

Cam called the repair shop one more time to check on the status of her car. Still waiting for parts. The loaner-soon-to-become-rental—if her car couldn't be resurrected—had grown on her. But she couldn't allow herself to get too comfortable with a vehicle that dependably started, blew cool air through the vents, offered a smooth ride, and had every safety feature she could ever want. All it was missing were the memories.

On to the Chester project. And more than one awkward conversation ahead with Eli.

As she navigated toward Chester's house, she relived Allison's homecoming the day before. What restraint it must have taken for Eli and Peg to do what Allison's condition required rather than what the condition of her *home* required. Who else did Camille know who would have been as cautious and caring?

Eli's experience with his grandfather had shaped him. As had the crippling emotional fallout his grandmother bore. Camille braked a little too hard for a stoplight. The car behind her honked its irritation. No collision. Not even a close call. Good. How would she have explained to the driver that she'd been distracted by the sudden compulsion to meet Eli's family?

Meeting at Chester's home rather than at the storage units served two purposes. Camille needed reassurance that he was continuing with his newfound strategies to manage what came into his house and stayed. And he needed the reminder that he was being held accountable to his commitment to himself and to his landlords.

He had coffee waiting for Camille and Eli. A month ago she would have found an excuse not to accept. But his kitchen remained clean. Dishes were washed as they were used. The accumulation on the counters had grown a little, but at least it was all kitchen related.

How many conversations with other severe hoarding dis-order clients had started with the revelation that the rooms of their homes could no longer serve the purpose for which they were intended? No room to sleep in the bedrooms. The bathtub was too full of closet-like items to be used for bathing.

No place to prepare food in the kitchen. No way to truly live in the living room.

Chester's home, though still cluttered by other people's standards, now functioned. His ability to keep it that way would call on all his internal resources in addition to the external resources Camille could provide through government services and ongoing psychological counseling.

"What's the first thing you do every day after you get dressed, Chester?" she asked over their introductory coffee.

"I don't know. Breakfast?" He glanced at Eli, as if looking for the "right" answer in his friend's face.

Eli shrugged.

"I'd like to suggest a small but certainly doable action to add to your routine," she said. "It won't take long every day. But symbolically it could be significant for you."

"I'm pretty sure I'm allergic to exercise."

Eli chuckled.

"Not what I was going to suggest. But also not a bad idea. Maybe you could work up to a morning walk around the block eventually."

He rubbed his knees, as if the thought made them ache.

"I would like to encourage you to open the drapes first thing every morning, as soon as you're up and dressed."

"I guess I haven't done that yet. Suppose I should."

"Routine. Habit. A good habit."

"Still feel a little *exposed* with the drapes open."

"I understand." She stood and made her way to the front window. "May I?"

Chester nodded, shoulders curling forward.

She pulled the drapes open slowly. Artificial light took a back seat to the sun's presence in the room. "What a warm, inviting home you have, Chester." She made her way through the room. "I hadn't noticed these pictures before. They'd been crowded out before. Where were these taken?"

"On our twenty-fifth anniversary trip to the Grand Canyon."

"That doesn't look like the Grand Canyon to me."

Chester joined her, Marlene's mug still in hand. "Everybody gets their picture taken with the Grand Canyon in the background. We found this gnarled tree with that heart shape where two of its branches must have gotten twisted around in a wind when it was still a sapling. As breathtaking as the wider scenery in front of us was, that small thing meant more to us at the moment." He stood in front of the picture. "That was the last trip we took together."

"Let me get out of the way," Camille said. "I love how the sunlight dances in the grooves of the picture frame. And I'm glad it has a place of prominence now in this room, in your memories."

"I know you're trying to prove a point, Dr. Brooks." His eyes turned down at the corners, but he was smiling. "I don't mind. It's a good point. One worth hanging on to."

"When you're finished with your coffee, we'll head to the storage units and see if we can't let that idea guide us in the decisions that are yet to be made. Okay?"

"Okay." His intention turned away from the photo on the wall to the wide expanse of the front window. "I'm not used to people being able to see in."

"No one's going to get close enough to the house to peer in the front window and see anything during the day, Chester. The light's stronger outside. But even if they did, what would they see?"

"That I'm living life. Having coffee with my friends."

"Yes."

He turned to the picture again. "And that I loved my wife."

"Yes."

He drained his cup and finished by running his finger along the rim in a slow circle. "We'd better get moving before that sun out there gets too hot."

"Good idea," Eli said, gathering their cups and heading for the kitchen.

"Young man," Chester said, "you give them at least a good rinse now."

"I'll have them washed, dried, and back in their assigned spots before you can grab your hat."

"You're on."

"His name's Tyson," Eli said, his back to Chester while the older man sorted through a collection of magazines.

"Whose name?" Camille returned to scrolling through text messages and emails, deleting those that didn't require a response.

"My brother. Peg. His birth certificate name is Tyson."

She looked him in the eye. He was telling the truth. "Like the famous wrestler?"

"No," he said, a wave of disbelief replacing the calm. "Like the chicken."

"Oh."

"And I think he deserves at least a chance to prove he has skills with the podcast thing."

"I don't doubt that." It was all so much more complicated than the way Eli's mind worked. *You have a need. I'll meet that need. Boom. Done.* And how long could that go on?

"He's probably not familiar with the kind of equipment Shyla had me purchase."

"He can learn."

"What about his regular job? How would the podcast recording and audio editing and all that goes with it fit into his schedule?"

"Do you want the help or not?"

It hadn't been said unkindly, but Camille's insides twisted. Who was he to insert himself into her every concern? What gave him the right to assume she had no other option than to rely on him? Okay, it might be true, but what gave him the right?

She wasn't the one who would suffer most if she pushed his assistance away. Her clients would. The podcast listeners, if that resource disappeared. It would cost her in pride and who knew how much financial investment, but he was standing there with what might be an answer—and all she could think of was how much she didn't want to say yes.

"Never mind," he said when she didn't respond. "I think that's my answer." He turned back to where Chester sat, thumbing through outdated pages that no longer mattered.

chapter nineteen

TWELVE SOCCER PLAYERS AND THEIR *coach huddled in the depths of darkness. Their Thai cave exploration after soccer practice had gone horribly wrong when monsoon flood waters rose, propelling them deeper into danger and farther from help. Their plan had been to spend an hour exploring the cave and then return to their homes, their responsibilities, their plans, their families. They'd planned to be home before nightfall.*

They'd tried to back out the way they'd come, but their exit was blocked by the rising waters. They searched for an escape route. There was none. They would have alerted their families, would have prepared, would have taken food with them, if their plan hadn't been to be gone no more than an hour.

Nine agonizing days later, they were located by a rescue team. Except for brief uses of a flashlight with limited battery power, they'd spent more than two hundred hours in complete darkness.

One rescuer died in the flood waters while attempting to save them.

When the boys emerged, they were shielded from light. Their eyes had temporarily lost their ability to adjust to subtle changes in light and dark. They'd been conditioned to the darkness. It's all they'd known for nine long days, or was it nights? Both looked alike to them.

The emotional darkness that enshrouds a person with a compulsive hoarding disorder keeps them from seeing. Normal to them is the darkness, the secrets and shame, the thick shadows of fear. Family members who attempt to flip on a light switch—"Dad, can't you see what you're doing? Mom, this is ridiculous. Open your eyes!"—blind the one who has known nothing but darkness for so long.

Mom or Dad may have intended an hour of collecting, accumulating, acquiring. When they saw the flood waters rising, they tried to retrace their steps but couldn't escape. So they dove deeper into the darkness, taking what little comfort there was from what they found familiar. Eventually they adapted to the dark so thoroughly that light seemed foreign. Distrusted. Unattainable. Blinding.

But there is hope. Reach out for the help that's offered. Family members, friends, realize that the rescue operation will need the assistance of experts who understand the labyrinth, the flood, and the intricacies of extraction.

Your loved one isn't resisting the light. He or she may be afraid of it.

An insistent tap on the window of the loaner car jolted Cam back to reality. She powered down the window.

"What are you doing in there?" Eli asked.

"Getting smarter," she said.

"Well, don't let me stop you from that." His grin erased any hint of snark from the statement. "Although, frankly, you're one of the smartest women I know."

"You don't get out much, do you?"

"You meant that as a joke, right?"

"Primarily. How's it going with Chester? I got an idea for a podcast and couldn't risk losing it."

"The show must go on?"

She turned off the engine that had kept her from sweltering in the car, stored her laptop, and stepped out onto the hot cement of the storage-unit pavement. "The show must at least try to go on."

"Look," Eli said, "I'm not going to pressure you. I'm offering options."

"Bossy with options. I like that. Could be part of your new branding effort for your business." She smiled. They were back on speaking terms. A relief. More relief than she expected.

"The heat's starting to get to Chester. I think he's ready to call it quits for the day."

"He's worked hard. Is your truck any fuller than—"

"We're making some progress. What he's been willing to part with today is rattling around in the back there. A little lonely. But it's something. Celebrate the small victories, right?"

"Right."

"Do you think we're done here for now then?"

She wiped at her brow with the back of her hand. She'd only been standing in the heat a minute or two and already felt its effects. "I have plenty to keep me busy."

"Me too." He rubbed the back of his neck, then wiped his hand on his coveralls.

"Eli, you must be dying in that." She wagged a finger in the direction of his cranberry jumpsuit. "On days like this, you could dress more casually."

"Dr. Brooks," he said, palm pressed to his chest. "I have an image to protect. Besides, my uniform has been my armor against creepy crawlies and dust of unknown origins."

"True."

"Do you want me to take Chester home?"

"You don't mind?"

"It would be a pleasure. The two of us could swap stories all day long."

She had no trouble picturing that. "Eli, could I have Tyson's number?"

"I'm telling you, he isn't going to be happy if you call him anything other than Peg."

"We'll see. What are his work hours? When would be the best time to reach him by phone?"

"He's working late this week. Usually sleeps until ten or eleven, if he can swing it. Sometimes grabs a nap early evening. So sometime this afternoon?"

"I'll try that. I'll see if he's interested in sitting down to talk about producing the podcast. The idea may not appeal to him."

"If I know my brother," he said, "he'll jump at the chance to try something new, especially something meaningful like this."

"Oh, and Eli?"

"Yes?"

"I'm still waiting for that invoice."

He laughed. "You know what they say about slow ponies in summer."

"No. What do they say? Eli? You're mumbling."

"Trying to make up an age-old nugget of wisdom that has ponies and summer in it. Give me a minute."

She watched as the two men pulled the garage door of the storage unit shut and climbed into the Awe-Done truck. Chester leaned his arm on the open window of the passenger side and waved at her as they pulled out.

Was that bulge under his shirt shaped like a small stack of magazines? *Oh Chester.*

"Sarah, it's me again. Cam. I've been thinking about you a lot. I figure the girls must be four by now. Time flies, doesn't it? Please give me a call back when you get a spare minute. Would love to talk and catch up."

Her fourth attempt. She might need to back off for a while. Even to her own ears, the messages were starting to sound like a team leader trying to build her downline for selling something—weight-loss magic, skin-care products, innovative cookware.

She'd wait. But she couldn't stop trying.

Sarah, don't let shame keep you from calling. I had to overcome mine.

She opened her laptop and started a pro versus con list about the podcast, determined to be honest with herself about all of it—the cost, the root of her motivation, the possibilities, and that interesting don't-yet-know-what-to-make-of-it collection of curiosities.

A sponsorship offer. Sponsorship. Check cashed already.

Losing a technician/producer but potentially finding another before the taillights of Shyla's moving van pulled out of sight.

Watching Allison progress faster than normal in part because the podcast had developed a layer of trust between them, virtual as it had been in the beginning.

The flow of ideas that kept coming even when she assumed she'd not have another thought worth recording. What could that mean?

And the nuggets of wisdom she almost tripped over every time she opened the Book she'd grown accustomed to dusting rather than reading. Another this afternoon. About so-called treasures rotting and rusting.

Motivation? She wasn't out to prove anything about herself or her abilities. Was she? No. She was desperate to make a difference. Cam paused in her list making. What propelled that sense of desperation? The need. So many families had no safe or affordable place where they could turn, or they weren't aware of the resources that could help. They slogged along in their pain and broken relationships, in their lack of information and understanding. And it was killing them.

She wasn't their saving grace. But if she could point them—

Point them to it. Pull back the curtain and let in the light.

Cam picked up the phone and added to her contacts list the number Eli texted to her. "Tyson (Peg) Rand." Time to make a phone call.

⌒

"Hey! Dr. Brooks. Thanks for meeting me here."

"Here" was not the quaint coffee shop or park bench she'd anticipated. It was a climbing facility. A rock wall—or series of rock walls of varying degrees of difficulty built around a courtyard with conversation areas, a central fountain, and an equipment kiosk.

From one of the conversation clusters, she'd watched him climb—one armed—to the top of an impossibly high wall, the muscles in his calves showing they were used to filling the gap of his missing limb. She held her breath as he momentarily let go of one handhold and reached for the next. He touched the top, then descended even more quickly.

Cam's mouth was still ajar when he caught up with her in the courtyard.

"Sorry to keep you waiting. I thought I could fit in one more climb before you got here."

"I'm grateful you're willing to take time out for this today. I know you're busy. And you work again tonight at the chicken processing plant?"

"Come on, Eli. You need new material. I suppose he told you my given name is Tyson."

"It isn't?"

"Love him like a brother, mostly because he's my brother, but the man needs to come up with some new material."

"You don't process chickens for a living?"

"Oh, that part's true. Right here. I manage this place. We . . . in a sense . . . help build confidence, turn the chicken-hearted into brave hearts. Plus, it's a lot of fun. Good gig."

"And your name's not really Tyson."

"It's a good name, but no."

"It's . . ."

". . . a mystery known to but a few. You can call me whatever you want, but I've answered to Peg since my last tour in Afghanistan."

"That's when—" She nodded toward the empty sleeve.

"I'm not uncomfortable talking about it, if there's anything you want to know."

The hairs on her arms prickled, almost mocking the fact that for Peg, only one arm would ever again experience goose bumps, sunburn, tennis elbow, a hug. For her clients, a loss like that might have sent them spiraling. Not Peg. Not now, anyway. "Are you willing to tell me how it happened?"

He scratched his head. "Always the first question anybody asks."

"You said it was Eli's fault?"

"He was involved. Yes. Ha!"

"What?"

Peg showed her the face of his phone. "He just texted to say, 'Do not tell her that story.'"

"Annoying, isn't he?" She slid on her sunglasses.

"In the finest ways."

Unusual thing for a brother to say. "Did you serve together in the military? Same unit?"

"No. We trained together. I . . . sowed a few too many wild oats, if you know what I mean. Our parents had about given up on me. Which is why I now never give up on anybody. If I could turn around, anybody can."

"But you both wound up in Afghanistan?"

"Yes. Would you like a bottled water or something? It helps that the courtyard is grass, but it still gets plenty hot out here this time of day."

"I'm fine."

"I'm getting one."

"Then make it two. Thanks."

He whistled to a young man—maybe fifteen—in a sleek black wheelchair. The boy performed alternating wheelies until he planted himself in front of them. Peg pulled a five from the waist wallet of his climbing shorts. "Two spring waters please."

The young man deposited the cash in a zippered pouch under his armrest and did a one-eighty. Peg pulled two icy water bottles from the small cooler strapped to the back of the wheelchair, tapped the lid secure, and handed her one.

"That's service."

"That's redemption. Brandon rarely got out of bed until his physical therapist suggested he hook up with the Coop."

Taken aback again. "Peg, I thought this was called the Co-op. Like, *cooperative*."

"Coop. Like Chicken Coop."

"You used Eli's marketing firm for your branding campaign, didn't you?"

"How did you know?" He chuckled, tucked his water bottle between his knees, and wrenched the cap open, catching the cap with two fingers so it didn't drop to the ground.

She opened hers the traditional way, which suddenly felt boring and too easy.

"You were assigned to different units?" she asked. "Or you served during different tours?" She wasn't a fan of plastic bottles but welcomed the hydration.

"Yes to both. I needed help. Discipline. Order." He drew a breath and considered the sky above her. "I needed to know my life mattered. That was probably the biggest thing. I had an appointment with a recruiter, but Eli could see I was chickening out. And he knew where I'd end up if I did. So he . . ."

"He forced you?"

Peg shook his head. "No, he went with me. Enlisted with me. Said he was going to see me through it. The man left everything."

"His trucking business?"

"What? No. Before that. His corporate gig."

Eli had a corporate gig before this?

"From the look on your face, I'd say you two need to talk."

"I agree," Cam said. "Life has been a little challenging the last couple of weeks."

"So I heard. About the podcast deal?"

"I suppose I should get to the point. I don't know if this interests you at all, Peg."

"Yeah, it does sound weird, coming from you. Just call me Cooper, okay?"

"Real name?"

"Let's say yes." The twinkle in his eyes wasn't all from the sun. "I am interested. Love a new challenge. And I still haven't shaken that drive to know my life matters. Doesn't have to be big. Just . . . worthwhile. You know?"

"I do."

"Investing in others. Nothing like it. If you think I can handle the challenge with my puppet, Mr. Invisible"—he nodded toward the empty sleeve again—"then I'm all in."

"I brought specs about the equipment." She pulled a thin three-ring binder from her purse. "Shyla sketched out the procedures she used, but I don't understand most of it. I was happy to leave that whole side of it to her."

He thumbed through several pages. "Seems fairly straightforward. Technology's amazing, isn't it?"

"If you say so."

"Dr. Brooks, when do you hope to start recording regularly again?"

"Shyla scheduled a rerun for this weekend. Hope to not miss next weekend's broadcast. I should mention that right now I can't pay you more than what Shyla was getting. I should have led with that since it might be a deal breaker for you."

"After all those years when everything I thought would make me happy wound up nearly killing me, I've chosen a different approach."

"Staying alive?"

"That's definitely part of it. A verse in Proverbs says, 'Those who live to bless others will have blessings heaped upon them, and the one who pours out his life to pour out blessings will be saturated with favor.' It's not the favor I'm after, or the blessings. That's all bonus. I'm working on living to bless others. Following in my older brother's footsteps. Haven't been disappointed yet. It's a good plan."

Saturated. That explains a lot about why when the Rand men are squeezed, nothing but good comes out.

Cooper grabbed his half-full water bottle with two fingers, flicked his wrist, and watched it tumble two times in the air and land on its bottom on the low table between them. He jumped to his feet shouting, "Hands in the air! Just don't care!"

Saturated. With just enough weirdness to keep them grounded.

chapter twenty

COOPER AND CAM SETTLED ON a recording date that worked for both of them, then parted ways. She was still two or three stories shy of the full Rand brothers' saga. But every conversation inched her closer to that goal.

Yes, she and Eli needed to talk. But when it came to distractions, he was one of the worst.

Welcome back to middle school, Camille. Your assigned lab partner this semester will be . . .

Back in her apartment, she repositioned her virtual professionalism hat and got back to work. Every hour she spent on keeping the podcast on life support was an hour she needed to recoup for her official assignments. And documentation. Endless documentation.

She considered drafting a resignation letter to Greta, the paperwork pusher. But that would have required more paperwork . . . and an alternate plan for paying her rent.

Instead she started a letter to Lia and Ryan, Allison's children. The words wouldn't come. How would she have viewed a letter like that in her childhood? But Ryan and Lia weren't children. They weren't preteens. They'd been hurt, likely felt abandoned, embarrassed, shamed, guilty, remorseful, artificially orphaned. Cam couldn't let their drama end the way hers did with her parents. Couldn't let that happen. If Allison's children thought they knew guilt and remorse *now* . . .

If it was within her power, she had to try to reconnect them with their mother, for everyone's sake.

Miracles like that weren't within her power. The reality hit hard. She could, however, help facilitate the bridge building. Or give it her best shot.

She opened the document again and fought to wrangle the elusive words. The screen remained blank until the power saver darkened it to save battery life.

Darkness wasn't the answer.

She moved her fingers across the trackpad to wake the screen. *Let there be light.*

Her phone danced on the surface of the coffee table when it thrummed. Had to be Eli, calling this late. No. Lia.

"Lia. I'm glad you called back."

"I owe you an apology for being so nasty to you yesterday. Was that yesterday?"

"Don't worry about that, Lia. I've been in your shoes. I get it."

"You've been in my shoes?"

"I don't talk about it often. But one of the reasons I became a clinical psychologist specializing in hoarding disorders was because of the childhood I knew with a hoarding mother and an enabling father."

"Now I feel all the worse for how I treated you on the phone."

"Please don't. I know those emotions. I know them all. May I ask why you called me back?"

The phone was too silent too long. "I got in contact with my brother."

"Ryan."

"Yes. Life has been so much . . . easier without our mother and her drama in it, you know? But she's never far from our minds, in kind of a tragic way, I guess. Makes me sad to even say that. And I'm all hormonal after giving birth, and I don't know from one minute to the next what's right."

"If I'd known about the baby, I would have waited to call."

"I . . . I don't think I can see my mom. Not now. I don't know when. You say she's better, but—"

"I need to interrupt you there, Lia. Your mother is making progress. But she's not better. That would be a false expectation and set you up for grave disappointment when you see her. She's still gripped by her hoarding disorder. But I have great hope. And I believe that part of her healing is connected to you and Ryan."

"I can't let you put that on me. I thought I could. Even when I called, I thought I was going to say, 'Okay. Let's get together. Let's talk. Let's hear what you have to tell us and reconnect with Mom and tell her we love her.'" The fragile voice disintegrated in tears.

"Take your time. And a deep breath."

"Dr. Brooks, I can't do this to myself. I have to protect myself from my own mother, sad as that sounds. Ryan said he'd talk to you. Maybe he's stronger than I am. I know his wife is all for it. She's been pushing Ryan since they got married."

"I'd be happy to talk to your brother." It was a start. Cam would have to be content with that much for now.

"I'll give you his number."

Was Lia already done with the conversation? "Thank you." *Keep her talking.* She might loosen up enough to give Cam something to build on. "Where is he living?"

"Near Atlanta."

Eastern time zone. Too late to call yet tonight.

"Lia, please hear me. You haven't said anything that I haven't felt. No condemnation. No shame. No guilt, okay? But I'd like to know I have your permission to call you if there's a change in your mom's situation or her health. Would that be all right?"

More silence. Faint sobs. "I don't . . . I don't know."

"Why don't you give me Ryan's number. I can pass information on to him if he's open to that. Do you two talk often?"

"Once in a while. Holidays. His birthday. Mine. We've agreed not to talk about the hard things."

But, hon, we can't get anywhere until you're willing to talk about the hard things. Lia obviously was far from ready. "I hear the baby crying. I'd better let you go."

"That's me. But yes." She sobbed again. "Here's Ryan's number."

Documentation: Late evening phone call from Allison Chase's daughter, Lia. Not open to discussing her mother's circumstances. Gave no hope that she would be soon. That door may be closed forever. Will attempt to contact Allison's son, Ryan, tomorrow. Ryan is married. Lia has a newborn. Allison doesn't know about either.

Some nights, peace and quiet was just plain lonely.

Every sound Camille made echoed in the apartment, magnified by its emptiness.

Nothing had echoed in her parents' home. Early pioneers could have learned a few tricks about insulation from her mother's ability to deaden noise, ward off drafts with stacks of outdated calendars, hide the exterior of the house with overgrown bushes. When she had to be home—no other option—Camille retreated to her room, a sanctuary, until her mother found reason to store "a few things" along the walls.

Cam's space had shrunk to half of a double-sized mattress, the bed frame long sold to pay for tag sale purchases.

For most of her childhood, she cocooned. And prayed for a way of escape.

Tonight, in an odd twist, she would have given anything if her teaspoon hadn't sounded so loud in the sink.

Determination was supposed to have been enough, adequate. She'd been determined to claw her way out of the rubble that defined her childhood and teen years, leave it behind as decisively as an immigrant changed citizenship. She'd taken the classes, studied the language, and claimed the new culture of freedom as her own.

And she'd signed up for the military, in a sense—fighting for *other* people's freedom with her degrees and experience and passion to keep families from turning out like hers.

But her "country" of origin would always be part of her heritage. The ashes of the legacy left to her stuck to the soles of her shoes and the crevices of her soul.

She couldn't fault Lia for her reactions. Cam empathized. She'd not only been there, she was still there, depending on the day and which way the wind blew.

Determination could never be enough. It depended too heavily on her. And she was still a little girl with a tattered suitcase and unwashed dress standing on the Ellis Island of emotional freedom, unable to read the signs, much less help others find their way.

Tomorrow she'd be strong again. Not tonight. Tonight she'd find a bench she could use as a bed, a rolled-up scarf she could use as a pillow, and fall asleep dreaming of a someday freedom.

Her pristine bedroom didn't welcome her any more than a magazine cutout could. What should have seemed evidence of victory instead represented the long miles she'd had to travel from home. The roiling of the sea voyage of school and work, the soul hunger of distance, and the unutterable homesickness when it all—they all—disappeared in billowing black clouds of smoke that made headlines and orphaned her.

She slid under the cool sheets too intimidating for bed bugs, laid her head on the pillow that smelled faintly of bleach, and waited for sleep to tame her thoughts. If she could remember what life had been like before The Accumulation began . . .

But most children didn't have clear memories that young.

"What did you do, Camille?" Her mother's voice pierced Cam's eleven-year-old ears like a siren.

"We can't live like this, Mom. Other families don't live like this."

Her dad walked in at that moment. Well, he crept in around the labyrinthine stacks. "Camille, calm down."

"How can you say that, Dad? How can you—*Why* do you put up with this? Help me, here. We need to get rid of enough of this garbage that we can eat at the table together, sit on the couch together, have friends over, like other people do."

Her mother's eyes glazed over. She was retreating somewhere Camille could never reach. "Mom, we can do this. I'll help you. Maybe we could get Uncle Matt to come in and help us too. He has a big truck."

"What's in that garbage bag, Camy?" Her dad's voice wasn't unkind, but even at eleven, Cam knew it was his no-nonsense talk.

"Stuff we don't need. We don't *need* any of this. Look at it." She opened the mouth of the bag and shoved it toward him. She knew better than to have thrown away any of her mother's "treasures." So she'd been careful to discard only worthless items. Styrofoam meat trays from who knew how long ago. Plastic takeout forks missing one or more tines. Junk mail. A disgusting bagful of her mother's used, carefully—almost religiously—wrapped sanitary napkins. Who saved things like that?

"These don't belong to you, Camy." Her dad handed the garbage bag to her mother.

"What do you mean? They don't *belong* to anybody, Dad! They're worthless!"

Her mother hugged the garbage bag to her chest.

"Mom, come on. Either they're worthless . . . or I am."

A glazed look still commanding her mother's once-beautiful face, the woman Cam most needed to love her turned her back and disappeared deeper into the house.

"Dad?"

"Give her some time, Camy. Give us both some time."

It doesn't take any time to tell your daughter you love her, that she matters. Two seconds. Maybe three. You don't have that to give?

chapter twenty-one

C AMILLE WOKE WITH A NECK ache, a spot she couldn't massage away. Nor could the superhot pummeling of water from her showerhead. The knot of tension had a foothold deeper than anything could reach.

But the light of morning dispelled a few shadows and recharged her internal solar panels enough for her to function. One of her first orders of business was also one of the hardest— the decision to pull the plug on her decrepit car.

Impatience wasn't pushing her to it. A simple text from the repair shop told her the parts she needed would cost more than the car's *Kelley Blue Book* estimated resale value. By double.

An easier decision than she'd thought, if it weren't for the cost and hassle of finding something else to drive. And closing the coffin lid on a rare happy memory.

Choosing another used car didn't threaten her. She was well versed in managing major purchases on her own, even flexing significant negotiating muscles when necessary. That was how she'd landed the apartment. She'd told the building owner what she could afford per month, which was several hundred dollars lower than the listing. "Take it or leave it," she said. "It's the best I can offer."

He took it. So she did. And other than the smoker two floors below her, it had worked out well.

But purchasing a used car—had to be used, considering the current unknowns in her career future—couldn't help but rattle a nerve or two. It'd be good to have a friend accompany her on the search, offer a second opinion, watch out for what she might miss.

Alas, no one fit that—

Yeah. She'd already thought of him. But car shopping was like asking a friend to help you move your grand piano up six flights of stairs. And this could not come off looking like she needed *him*. She needed advice. Two different things.

"Eli, good morning."

"You sound especially perky today. Is it okay to call a PhD perky, Dr. Brooks?"

"Why don't you ever call me Camille? Or Cam? The letters behind my name are a foot in the door in certain circumstances. They don't say anything about my character."

A long pause followed. "I've noticed that. Appreciate it, actually. Your character speaks for itself."

Okay, Eli. You just made my question harder. "I'm . . . looking for some advice."

"Well, I like it."

"You like what?"

"Your hair. I think it looks great. I like that streaky thing you have going."

She held the phone to her chest while she composed herself. A night like the previous one, and he'd gotten her to laugh a few sentences into their conversation. "You mean the highlights?"

"Yes. Those. Anything else I can do for you?"

If joy were a commodity, he could make a fortune, if he weren't alternatingly irritating. "Any chance you have a spare minute sometime today to help me find a good deal on a used car?"

"Bruno bit the dust, did he?"

"I always thought of her as a she."

"Hmm. Interesting."

"And yes. I got the estimate for repairs. Worse than I thought. It's time to pull the plug."

"Do you have something in particular in mind? I can do some internet research."

"So can I, but time is of the essence here."

"Hold on. I may have a lead."

Why did that not surprise her? "I haven't even told you what I was looking for yet."

"I have a few connections locally."

"Not looking for anything in white with a cranberry-colored logo, Eli."

"There goes that idea. And yes, you need something that gets better gas mileage."

Did he just chortle? Was that chortling she heard?

"I was about to call you," he said. "Did you hear from Chester this morning yet?"

"No."

"He's nursing a summer cold or something."

"Could be allergies or asthma from the dust and mold spores we've been stirring up." Always a danger. Like second-hand smoke.

"Could be. I kind of gave him permission to lay low today. Told him I'd clear it with you, of course."

"So that means . . ."

"I know a great place that serves a lumberjack breakfast. And it's not far from the car dealership I had in mind."

"I already ate," she said, eyeing the last blueberry.

"So did I. Your point?"

She did the right thing by calling him, didn't she? "What if we skip breakfast and go straight to car shopping?"

"What if I eat and you talk about the features you're looking for?"

"That could work."

"I'll pick you up in thirty?"

"I can take the loaner one more day and meet you some-place."

"However, if you need to drive a new vehicle home . . ."

"Eli, you seem overly optimistic that I'll find a good option yet today."

"Confident bordering on overly optimistic. Works for me."

Could she say the words? Deep breath. "Works for me too."

⟋

All of life is a muddle of comedy and tragedy, drama cake with joy-jam filling between the layers. The human heart's ability to flip between textures is schizophrenia at its worst, managed chaos at its norm, exhilaration at its best. We cry at weddings, find moments of laughter at funerals, minimize our successes, and craft riveting stories from our failures.

Even hoarder piles tell stories. "I touched this. I gained that. I ac-quired this. I purchased that. I hug this tight. I have. I have. I have. My things protect me." Even when they don't. Even when the very comforts that accumulate are the source of spoilage and rot. Mold. Mildew. Crowding out the things and people that really matter.

Few trapped by a hoarding disorder would say, "I choose my possessions over you." They would insist it's not true. Scream it. Die on a hill of refuse trying to defend their claim that their children and spouse and sisters and brothers matter more. It's an illusion darkness creates. But darkness is indefensible. It hides and mimics and distorts. Only light tells the truth.

Only light.

⟋

Camille scanned the street both ways. It was anyone's guess from which direction Eli might appear.

210

Yes, Cooper. I do appreciate technology. It allows me to capture my thoughts in a document while I wait for your brother. This last batch of words? I think they were for me.

What a pair, those two. Any family resemblance was internal. Her career path didn't often afford her much contact with healthy family dynamics. She'd been well into her teen years before she even knew what that meant. Now, the parameters of her job meant dysfunction came in daily doses.

Out of her norm, she stopped for a moment to pray for Lia and Ryan. The least she could do right now. Or was it the most?

A car pulled up outside her building and into the ten-minute parking slot. She gave it little thought until the driver stepped out. Eli. She wouldn't have the distinguished luxury of riding in the passenger seat of a trash truck today. *Huh. Fun.*

It made sense that Eli owned a regular vehicle, but it hadn't occurred to her to picture him in anything but his Great White Shark.

This one didn't seem like a good fit either. A little more refined than she would have expected. Sleeker. Definitely not utilitarian. More her style.

Her style. *Eli, what have you done?* "Eli, what have you done?" The words wouldn't stay inside where they belonged.

His grin did nothing to assuage her concern. "I brought you something to test drive. This may not be 'the one,' but a few miles of city driving followed by a few miles of country driving should tell a lot. Here are the keys." He tossed them to her—high—as if he knew she'd catch them or die trying.

She settled behind the wheel. "Give me a minute to orient myself."

"You have nine."

"Nine?"

"It's only ten-minute parking."

She located the turn signal, observed the dash readings, adjusted her seat belt, mirrors, and headrest. Then she lowered her sunglasses over her eyes and signaled to pull into traffic. The car smelled new. It couldn't be. He knew better than to show her something she'd fall in love with but couldn't afford. Didn't he?

The engine did that purring thing car aficionados talked about. She'd been grateful when her beater car had made any sound at all. It hadn't for too long.

"Eli, where did you find this?"

"Not far."

"I should have checked the sticker on the window before I even got in. What year is it?"

"It's two years old."

She checked the odometer. "Ten thousand miles? What's wrong with it? Why so few? No, more importantly, how much?"

"You see, there's a story behind it."

"Shocking."

"But it's probably best if we give it some legs, some room to roam. Let's take this exit and see where it leads us." He leaned back against the headrest and crossed his arms. And stayed in that position.

"Eli." She glanced his way again as the exit led her onto a quieter stretch of road, away from the city. "Eli, aren't you going to watch where I'm going?"

"No need. You'll find your way. I'm listening."

"To what?"

"The sound of silence. No clunks. No rattles. No shimmy. No exhaust roar. No knocking. Peaceful, isn't it?"

"It doesn't look like it's two years old. Or like it has more than a dozen miles on it."

"I had it detailed the other day."

"It's yours?" This would never work. What was he thinking? She was not about to owe Eli more money than she already did. He could not manipulate her into—

"No. Well, it used to be. For a few miles. Then I gave it to my grandparents. But as you can imagine, Papaw has no use for it anymore. And I doubt that Nana will drive again. She'd better not, in her state."

She'd have to meet his family. The idea both energized and unnerved her. "So it's basically yours."

"Nana's."

"Do you still owe on it?"

He sat forward but said nothing. She focused on the road.

"I don't do debt," he said with finality.

"Oh. It was inappropriate of me to ask."

"No. It's good to have that in the clear. I don't do debt either direction, owing or asking anyone to owe me."

People really lived like that? How was it he had a *fleet* of trucks without owing anything? Maybe his business was separate from personal in that regard. That would make sense.

"I can't afford a car like this, Eli. It's not that it's over-the-top luxury. It's just a really fine car. And I know without asking any more questions that it's out of my price range, especially this year."

"You're really attached to that beater, aren't you?"

"More than you'd think. Some happy memories of road trips with my parents in a car much like that one. They were . . . different on the road."

She didn't elaborate and hoped he wouldn't ask.

"I really didn't mean to push," he said. "I'm an exuberant."

"Y-y-yes. That's a good analysis."

"I score high on the problem-solver personality spectrum."

"Not at all surprised. And it's appreciated." *Most of the time.*

"But not now?"

"Eli, what am I supposed to do with this? You're showing me a car I can't afford but need. You won't tell me the price—like a used car salesman ready to pull a magic calculator out of his pocket. You don't believe in debt . . ."

"That'd be a weird thing to *believe* in. Debt."

Her stomach soured. Blueberries at war with each other.

"I'm going to watch for a place to turn around. I can't keep doing this."

"I know a place up the road about another half mile that would be a safe spot, if you insist."

She should have gone by herself to a cheesy car lot or found something online like savvy people did these days. She shouldn't have involved Eli.

"No wonder you have such a hard time connecting with God," he said, more concern than condemnation in his voice.

"Oh. You want to go *there*?" And she'd thought he'd be a good source of advice.

"It's hard for you to ask for help. You do it, but you don't want to. You're not embracing the idea that giving is his nature and that you are worth being a recipient of what he gives. Even if it's outrageous."

"Psychoanalyzing the psychologist. What could go wrong?" Her jaw tightened.

"Observation. You pour yourself out. You go way beyond what's expected of you. But for some reason, you've lost the joy of receiving. And in turn that dampens the joy of giving."

She didn't wait for his "great" idea of a "safe" place to turn around. She pulled to the side of the road, fumbled for the hazard lights—too bad they didn't come in extra-hazardous—and faced him, arms crossed.

"Look," he said, "before you start in on me, I wasn't going to *give* you the car. I mean, not outright."

"Oh, Eli."

"I like bartering. Everybody wins. But I don't think I'm wrong about your losing the joy of receiving. Am I?"

"Yes. You're wrong." Her mouth worked hard before the words came out. "I never had any to start with."

He lowered his head. She'd stung him. He didn't raise his head but reached out, put his hand on her shoulder, and sat like that a disturbingly comforting long time.

chapter twenty-two

CAMILLE HAD BEEN CAUTIOUS, BUT when it seemed right, she'd often put a hand on a client's shoulder or arm, unaccompanied by words. She hadn't known how undoing the expression of tenderness could be. How warming and tethering it could feel.

When she looked at the spot on her shoulder where his hand rested, he removed it. She regretted looking.

"It's not that I've had no experience being on the receiving end of someone's kindness, Eli." Nerves or some other emotion pushed out a strained laugh. "A lot of it within the last few weeks, actually. It hasn't been what you'd call a lifelong pattern."

"I'm sorry."

"Don't be sorry. It's not your fault." She laughed harder at that.

"I'm sorry I couldn't have . . ."

"What?"

"Couldn't have met you sooner."

Okay, time to turn this car and conversation around. Despite the hazard lights, cars and trucks passed them inches away, traveling too fast. "You mentioned a wide spot up ahead a ways?"

"Around the next curve. You'll see a stand of pines followed by a stand of birches. You can pull in between the birches."

Hazard lights off. Gear engaged. Drive.

Drive, Camille. Don't think.

If she'd thought, though, it would have made sense that the turnaround spot was the driveway to a property with a big wooden sign edged in and supported by river rock. *The Rands*.

"Before you say anything," he said, "it really is a nice wide driveway, isn't it?"

A nice wide driveway that formed a straight path through the trees until the scene opened to a lush lawn and circle drive in front of a stunning lake house.

"This is your place?" she said.

"The old homestead. We should probably stop in and say hi."

"Probably should." The warm spot on her shoulder itched. Could be developing a rash.

"Looks like the car knew its way home," he said.

"Amazing instincts for a hunk of steel and plastic."

He exited the car. She followed.

"You seriously live here, Eli? Oh wait. Yes. You do." Two matching Great White Sharks with cranberry lettering sat on a concrete pad near the edge of the woods. "You live here."

"My parents and Nana have the big house. Peg and I share the carriage house." He pointed to what qualified as a moderately sized home on the other side of where the wide drive kept going toward the lake's edge. "The carriage house was where Papaw and Nana lived until . . . until he died."

"This is beautiful." Undeniably.

"An old farmhouse stood here for years. It was collapsing around my grandparents' ears. So I—we built this in its place. It's served our family well."

"I imagine it has."

216

"Come on in and meet the folks." His energy was returning. "We missed breakfast, but lunch can't be far away."

Double doors opened into a foyer completely outdone by the view of the lake beyond the great room. All windows, lakeside. A deck that seemed to stretch far beyond the wall of windows in both directions.

And clutter. Not the hoarding kind, but enough to set Camille on edge.

"Mom? Dad?"

"In the kitchen."

The response was so homelike that Cam's heart muscle caught on a rib for a moment.

"Hey!" Eli embraced his mother, a sturdy woman with a deep tan and bright-blue eyes. Her prematurely white hair—she couldn't be that old, considering the youthful appearance of everything else about her—was cropped short and spikey. Stylish. Cute on her. She had her hands in dishwater but didn't seem to mind dripping onto her floor and Eli in returning the hug.

"Eli, my boy!" The gentleman at the small table near the window stood and approached them. He had a many-lured fishing hat propped at an odd angle on top of his head and the weathered hands of a longtime outdoorsman.

"Dad, Mom, I'd like you to meet Dr. Camille Brooks, PhD."

"She's the one?" his dad asked, reaching for a handshake.

"Yes, Dad," Eli said with uncharacteristic caution. "She's the one . . . who . . . is looking at Nana's car."

"Great. I know you'll love it," his mother said. "Not many miles on it."

Camille's internal sigh wasn't audible, she hoped. "I see that. You have a beautiful home."

Eli's mother looked at her son. "We do. Thank you." Turning to Camille again, she asked, "Can you stay for lunch? You've heard of catch and release? My husband believes he's the king of catch on demand. I tell him how many fillets we'll need, and he makes sure that's how many we have to serve."

"I don't think I have time today to stay for lunch, but I appreciate the offer. I need to get back to work. Soon."

"Some other time then?" Eli's mother asked.

Eli's shirt sported wet, soapy handprints. No one appeared to mind. "I thought I'd introduce her to Nana."

"Great idea, son." His father grabbed a pole that was leaning against the door that led to the deck—which did indeed wrap around the angles of the house—and waved a "see you later."

"How is she, Mom?"

"Woke up brokenhearted. Like every day. Go on over there. Dr. Brooks, don't expect too much. She may not even talk to you. Some days you'd think she couldn't. Then other days . . ." The thought trailed off, and Eli's mom returned to her sink duties.

Eli grabbed an apple from the bowl on the island and tossed another to her. Which she caught. "Come on. It's time you met my nana."

They exited the kitchen through the great room again and crossed to a split hallway. One led right, away from the water. The other led them closer. Eli tapped on a door at the end of the lakeside hallway. "Nana? You up for a little company?"

He didn't wait for an answer.

A wisp of a woman sat in a blue wing chair by the window, staring at the lake through a narrow opening in the drapes, stroking a chenille cat as if it were real. She didn't stir when they entered, didn't acknowledge their presence, not even with her eyes.

"This is my friend, Dr. Brooks."

He left off the PhD this time. Good.

"She's the one I told you about, the one who's helping so many people like Papaw. You and I listen to her podcast together. Yes. This is the one."

Nothing. Not even a twitch. Cam was twitching enough for both of them.

"Let me open these curtains, Nana. Dad's out fishing. You can probably watch him take off in the boat."

She turned her head away when the room flooded with light. "Hurts my eyes."

"It'll take a little getting used to, Nana. Give it time."

"I should have stopped him," the frail voice sputtered.

Eli turned to Camille. She drew closer to the wisp in the chair. Her heart clenched for Nana, for Eli, for what had happened to all of them. She sat gingerly on the edge of Nana's bed, which put her within inches of the woman.

"Sometimes," Cam said, "we can't stop people from harming themselves, no matter how hard we try or how passionate we are about it. All we can do is . . ." What? What came after "all we can do"?

She leaned on the arm of Nana's chair. "All we can do is love and preserve and honor their memory."

Why hadn't she thought of that a lot sooner? When it might have made a difference? Or could it still? If not for her, for others?

Nothing changed. Sunlight reflecting off the serene lake continued to bounce around the room as if it were happy to be alive. And the woman in the chair shrank deeper into its cushions.

"Dr. Brooks and I have to get back to work now, Nana. I'll stop in later tonight and maybe bring you a lemon slushy from the drive-through. Okay?"

No movement. No change. A pool of darkness struggling to fight off the light.

Eli closed the door behind them with a soft click. He shrugged at Cam when they stood in the hall.

"You're doing all the right things, Eli. Loving her. Talking to her as if she wants to hear. Not giving up on her."

"That's the barter," he said, his chin tipped slightly upward.

"The use of the car in exchange for your help trying to bring her back to us."

"You know I can't promise a thing like that," she whispered.

"Didn't ask for a promise. Just that you'd try."

—

He drove on the way back to the city. Neither of them said much.

The ten-minute parking spot in front of her building was free again, a rarity. He slid the gear shift into Park and exhaled hard, but still said nothing.

The ball was in her court. She should tell him she would not be manipulated into taking on a new client, even if it was his grandmother. And even if Cam's locked-tight heart hadn't developed a crack where compassion leaked out. "Is the offer still good?" she asked. The rash on her shoulder had stopped itching.

"About the car? Yes."

"I'd be grateful to have temporary use of the car in exchange for conversations with your Nana, until it's clear I've exhausted my resources or she no longer needs what I might have to offer."

"That would be great. Just great. The title's in the glove compartment and—"

"Temporary use, Eli. I'm not sure I could afford the insurance alone."

He smiled for the first time in too long. "Agreed."

"Eli?"

"What?"

"You and your family could have flat out paid for my services to work with your mom, couldn't you?"

"Yes."

"But I needed a car. So you—"

"That's how I saw it."

Was it possible that on some people niceness could be a

vice? It seemed like a pretty deeply rooted obsession with him. She'd seen it in five minutes with his family too. "Eli?"

"Eight minutes before they kick me out of here."

"The keys?"

"Oh. Yes." He handed them to her but didn't move. "Hey. I seem to be in need of a ride home."

"Seems so. Want me to call you an Uber? Or I could drive you home and you could treat me to a lemon slushy on the way."

"Lunch first. I don't do well if I skip lunch. Hangry doesn't begin to describe it."

"We can't have that. Do you mind driving so I can catch up on some work?"

He grabbed the keys back. "Not at all. Do you mind if I . . ."

"What?"

He thought for a couple of seconds. "Sing. Do you mind if I sing all the way?"

"Yes." She pointed to her phone. "Yes, I do."

"Right. Work."

He pulled into traffic, as she had earlier that morning.

"Speaking of work, do you have any? I know Chester has been keeping you busy and Allison's a project that'll take some time. But you seem to be unusually available."

"Another life goal of mine."

She had a feeling that wasn't flippant. He was serious. "You didn't answer the question."

"Do I have work?"

"That one." She stopped scrolling through a cadre of emails that needed attention.

"You've seen my fleet of—"

"Not going to get a straight answer, am I?"

"When I'm ready to talk about it. Let's just say I'm not who I once was."

She leaned forward so she was sure he could see her peripherally. "What's keeping you from being ready to talk about it?"

"What is it always? Fear."

"Of what?"

"Having to admit out loud who I was, what I'd become."

She'd heard it all. Surely he knew that. Nothing could shock her. "Drugs?"

"No. That was Peg."

Cooper. "Alcohol?"

"Quit guessing, *Dr.* Brooks. I'm not . . . I'm still processing some things. I don't have it all worked out yet."

"Some people say I'm a good listener." She slid the phone into her purse.

"Can we call a moratorium on unsolicited counseling for a little while?"

"Can we call a moratorium on unsolicited helping?"

"Point and counterpoint. Nicely played."

"Thank you."

If her phone hadn't rung, and if it hadn't been Sarah, they might have gotten somewhere.

"I have to take this call, Eli."

"Please do."

"Sarah? Good to hear from you. So glad you called."

"This isn't Sarah. I'm Rachel. I'm four. I have Mommy's phone."

"Well, hi, Rachel. Nice to meet you. Where's your mommy?"

"On the floor. She punched the buttons for me but she's not moving now. And I'm scared."

Cam couldn't have felt more gutted if she'd been rammed with a dagger. She hit the Speaker button so Eli knew what was going on. "Rachel, honey. What's your address? Do you know your address?" *Do I have it in my contacts? Yes, I think so.* "I'm going to call 911. They'll take care of your mommy for now. I live far, far away from your house. But 911 will come right away."

"Ruthie's crying, and I can't make her stop, and I can't make Mommy get up and do something about it."

Eli pulled into a parking lot and turned off the motor. He rubbed the back of Cam's shoulders while she talked.

"Rachel. Honey, listen to me. I need to call 911."

Eli pulled out his phone and dialed. "Keep talking to her," he whispered.

Cam took a breath and addressed the little girl. "They'll probably want to talk to you. But I'll stay on the line with you too, okay? When the policemen get to the house, you let them in and tell them everything about what happened."

"I'm so scared."

"It won't be long and someone will be there. A few minutes. Do you have neighbors next door? Or across the street?"

"They're at work. They're always at work."

"Rachel, you're a strong girl. You can do this. Hang on a moment while I give your phone number to my friend."

"Okay." The small voice shook like a puppy caught in freezing rain.

The numbers on Cam's phone swam in front of her eyes. "Eli, can you read the contact number?"

He informed emergency services what was happening while Camille racked her brain for the name of the town in which Sarah and her girls lived. Cam had never written, hadn't had a need to get her address. Emergency services would have to pull it from the cell phone number.

While they raced to the scene, Cam and Eli kept Rachel talking. Eventually the little girl handed the phone to a policeman who'd accompanied the EMTs.

No longer needed, Cam fell against Eli's chest.

chapter twenty-three

N
EED ANYTHING?" ELI ASKED. "CAN I get you . . . Can I make tea?"

Camille stared at the too-empty wall across from her traditional spot on the charcoal couch. *A question waits for an answer. That's how this works. He needs an answer. Expects an answer. Tea or no tea? A simple question. Where were the words?*

"I'll make some for myself, if you don't mind, Camille. You may decide you want some too."

"I thought I already knew *the* most helpless feeling. When my parents died. And I was five hundred miles away at school. But I was also the only one affected."

She heard the sizzle her electric teapot made when revving up.

"Doesn't come close to this. This wins."

"You've done everything you can. Now it's up to the professionals on the scene. Peach or jasmine?"

So she *was* talking aloud. *Rein it in, Cam.* "I have a honey-plum variety in the drawer."

"Yes, I see it. Wow, alphabetical tea. Filed under both honey and plum."

"'Professionals on the scene.' That's almost exactly what the dean of students said to me when she called me into her office." Why would her mouth not obey and stop talking? "The school helped with arrangements so I could get home. Well, to the lot where my home had been."

"You haven't told me what happened. I guess I didn't realize that both your parents died at the same time. Can't imagine."

His voice behind her, where she couldn't see him, offered a layer of comfort, but not enough, like a too-thin blanket midwinter. There, but not enough to stop her shivering.

"Do you think they'll call soon?" she asked, as if he'd know.

"I'm sure they will. The girls are safe with their grandparents. Your friend's on her way to good medical care."

"Do you think I should book a flight? Maybe I should fly out there."

"You don't know what you're walking into yet, Cam. She might need surgery or . . ."

"Right. *Or.*"

He sat beside her, the weight of him barely jostling the couch cushions. She could smell the tea before he set the cup in front of her on the coffee table.

"Do you have coasters?" he asked.

"No. I clean up spills and drips as they happen." Leaden voice. Flat words. Not thinking.

"Too much clutter, huh?"

"That's unkind." She glanced at him sideways. Couldn't have been her most flattering look.

"I didn't mean it to be." His brows furrowed, intensity growing.

How could he be so insistent on pestering her for her family secrets and so closemouthed about his own? She looked away. Stared at the phone. Dared it to ring. Then it occurred to her. "You don't know about Sarah."

"No. Do you want to talk about her?"

"It's why I snapped at you. I'm sorry. The word *clutter* can be a trigger for people. Sarah reached out to me a couple of years ago, and I didn't follow up. Not then. I think she's dealing with compulsive hoarding, Eli. I think her boyfriend leaving her pregnant with twins may have been her entry wound."

"She told you?"

"I saw a picture on her phone. One she claimed she hadn't meant to show me. I think it was a cry for help. And I might have been able to make a difference if I'd answered her cry."

Eli leaned his forearms on his knees. "No matter how many we help, we still mourn the ones we can't."

"Every day."

"And that can cripple us if we let it."

She sighed. "Are you talking about you or me?"

"Both of us." He let the answer hang in the air between them, then said, "You were there for Sarah's little girls in a powerful way today. They needed you, and you were there. And in a sense, that was directly meeting Sarah's need. She had her daughter call you. She knew she could count on you."

"*The* most helpless feeling." The tea scalded her tongue, but its fragrance soothed.

"Tell me about your parents."

"Oh, Eli. Not now."

"It might distract you until that phone call comes." He nudged the phone a little closer to her.

She would have slapped his hand if he'd pulled her phone farther away. It was as if he knew she was willing it closer.

"You know the part about my mother being a hoarder. Class five. An overachiever in that department."

"I've heard you talking with Mrs. Chase. You've given a few hints to that end."

"One of our biggest fears is for the safety and health of our clients. Falling. Being buried under their possessions. Infections. Disease. Breathing difficulties."

"And the inability of rescue to reach them in crisis."

She drew her legs up underneath her. "My mother and I had innumerable arguments about that. She was so filled with anxiety, but that's the one thing she refused to worry about. I never understood the way she thought."

"What happened?"

"More than one incident, as you can imagine. Dad got a concussion from a tower of worthlessness that fell on him one day. He lay there where he fell until I got home from school. Mom couldn't move enough of what was between them for her to help him stand."

She didn't flinch when Eli laid a hand on her shoulder. She didn't have the energy.

"The night of the fire, he got out. I don't know if he was near the front door or what. Neighbors heard him scream for help. They called the fire department. But you can imagine how fast and hot that fire burned with all the fuel it had."

"And your mother was trapped inside."

"She'd made our home a bier—piles of kindling waiting for a spark. They say it was electrical, not intentionally started. I'll never know for sure. I'd caught her fraying the ends of extension cords before to collect the flakes of plastic."

"Oh, Cam."

"A neighbor said Dad got real calm when he heard the sirens in the distance. Eerie calm. And he headed back into the house."

"No!"

"Not running, like a person would if he misguidedly thought he could save her. I think he knew that was a lost cause."

"What, then?"

Cam felt as if she were being asked to pop the lid of a plastic tote full of hoarded emotions. *Resist. Resist!* "I think he didn't want her to die alone."

The stillness in the room was a gift. She'd laid it out there to another human being. Anything he said after that wouldn't have been the gift his silence gave her.

When her tea was gone, she unfolded her legs and stood. She flicked on the light switch for the pendants over the island. Their Edison bulbs fought hard to be noticed with the late-summer sun still strong at this hour. But she left them on.

Sarah's mother called at 6:17. Cam had noted every passing minute until the phone rang. Sarah was doing well. The girls were shaken but, like all resilient little girls, were bouncing from concern for their mom to concern about missing gymnastics class.

"Thank you for being there, Camille," Sarah's mom said. "You may have saved her life. She's getting IVs and all kinds of tests, but she's going to pull through. They assigned her a social worker, and one for the girls too."

"The police wouldn't tell me much about what happened."

"She hadn't been eating. On purpose, I assume. There was plenty of evidence that the girls had been subsisting on a wide array of fast food. I . . . I don't think she could even use her kitchen."

The woman's voice quavered. Cam waited.

"I should have taken those girls out of that house. I should have insisted. It was squalor. Just plain filth. My own daughter." Even long distance, the tears were evident.

"Did Sarah ever tell you about what I do for a living?"

"She listens to your podcast. I started listening too, although I never told her that. I thought it might help me help her."

"You don't need to hear any advice right now. Your being there for the girls and for Sarah matters more than anything. But if you ever do want to talk . . ."

"I do. I need to. After we get through this, whatever it is. Thank you."

"I'm relieved she's going to be okay."

"Physically."

"Please don't give up hope for the rest of it too. You have my number now. Call anytime. And I'd love to talk to Sarah when she's up to it."

"I'll let her know. I'm not sure I'm equipped for this."

"You love her. Let that lead the way."

Camille's muscles uncurled from their tense state. The immediate crisis was over. She let her shoulders relax, surprised at how far they moved when she intentionally let go.

Eli's face was hidden by his hands.

"Are you doing okay?" she asked. Where were his thoughts? His papaw? Nana? The secrets he had yet to reveal?

"There's always a cost," he said, his customarily smooth voice gravelly now. "Always a price to pay for caring."

"Sarah's mom—I wish I could remember her name—sounds like a strong woman. She'll get through this."

"I was thinking," he said, "about you."

"Me?"

"What it costs you to take on these people's pain every day. You signed up for this. You . . . volunteered. And you know the statistics. You know how few will conquer their addictions, how few will stay hoarding sober long term. You're counting on your clients to break out of statistics prison. But you do it anyway. It's remarkable to watch, but it's disconcerting too."

Where was he headed with this train of thought? "It comes with the territory, Eli. I can't not care."

"I know."

"And that was a double negative, so you know I meant it."

The smallest smile tugged at the edges of his mouth.

If she knew one thing as a psychologist, it was that resolution was rarely swift. This wouldn't be the end of the river into which they'd waded. "I still need to get you home, young man. It'll be dark soon." She took her teacup to the sink and turned on the faucet for superheated water.

"Cam, as much as I'd like to introduce you to the Dairy Barn's lemon slushy, I think I'll call my brother to come get me."

Had he been shaken by all this more than she realized? Maybe she'd found his Achilles' heel. Hyper-compassionate. Hyper-empathy syndrome, to be exact. Her heart was still racing, but slowly dropping to a range closer to normal. She couldn't read his mind and wasn't sure she had the right to ask. "If that's what you prefer."

"I'll see you in the morning at Mrs. Chase's."

"You're welcome to wait for Cooper here, Eli."

He turned toward her then. "He broke down and told you his name. That chicken. Thanks for the offer, but I'll wait out in front." He thumbed his phone and headed for the door.

And she was left with a hollow spot on the couch and an empty cup with his fingerprints on the handle.

chapter twenty-four

RAIN. THE DRIPPY, LAST-ALL-DAY KIND. One time when an eighth-floor view didn't help at all. Cam stepped away from her window to the street, for a moment imagining she saw Allison's reflection looking back at her. Allison wouldn't have to try too hard to find an excuse for pausing her progress today. Camille had seen it before—the look of despair at the idea that a hoarder's belongings would not only be hauled from the home but submitted to rain damage.

It made no rational sense. Most of the items Allison needed to dispose of immediately were already damaged, warped, water spotted, soggy. Rain would not destroy what was already beyond hope. But the attachment to items, the compulsive attitude toward inanimate objects, changed normal expectations and responses.

"That seems like something you need to throw away, doesn't it?" she'd said to many a client.

"But it *depends* on me. I can't bear how sad it will be if I let it go. Like I abandoned it."

Not an unfamiliar perspective. Too often, as in Allison's

case, her disorder had caused her to lose her attachment to what she most loved—Lia and Ryan—while clinging to objects that gave false comfort and could not love her back.

But without professional help, she might never see the disconnect.

And without the podcast, Allison might never have gotten professional help.

Who am I trying to convince? Me? Greta wasn't listening. But Camille couldn't deny facts and figures. She needed to collect an impressive hoard of—She needed healthy numbers, tangible evidence, or the podcast would disappear.

Either that or the podcast could stay and her paying job would vanish. Every day that seemed a little less disaster-like.

More and more the lure of working independently tugged at her. But that would require capital and a business model she hadn't yet created. She had no margin financially. As frugal as she'd been and as hard as she'd worked, she couldn't avoid school loans that still nagged like a sink full of dirty dishes. Not that she'd had a sink full since leaving home. Taking years to develop a self-sustaining private practice wasn't an option. Not yet.

Getting on Greta's good side—*she had one, didn't she?*—had to be a priority.

But forcing the numbers game or seeking out clients who weren't ready to accept help solely so she could pad the results was not going to happen.

Continuing to create content, giving all she had in her to the clients already assigned to her, and upping her marketing game for *Let In the Light* couldn't hurt.

Marketing. *Word of mouth is still number one.* But hoarders and their families were among the most tight-lipped about their circumstances. She was living proof. Expecting them to post on social media, "Hey, you have to subscribe to this podcast! It could change your life. It changed ours!" would not be her organic reach.

"Open to any and all ideas," she said, trusting God knew she was talking to him, not the walls.

Decision-making is a life goal for a young person on the way to adulthood. "I can't wait until I can decide for myself."

For a person dealing with a hoarding disorder, decision-making is tantamount to torture. As possessions accumulate, the act of deciding to acquire is relegated not to the specific region in the frontal lobe of the brain designed for that task but to parts of the brain not equipped to weigh pros and cons, evaluate consequences, judge impartially.

The addictive nature disconnects wiring and solders together new paths that flow freely but bypass reason. It takes to the extreme the same impulses that compel alcoholics to fall off the wagon or turns "a little something" into devouring an entire bag of Oreos.

Are choices involved? Does a hoarder choose to hoard? Yes. In the beginning. And some would argue that every act of hoarding or any other addiction involves decision-making.

"I will go online. I won't go online."

"I'll save this. I won't save that."

"I'll set this aside for later. I'll decide now."

"I'll satisfy my craving. I'll ignore or starve or turn a deaf ear to my craving and make a wiser decision."

But the internal mechanism for making those choices is skewed. Until the wires are untangled, nothing sensible makes sense. When power is abdicated to the addiction, the addict is subject to it, unaware that no papers were signed, no contract initialed. It was in a way a hostile takeover. But it is possible to reclaim the right to decide. Not without collateral damage. Not without emotional bloodshed. And rarely without family support.

"What would you like to do with this, Allison?" Camille used her "I'm on your side" voice, but the slump of Allison's shoulders said she wasn't buying it.

"It's part of a set," Allison said. "The others are around here somewhere."

"How long has it been since you saw the rest of the set?"

"Don't get me flustered. It's been a while, but I know they're here."

Eli shot a sympathetic glance through the doorway from the kitchen, where he'd been given permission to gather empty cans for recycling.

"Tell me the story behind this pine cone, Allison. I'd like to hear about it."

The woman pinched the bridge of her nose. "My kids used to bring me pine cones from the park when they were little. No matter how many times it happened, they always seemed surprised their hands were sticky with sap at the end of their excursions."

"Did you start saving them with the first one?"

"Yes. But life got busy, and I told them to stop."

"Oh."

"I told them they were nothing special and they were making a mess. I said that. That their gift was nothing special. What kind of mother does that?"

Such tangles. "It sounds as if you almost instantly regretted it. You kept what they'd brought."

Allison sank into her chair—her go-to refuge when overwhelmed. "Not because they had any real value. But because I'd made my kids think they didn't. I don't dare throw them away. You see?"

"That was years ago. This one's crumbling to dust on the edges. It doesn't smell like pine anymore. It smells more like regret."

"I suppose it does."

"If we could find something here that was a positive memory of you and your children, do you think that would be more valuable to hang on to than something that intensifies your regret every time you see it?"

"I deserve the reminder of what I did."

"How is this serving you?"

"Serving me? I'll never turn down a gift from one of my kids, or any kid, again. That's how."

"And that conviction is driven deep inside you, isn't it?" Camille watched for muscle movement on Allison's face.

"Deep inside."

"So it has served its purpose. It taught you a life lesson you'll never forget. It did such a good job that you didn't even have to have this pine cone and its friends near you to stick to your determination not to let that happen again."

"But what if I forget?"

"How can you? A pine cone in the forest eventually becomes mulch, fertilizer for what grows on the forest floor. This one has already become mulch. It's fed an important truth that is growing inside you. Something took root. A new way of looking at small, meaningless gifts from children. I would guess that you can't pass a pine tree without a reminder."

"So it worked itself out of a job?"

"That's a great way of looking at it."

"Keep the regret. Get rid of the reminder of the regret?"

Camille laughed. "I think I'd rather word it, 'Keep the life lesson. Get rid of the spent reminder and the regret it once represented.'"

Allison rubbed her finger against the grain of the cone's scales. More crumbled in her hands. "That tree in the front yard looks like it could use some mulch."

"I agree."

Eli joined them. "Do you want me to hunt down the rest of the pine cones?"

Mr. Exuberant. "I think we'll take care of this one and discover the others naturally as we come to them."

"Got it. I'll . . . get back to work in the kitchen."

He'd been uncomfortably quiet since arriving a few hours earlier. Cam never thought she'd accuse Eli of being uncomfortably quiet. Ever. What was going on in his mind?

And why was she letting him distract her? They had a houseful of clutter to clean out—one pine cone at a time, apparently.

"Allison, let's see if we can make a dent in some of your books. We only have a couple of hours before Kimberly and her team get here. Then Eli and I will need to move on to another client for the rest of the day. If you and I can establish a system that works for you, Kimberly can take over and implement your plan. And you can always call me if you have questions. Sound good?"

"My books are off-limits."

Not unexpected. "Which are your favorites?"

"All of them."

"Then you might be in favor of an idea I have."

Allison tilted her head, as if trying to make sense of what she thought she'd heard. "What is it?"

"I suggest we turn the third bedroom into a library. It's possible you have duplicate books here, and if so, I'm sure you're probably ready to let someone else benefit from the duplicates. But we'll try to keep all that we can. On shelves. Organized. So you can find them or just walk into that library room whenever you want and gaze at them."

"You're not going to make me throw them away?"

Camille picked up a nearby copy of a classic amid the piles of accumulation carnage. She ran her hand over the textured cover. Allison reached as if to grab it from her, but stopped.

"We may find books," Cam said, "that are water damaged or mildewed. Some of those can be treated. Others may not be reclaimable. But I can tell that you've taken particular care of your books, even if they are currently in a jumble of stacks."

"I always dreamed of having my own library. That's what this was supposed to be when I started collecting. I ran out of shelf space a long time ago, so . . ."

"So that will be one of our first orders of business. Getting your third bedroom converted to a library, lined floor to ceiling with bookshelves so you can care for them as you've always wanted, keep them from bending, breaking, getting lost or damaged."

Allison's eyes filled. "No one's respected my things before."

"I'm not advocating your acquiring more books right now though." Cam made sure Allison could see the mirth on her face.

"I'd wonder about you if you did."

Good. Sense of humor showing itself today. "You have a significant collection already. They're not organized, so they're not as accessible as you need them to be. But because they're that important to you, we will make room for them."

"Can I have a chair in there too?"

"Of course. A reader needs a reading chair and a good lamp. Can't read without good light."

Allison let her head fall back against the headrest, then popped back up. "Not this chair though. It's not reading comfortable."

"You and I will create a lovely reading corner for you, Allison. I think it may well become your favorite room."

"I can see that."

And now for the punch line. "In order for us to do that, in order to make room for these books, we'll need to completely empty that third bedroom."

Allison's eyes widened like a toddler seeing fireworks for the first time. And hearing the sonic boom. "I can't imagine."

"You can do it. You're prioritizing what matters most. Not what *matters*. It all does. But what matters *most*."

"Yes. And then when it all looks pretty, maybe Lia and Ryan will come for a visit? Lia can have my room, and Ryan can take the second bedroom when it's fixed up, and I'll sleep in my reading chair. I won't mind."

I'd give anything to be able to promise you that, Allison.

chapter twenty-five

ELI CLIMBED INTO THE PASSENGER seat of her smells-like-new car. They planned to leave the first truck of his fleet at Allison's for Kimberly and the team to fill while Camille and Eli worked with Chester. Cooper and Eli had dropped the second truck at the storage units predawn.

"Is that Ivan?" Eli asked as Cam reached to start the car.

"It is. Do you think he wants to talk to us? He's just standing there."

"Looks a little lost."

She unbuckled her seat belt. "Are you coming?"

"I guess I am."

"Ivan, I'm Dr. Camille Brooks. We haven't officially met. But I've heard about you, and I've seen the evidence of your kindness to Allison. Thank you."

Eli shook his hand. "Eli Rand. Nice to meet you, Ivan."

"I usually try to stay out of Allison's way," the older gentleman said, hat in his hand, rain dripping onto his receding forehead. "But I wondered if there was something I could do. To help."

Camille shielded her eyes from the rain.

"Bad timing on my part," Ivan said.

"Your reputation precedes you, Ivan. You have impeccable timing," Eli said. "Ordinarily."

Cam elbowed him. "Can we talk on the porch and stay a little drier?"

"Sure." He sauntered toward the porch on which he'd so often stood, near a door never opened to him.

"Lots of . . . activity here lately," he said. "Allison's okay?"

"Better than she's been in a while, Ivan." Cam shook rain from her hair.

"Good. That's good."

"You've been so faithful to her," she said. "I don't know many friends who would have not walked away a long time ago."

"Not in my nature," he said, slapping his hat on his thigh and repositioning it on his head. "I know she's been hurting. I know what she's living with in there. I don't understand it all."

"Few do," Camille said. "But God bless you for continuing to show up, mow the lawn, bring small treats."

Eli stepped forward. "Do you clear her sidewalk and driveway in the winter too?"

"It's not much. But it's something. Everybody has something they can offer another person, right?"

Cam put her hand to her chest. "Please know how much I appreciate it. It's good to know you're looking out for her."

"You don't think I should mind my own business? I'm not making things worse?"

Eli and Camille exchanged glances. She said, "You have for a very long time made life better for her, even when she hasn't been able to express it to you. She notices. You matter. And I believe that one day she'll find her voice to tell you so."

"Sometimes when she opens the door a crack, I hear her whisper, 'You old fool.' I ignore it. I know that's not who she is deep inside. She's a wonderful woman going through a tough spell."

"A very long tough spell. Yes, Ivan."

"If it makes you feel any better, Dr. Brooks calls *me* an old fool too." Eli seemed especially proud of himself for that one.

"Eli, do you prefer to wait in the car?" She nodded that direction.

"No, I'm good."

That smile. That irrepressible, exasperating smile.

"I wonder," Ivan said, "if I could give you my phone number, in case she should ever need something. Or if you do. I don't look it, but I'm strong."

"I'd love to have your number," Cam said.

He handed her an envelope with his number in the upper left-hand corner. "I wrote her a little note, if you ever think it's an appropriate time to give it to her."

"You're a remarkable man, Ivan Probst. I'll watch for the right moment."

"Thank you. So you two were heading out?"

"I have another appointment. We do have to be going. What brought you here on a day like this?"

"Once in a while I check the rain gutters for her. Make sure everything's working like it should. Best day to tell is a rainy day."

Eli shook Ivan's hand again. "We won't keep you from it then."

"Feel free," Cam said, "to stop by again when we're here. You may have insights that will help me in addition to what you're doing to lift her spirits."

"I'll do that. You have a great afternoon."

A few blocks into their road trip to pick up Chester, Eli asked, "What were you doing when you were eight years old, Cam?"

His out-of-the-blue question prickled the back of her arms. She cranked the air conditioner to a cooler setting. Hard to keep ahead of the humidity with a steady, warm rain like that. But cool air and rain dampened clothes are an awkward combo.

"Why do you ask?"

"I'd started my first business."

"At eight?"

"First official business. The others were testing the waters."

"What kind of entrepreneurship does an eight-year-old aspire to?"

"I made Dutch apple pies and sold them door-to-door."

"At that age?"

"What can I say? I was gifted. Do you mind if I turn the air conditioner a little warmer?"

"Go ahead. Did you think that a kid might need a permit for a business like that?"

Eli sighed. "Could have pulled it off if I hadn't decided to advertise on an abandoned billboard."

"Eli!"

"Cooper did the climbing. I just told him what to spray-paint up there."

"How much of this is true and how much is imagination?"

"True. All of it."

"You must have given your mother fits."

He turned in his seat. "That's exactly the word she used. Fits. For a while, Papaw called me Fitz. He got a kick out of that."

"I take it when the apple pie business crumbled . . ."

"Ah. I see what you did there."

". . . you created a new business venture?"

"Several. Always had some moneymaking venture going. What were you doing at eight years old?"

A knot formed in her stomach, harder than a plum pit. Buried deep, but real. "I was begging my parents to let me go, to let me live with a foster family."

The nearer they drew to Chester's house, the thicker the silence grew. Over the noise of traffic and the splatter of raindrops and the *squee-gee* of windshield wipers, she could hear

Eli breathing. Breathing louder on the exhale than the inhale. She'd derailed his train of thought. Why did she resist getting it back on track?

She was over it. Her eight-year-old self had survived not getting her wish. As much as she wanted to know where Eli had been heading with his entrepreneurial escapades from his youth, he didn't appear eager to reintroduce that subject.

Look, Eli. You have to understand that it's okay now. I lived through it all. It's over, that season of my life. It made me stronger. Moving on.

Yeah, she wasn't convinced either.

———

A great conflagration of meaninglessness.

That was the phrase that popped into Cam's mind unbidden when she and Chester stepped into the storage unit *du jour*. Chester sucked in his breath. She didn't dare.

"Chester, tell me how you're feeling."

The rain kept coming, filling in the gaps between bits of conversation, reminding them that the sun wasn't shining, everything damp was about to get damper, and hauling would be more miserable than it normally was.

"It's darker than usual."

"The bulb overhead doesn't shed much light, but maybe Eli has a flashlight or two in his truck."

Eli backed Great White 2 to the entrance of the unit. It nearly filled the space, blocking out even the subdued daylight. But it would minimize trips dodging puddles.

Chester shrank back against one wall. "Too dark."

"I know. We'll fix that. Eli? Flashlights?" She popped on her phone's flashlight for immediate relief. Its stark blue-white light cast monstrous shadows amid the great conflagration of meaninglessness.

"Coming up." Eli squeezed between the side of the truck and the unit's garage-like doorjamb.

"Chester? Where are your thoughts right now?" Camille joined him against the wall, shoulder touching his.

He shielded his eyes, as if the valiant light in the space were too bright. "Shame. Look what I've done to myself."

Eli approached with two industrial-sized flashlights but paused several feet away.

"Shame isn't a new emotion to you, is it?" Always measuring words. Always testing the weight of the ice on the pond for stability.

"No. Lived with it a long time."

"The problem is that it's outdated now. Shame outgrew its welcome. You tried to evict it long ago, but it refused. The fact that we're standing in one of only a couple of remaining storage units is a tribute to shame's defeat."

"That was profound," Eli said.

She shot a "no jokes, Eli" look his way.

"No, I mean it really is profound. I'm going to remember it. You too, Chester?"

"A tribute to shame's defeat," Chester said. "What do you do with a defeated enemy that keeps hanging around like he owns the place?"

Hope rose, as if the battery on her phone's flashlight surged. He was starting to think more clearly about his motivations, his reasonless reasons, his true enemies. And they weren't inanimate objects. "It will help when you can turn in the keys for these storage rentals, when this part of the process is finished."

"I still fight the urge to surround myself with things. I know . . . I know, Dr. Brooks. You said it would be like this. And I'm working on the coping strategies we've been talking about. But I don't know if I'll ever graduate from this school. Do you think I'll ever be free of the memory of who I once was?"

Eli flicked on one of his flashlights and propped it on a

nearby stack of the yet to be addressed. "I don't know about you, Chester, but I'm counting on it."

"Who *you* once were?" Chester said. "What? Star athlete? CIA operative? Spy for the . . . huh . . . fashion industry?" With a rare glint in his eyes, he gestured toward Eli's now dusty-red coveralls.

"I had my own hoarding issues."

"You?"

Camille bit her lip hard. It was about to come out—the reason why she needed to keep her distance from Eli Rand. An excess of kindness but saddled with a hoarding history she could not afford to consider. Didn't dare let close. Didn't want to hear.

Okay, she did, but it would likely change their relationship, such as it was. Was it selfish of her to now want to prolong discovering what it was that made Eli Rand all wrong for her?

"Men, we have a few hours to work. We should get started." She didn't wait for a response but grabbed a clear garbage bag from the back end of the truck. "I'll collect the items you want to donate, Chester. Eli, you'll be in charge of the unsalvageable?"

He hesitated. "I always am."

"And, Chester, you can use this cardboard box for what you intend to reintroduce to your house. We want to continue to honor your concern that we not accidentally throw away something of true value. And you're developing a great sense of what constitutes genuine value. Sound like a plan?"

Chester slowly stepped away from the wall. "I never thought I'd have a hard time finding something worth saving."

"Except yourself," Cam added. "You're worth saving."

"How many saves do you suppose God has?" Eli asked during a midafternoon break in the action.

Chester wiped his brow, leaving a dark smudge across his forehead. "What made you wonder that?"

"Those talent shows on TV. The judges are given a 'save' they can use when they're especially interested in a contestant who might not have made it through otherwise. One save per judge or per season. Wonder how many God has."

"Unlimited?" Chester said.

"That's what I was thinking. Puts a whole new slant on shame and regret, doesn't it?"

Camille took an extra-long sip of water from her BPA-free bottle.

"I like how you think," Chester said. "You're a taller, sometimes smellier, and a lot hairier version of Dr. Brooks."

Should she thank him? Or put a stop to this conversation?

"Except for the smelly part," Eli said, "I'll take that as a compliment."

"She must use more expensive deodorant," Chester said. "No offense, Dr. Brooks."

"We're working hard here, my man." Eli tossed an M&M from his trail mix—new gloves firmly in place—toward Chester. It fell at Chester's feet.

All three stared at the treat lying on the storage unit floor. A bright-yellow spot in an otherwise stifling, refuse-strewn environment. Like Eli. A bright spot. Apparently hanging out with compulsive hoarders had drained all *her* logic too.

"I'll get that on my next pass," Eli said.

"Good idea." Camille kicked it to the side with her foot.

chapter twenty-six

ALTHOUGH HER ROLE WAS—ON paper—less hands on than what Camille had been involved in with both Allison and Chester, she couldn't imagine not getting her hands dirty—as long as she was wearing gloves. She needed tangible evidence that she was making a difference. She'd snapped a few pictures, with Chester's permission, for documentation, but Greta wasn't the only person who needed proof.

Truth be told, she needed it.

When Eli again volunteered to drop Chester off at his house, Cam didn't hesitate. She could compartmentalize for only so long before the need to purge the knot of thoughts, ideas, and tasks.

Her apartment said, "Come in out of the rain." *Needs some pops of color.* Light-gray bare walls, gray couch, a third tone of gray in the drapes framing the window . . . That was the color she'd left outside. What would happen if she purchased a red throw pillow or two? Or red and white?

Sleek could be both classy and cold. Uncluttered spoke calm

to her soul. But she daily, sometimes hourly, erased evidence that someone lived in the apartment.

A pop or two of color.

One online purchase does not a hoarder make. She opened her laptop and pulled up a popular home décor website. Pages of pillow options scrolled past. She lingered over three that caught her eye. A nubby chenille, a smooth silk pillow with a compelling sheen, and a black-and-red buffalo plaid.

She moved the buffalo plaid to her shopping cart before she could rethink that option, then clicked for more info on the nubby chenille. Interesting. The color options were black, gray, and . . . yes, cranberry.

She chose the cranberry.

Two pillows. Enough for now. Maybe ever. But the room already seemed brighter.

Her routine was off. She always showered first. Time to get her head back in the game.

<hr />

Outside my childhood home, in the back yard where few people ventured, stood an unsightly bush, nondescript, invasive. It didn't flower. Its leaves were jagged in an unpleasant way. It had no definable shape to it. And it resisted most normal methods of dealing with an overly bushy bush.

My parents didn't mind it. They easily or maybe intentionally overlooked it. But I couldn't. It stood outside my bedroom window and scritched at the siding and glass in windstorms and blizzards. A child doesn't need much more than that to induce endless nights of insomnia.

One day I realized that if the bush were to disappear, I'd need to take on the task of removal. I wouldn't recommend a child of ten or eleven wield a sharp lopper, but I claimed to be—and felt—older than my age. So I lopped off branches until only a stubby lump of shredded wood remained. Success. I hauled the branches to a pile of brush at the back of our yard. We always had a brush pile, even though no one but me was interested in landscaping.

And for three seasons, even though other things interrupted my sleep, the bush's talons did not.

But during a late-summer storm, it tapped against the side of the house. Scraped. Clawed at my sleep. It had grown back, fuller than before. Why do good things grow slowly and the unwanted too rapidly? Chin hairs come to mind. And regrets.

I tackled the bush with unbridled vengeance after the storm passed. The ground was soft from recent rains, which aided the efforts of shovel and spade. I would not just cut it down. I would dig it out.

Three seasons passed. After all that hard work, the bush revived. Diligent as I'd been, I missed a root. The bush needed no more encouragement than that.

A compulsive hoarding disorder defies many conventional mental health treatments. It's particularly resistant to uprooting. Where that knowledge might at first seem discouraging, it has another side. Setbacks are not a sign of defeat. They signal a need to dig deeper. For those of us who are friends with, in love with, married to, or children of hoarders, it reminds us that the process will not be easy, uneventful, or quickly solved. Those who are in it for the long haul and willing to do whatever it takes, including family counseling, are likeliest to be standing near when a season comes with no sign of unwanted growth.

After my first sleepless night, I learned several important truths. The bush would not disappear because I wanted or willed it to. It was unaffected by my hollering at it. Throwing it a good thought (or a bad one) from time to time did nothing. And no matter how many names I called it, it didn't leave.

The only way to be free of it was hard work, over time.

May that strengthen you, listener, for the long haul.

Cooper had proven himself a quick study regarding podcasting. He took to the technology side like the challenge of rock climbing with one arm. Relentless, unfazed, willing to look for an alternate if the first path didn't work.

The Rand men shared a disturbingly similar sense of humor and fun. But Cooper's seemed tempered, more reserved. A pleasure to work with, Cooper didn't make it as hard for Camille to keep work and friendship separate entities.

In one session they'd managed to record a month's worth of podcasts. He had them edited in two days, fitting the project around his host of other interests and work. With her blessing, he'd been in contact with Shyla on a few questions about the audio editing and his idea to freshen the intro and outro music.

Camille knew the danger of going too long between contacts with friends. While waiting for Kimberly to return her call about the schedule for Allison's ongoing cleanup campaign, she called Shyla.

"I miss cupcakes," she began.

Shyla's laughter reached across the miles like a hug. "I do too. Jenx doesn't bake much anymore. Nice to hear your voice. Over the phone rather than over cyberspace."

"Do you still listen in?"

"I may have walked out on you, but I'm not abandoning my interest in what you're trying to do. What you are doing."

"Shyla, you're good for me."

"And you for me."

"How's it going out there?"

"Hot and humid."

"Other than that?" Cam noted that her air conditioner wasn't kicking in as often since that last heat wave. Soon, more than a handful of leaves would be turning, pushing too fast toward another winter.

"I have news," Shyla said.

"Let's hear it."

"We've been approved as foster parents for Jenx's niece's baby."

"That's wonderful, Shyla." Cam's heart seemed to turn from

side to side, like a restless child refusing to settle for a nap. Had Shyla told her they'd considered fostering?

"Did you sell my armoire yet?"

Same Shyla. Cam wondered if she'd started wearing her long micro braids on top of her head because of the southern temps. "No, I did not sell it. It's in my bedroom."

"What's in it?"

"Inside?"

"I'm curious what you're storing in there. You, Ms. One Spoon Is Enough, Thank You."

"I own more than one spoon. And for your information, I'm keeping books on one shelf."

"Books, plural?"

"Shyla . . ."

"Camille . . ."

Cam could hear the healing in Shyla's voice. Not healed, but healing. *Like the rest of us.*

"So what do you think about Cooper? Is he going to work out for you?"

"Your instincts were good, Shyla. He's a quick learner. And you set him up for success with the notes you left for him."

"I like what I've been hearing. He has a deft touch with details, little audio-editing details others might not notice."

"Oh no."

"What?"

"I've been waiting for a call from Kimberly and her team. This is her calling me back."

"Listen, I have to go anyway. It's an hour later where we are."

"One time zone apart is better than two. I'll call you back soon. Good to hear your voice."

"Yours too. Now, catch Kimberly's call before she hangs up."

Arrangements for the next afternoon's session with Allison complete, Camille ended the call with Kimberley. In her haste, she'd forgotten to tell Shyla about the pops of color. Next time.

She repositioned the new throw pillows on her couch. Two-day delivery. Amazing.

"You betrayed me!"

Cam held the phone away from her ear as she punched the keycode into the pad. "Allison, calm down. What's going on? Where are you?"

"At my house. Where I always am." The words were laced with venom.

Camille hadn't even gotten through the door to her apartment after her monthly office-hours meetings with Greta and her cohorts. Cam still reeled from a growing lack of respect for her methods, and Allison's angry words hit especially hard.

"What's happened? Whatever it is, we'll deal with it."

"You can't fix this. Nobody can fix this. Ryan is here."

"What?" She turned to head back down the stairs to her car. "Your son's with you?"

"He's not with me. He's with a woman, and they're standing on my front porch. I can't let them in here."

The pops of color on her couch seemed suddenly garish. She turned her back to them and addressed her client. "Yes, you can, Allison. Talk to them."

"Oh, they rang the doorbell all polite and everything, but this is the worst possible thing that could have happened. I don't know what to do."

Allison's sobs rattled Cam's rib cage as she relocked the door and pounded down the stairs.

"Would you let me talk to them please? Let me talk to Ryan." She'd hang up and call him herself, but she couldn't afford to leave Allison tetherless right now.

"No! They're going to want to come in, and I'm not ready. I'm not ready."

"Allison. Please trust me. We'll work through this. Let me talk to him."

"I'd have to open the door a crack."

"You can do that. You can do that much."

"I don't want him to see inside."

Think fast, Cam. This woman is on the ledge, and you might not get her back. "Would you just ask him to stay there until I arrive, then? Don't send him away until I get there."

"Oh, tell him yourself, traitor."

One more flight of stairs and she'd reach the parking garage entrance, if she were still breathing. Allison hadn't hung up. She could hear her making her way through the living room, unlocking five locks—*click, click, click, click, click*—and the door creaking open that proverbial sliver.

"Allison?"

"This is Ryan. Ryan Chase."

"Ryan. I'm so glad to have a chance to talk to you. I'm Dr. Camille Brooks, your mother's clinical psychologist."

"You didn't tell her you'd contacted us."

"No. And please don't mention Lia if your mother's listening. Is your wife there with you?"

"Yes. Nicole is a great motivator. She insisted we come. But after this welcome . . ."

"Ryan, I'm about twenty minutes away. I know that seems like forever right now, but can I please ask you not to push for your mother to let you in just yet? I need an opportunity to talk to both your mother and you and your wife."

"Twenty minutes?"

"Would you rather meet me somewhere? I don't want to leave your mother alone for long, but . . ."

"We can stay here on the porch if she'll let us. If she won't call the cops on us for trespassing. This was my home, Dr. Brooks." He huffed. "I thought she'd be happy to see me. I guess that was pretty naive on my part."

"Trust me. She won't call the police on you. Hand the

phone back to your mother so I can have a word with her. If you're willing to wait, I'll be grateful."

"I should have called you first. I'm not surprised she doesn't want to let us in. But I did think she'd want to see me. Can you imagine what that feels like?"

"Exactly how that feels. Yes. Can I talk to Allison?"

Camille negotiated the car out of the parking garage with the call now coming through the car's speaker.

"What do you want?" So much venom.

"Allison, we've been through a lot together. Don't give up on me now. Trust me one more time. I'm on my way. You can stay put in your house, and they'll stay out on your front porch. They won't try to pester you to let them in. But I'd really like to meet them. And they've come a long way."

"How do you know? I don't even know where Ryan's been living."

"What were you doing before they showed up?"

"I was washing my hair in the kitchen sink. The shower's stopped up again."

"Why don't you finish doing that. By the time you're done fixing your hair, I'll be there."

"And what are the odds I'm going to let *you* in?"

~

Ryan and Nicole must have taken an Uber or Lyft from the airport. No car sat in front of Allison's home. The two people in the metal chairs on the small porch looked about as miserable as two people could be on an ideal summer day with a cool breeze blowing and an abundance of flowers blooming in the window boxes.

Ryan was easy to recognize from Allison's pictures of him. Nicole—concern all over her face—sat as gracefully elegant as one could in a rickety metal chair. Both stood as Camille approached.

"Dr. Brooks?"

"Ryan, it's so good to meet you. Nicole? A pleasure."

"Did we ruin everything?" Ryan asked. "I thought she was doing better."

"She is. She's made great progress. Much more to go, as you can imagine."

"We shouldn't be here." He sighed and turned in a circle, as if completely lost.

Camille ran through myriad responses. Only one seemed to fit. "You definitely should be here. When Allison has gotten over the shock, whether that's yet today or a month from now, she'll be grateful you came. I do wish I could have had time to prepare you for where she is in this process."

"Should we leave?"

Nicole held Ryan's arm to stop him from pacing.

"I honestly don't know yet. She's . . . as you can see . . . upset. More with me than with you, I think."

"When I moved, I didn't tell her where I'd gone."

Cam watched his wife's fingers dig deeper as Nicole squeezed Ryan's arm harder.

"What kind of son does that?"

"I'm sure there are apologies waiting on all sides of this. But right now your mother is in a full-blown meltdown, so . . ."

"I am not." The sound of her small voice was both welcome and frightening. How much had she heard?

Camille made her way to the crack in the door. "Allison, Ryan and his wife have come a long way in hopes of seeing you."

"He's married? Would have been nice to know that."

"We all understand that you're hurting, and we get it that surprises are hard for you. I've met Nicole. She's a lovely woman. I think you're going to want to meet her too." *Nicole was the motivator.* "She's a woman of deep compassion, Allison. Your daughter-in-law wants you and your son to connect again."

"Can they wait until . . . until the house is . . . until my collections are . . . more organized?"

"What if they sat in the kitchen with you? It's so pretty and bright in there now. It's not like Ryan hasn't seen the house before."

"It's what made him leave in the first place."

"You and I know it was more than that. Just like your disorder is more than a collection."

"Mom," Ryan called over Camille's shoulder. "We're not here to judge you or change you. I . . . I miss you."

"Like you have for the last how many years?"

"Yes. Every day of all that time. I missed you. And I want to do what I can to help."

Camille turned away from the door to whisper to Ryan and Nicole. "Helping may not mean convincing her to get rid of her things. The biggest help you can be to her right now is to accept and love her as a work in progress."

Nicole stepped closer. "I've been doing a lot of reading. I minored in psychology in college, which I know doesn't mean much when it comes to this. But I'm committed to listening. We're both committed to letting you lead, Dr. Brooks. Which we should have done in the first place."

The gentleness in her voice and the way Ryan leaned on her told Camille their mission in coming was not adversarial. They wanted to do the right thing, if they could figure out what that was. And if Camille could.

"Are they still here?"

"Yes, Allison. They're not going anywhere."

"Dr. Brooks?"

"What?"

"If I lose them forever, it's on your head."

As if there weren't enough at stake. As if she hadn't just been pummeled by the decision makers waiting for her to mess up big. As if she were an expert in family glue.

"I'm willing to take that chance. Allison, please let us in."

chapter twenty-seven

THE FOUR OF THEM SAT at Allison's small kitchen table. Nicole's eyes were still wide from her foray through the living room. And she hadn't seen it at its worst.

Allison sat stiffly, her hands clasped in front of her on the table, her hair wispier than usual, jaw set. Before Camille could begin what she hoped wouldn't sound like a speech, Allison's expression dissolved. Face contorted, she sobbed like a little girl lost in the middle of Walmart.

"Oh, Mama." Ryan crossed to her, lifted her from her chair, and held her in his lap as if she weighed no more than an infant. "Mama. I'm so sorry. I'm so, so sorry. I didn't understand."

Nicole scooted her chair closer and rested her head on her husband's shoulder. Camille leaned her elbows on the table, laced her fingers together, and pressed her clasped hands to her mouth to staunch her own flow of tears. She needed to remain professional. Caring, but distanced enough to let this happen organically. She was an observer, not part of the family.

In a sense, she'd never really been part of anyone's family. How much of that was her fault? The scene in front of her could have been Cam with her own mother in her lap, if she'd known.

Two hours later, all tears spent and a tentative truce enforced, Allison indicated she'd reached her limit of raw emotion.

"We're staying at a hotel not that far from here, Mom," Ryan said. "Our plane doesn't leave until late tomorrow afternoon. We'd like to come by again in the morning if that's okay with you." He looked at Cam for confirmation.

She shrugged as unobtrusively as possible. Who knew what Allison would be like in the morning? "What do you think, Allison? Would you like us to call first?"

"I have a full day planned."

Camille tilted her head Allison's direction.

"I guess a short visit. If you call first. And just here, in the kitchen. No tours. No gawking. No 'Mother, shame on you' or 'Oh, Mother, how could you?'"

"That's not in my vocabulary anymore, Mom."

"Okay then."

Ryan kissed his mother on the head. "Mmm. Smells like those yellow plums we used to pick from the tree in the back yard. Nice." Then, "I love you. See you tomorrow."

Allison sat unmoving for a moment, her lips pinched, new tears forming. "Love you too, son. Nicole. That's a pretty name. Tomorrow, you can tell me about Lia."

And the fragile bubble burst.

Lia.

Ryan and Nicole agreed to meet with Camille in the restaurant on the first floor of their hotel for dinner. They needed a speed course in compulsive hoarding disorder and the long, slow crawl toward freedom.

She found herself parroting much of what she'd been

saying on the podcast, which was oddly comforting. If it was a resource *she* turned to, maybe others would too.

"I always felt like I had to be the parent," Ryan confessed over his steak dinner. "That's a heavy load for a teen boy whose brain cells haven't fully matured yet."

"That's a common concern," Camille said. "And not an easy one to either live through or think back on."

"Now, of course, I regret all the times I could only see Mom's hoarding through my own eyes, how it was affecting *me*, inconveniencing *me*. I couldn't have friends over. Made up all kinds of excuses for why. Dad was not there a long time before he actually left. I thought he was being so unfair. Then I turned into him."

"Ryan." In her always gentle way, Nicole rubbed his arm and consoled him with her presence and patience.

"It was more than just inconvenience, Ryan. Your life was radically altered by your mother's disorder. But if you're like most of us, you weren't ever sure how much of it, if any, she could control."

"And I guess I was afraid that it was contagious. Or genetic. I'd gotten so used to the mess that I didn't care anymore. I found myself tossing used plastic cups in a corner, just like she did. Digging a nest in a pile of clothes to sleep at night. Spending more than I made at my part-time job and . . . finding unhealthy ways of paying for what I couldn't afford. I left for my own sanity and to keep me from a lifetime of that." He pointed over his shoulder as if they knew he meant his mother's house. "Tell me it's not genetic."

Nicole piped up. "Ryan, even if you'd started a habit that could have led to something more serious, that is not who you are anymore. You're so conscientious. So careful about wastefulness or excess accumulation."

"There are biological and psychological components to a disorder like this," Cam said. "We're discovering more about the brain and how it works, how addictions of various kinds are passed on or simply adopted when a child grows up in an environment like that. But it sounds to me as if you have fought off those patterns of unhealthy thinking, many of which your mother is just beginning to understand."

"Disposophobia," Nicole said.

"Other than in official reports, I don't use the scientific term for compulsive hoarding disorder. And never with my clients. It sounds like a cartoon joke. Or as if the client is suffering from a fear of garbage disposals. And it's not a laughing matter."

"No," Ryan said. "It is definitely not a laughing matter."

"I asked Lia how much she knew about her mother's disorder." Cam took a drink of water before continuing. "I should have asked her a different question. 'How much do you *understand* about your mother's disorder.'"

Nicole leaned forward. "How long has it taken you to understand it, Dr. Brooks?"

"A lifetime. And I'm still learning."

A pile starts with one. One item. One disappointment. One heartache. Two? Still manageable. Three? Four? And when one melts into another or is interlocked by a common thread of despair? And when depression or anxiety means there is no more steady hand to keep the pile from tipping?

Those of us who work with people with hoarding disorders and other compulsions know that we're playing Jenga every day. And so are our clients. Whether they're placing a new injury on the pile, a new acquisition, or trying to remove one, it can all come crashing down, depending on what else is leaning on it for support.

Imagine living as if your entire life is a game of Jenga and every collapse is not merely the end of a game but the death of something inside you. Imagine watching the tottering pile increase, unaware that it is your own hand adding to the pile. Imagine pulling out one block but it's never the right one. Never.

Now imagine a family member breathing down your neck, shouting at you to hurry and take your turn, pounding on the table in disgust, slamming the door in frustration on their way out of the house.

That's the life of a hoarder.

But now imagine acquiring skills to reduce the pile, new ways of processing information about the physics and dynamics of how the blocks are stacked. Imagine family and friends steadying the table, quieting the noise, waiting until . . .

That's the life of a hoarder on the way to freedom.

Camille's fingers hovered over the keys of her laptop, tempted to do her own investigation of the Curious Case of Eli Rand. Paranoia. It was her paranoia that made her doubt his intentions. Shyla had vetted him already. Cam still had a long way to go in trusting people, especially those who treated her with respect.

How twisted was that? She'd sought it all her life. Begged her parents for it. People-pleased her way through college. Dodged more than one bad-relationship bullet for lack of respect. And the one man who acted with nothing but integrity and honor toward her made her nervous. Go figure.

Her phone pinged. He must have been somehow tuned in to her thoughts. More than a little scary. He'd sent a text message letting her know Allison's shower was fixed.

It was no secret Eli Rand was a flawed human—just flawed enough to be believable. Why was it so hard for her to let down the heart guard she'd spent years erecting? If she were to fill out a Ten Most Wanted Character Qualities for a potential relationship, she would list what she valued most. No one she'd met ticked off more of that list than he did.

But a relationship was a risk. Always. Letting her emotions out into the light? Dangerous. And her track record proved that loving her was too much to ask of anyone, even for her flesh and blood.

Loving? Who said anything about loving?

⟋

Eli's mother let her into Nana's room for their first official coaching visit, although Camille held little hope that any actual coaching would take place. But that was the bargain, the barter. Camille had dependable wheels in exchange for sitting with Eli's nana and trying to woo her out of the mental state that held her in an inaccessible turret.

Impossible situations didn't shock Camille anymore. But for some reason, the idea of failing to make a difference for Nana loomed as a professional failure of epic proportions.

"Would you like me to get us some tea, Nana? Is it okay if I call you Nana?"

No response.

"I'll make tea," Eli's mom said, backing out of the room at the end of the hall.

"I've enjoyed getting to know your grandson," Cam said. It seemed the right thing to say, until after the words left her mouth. "He's certainly had a wide variety of life experiences, hasn't he?"

Nothing.

"I'd so love to hear what he was like as a child. He adores you. The whole family does."

No movement. The older woman blinked so seldom and so slowly, Camille watched for a pulse in her neck to assure her Nana's heart was still beating.

"Maybe one of these days, you'll grace me with a few stories I can use to . . . get his goat. You know his sense of humor. A little over the top, but he almost can't stop himself from making people smile." How far dared she go with this thread of one-sided conversation?

"It's been a joy to meet Cooper too. Two fine grandsons you have there, Nana. Cooper is an inspiration. What do you remember about Cooper as a little boy?"

Silence. But the woman drew a deep breath with an endless exhale.

Last breath? No. Maybe that was Nana's way of signaling the end of her patience with Camille.

"Do you like to listen to music? I have several playlists here on my phone. What would you like? Something soothing?" Camille did a quick calculation. Nana would have been in her forties in the 1970s, late thirties at the end of the 1960s. She scrolled through looking for—No. Who knew what memories that might stir of Nana Rand and her husband. How would Nana feel about church music? Hymns?

Cam scanned the room for an mp3 player or turntable or stack of cassettes or CDs. Nothing. Maybe music wasn't the battering ram to break through the wall around Nana's heart.

At the pace they were going, she might not discover what would break through before Nana really did breathe her last.

chapter twenty-eight

SHE CHECKED HER WATCH. AN hour before another date with Nana. Eli had said one of the only fragrances Nana responded to anymore was lemon. No time to make lemon bars or cookies. And Cam didn't have the ingredients on hand. It probably wasn't a good idea to stop and get her a lemon candle. But maybe a lemon diffuser. Electric base. The woman had years' worth of stuffy and musty to breathe out.

They'd met two times since that first visit. Nana hadn't left her room or her chair. It might be a long time before she was willing to listen to the encouragement Camille tried to offer. For now, the conversations were one-sided and usually focused on the way the light danced on the water outside her window or the antics of her grandsons. Eli provided her the most material.

For an independent woman with every reason to keep it that way, Cam found her thoughts too often drifting to Nana's oldest grandson. Eli's mom wasn't helping. It was as if she orchestrated reasons for them to be together outside of the normal workday.

"Camille, I'm trying a new recipe for a health-conscious

pot roast. Would you mind joining us for supper and giving your opinion?"

Where was this headed?

"And then, Dr. Brooks, I wonder if you'd mind filling in as the fourth in our Scrabble game tonight. Cooper has to work, and it's just so much more fun if we play teams. I have dibs on you. You know words."

But your son is the one with a competitive nature, Mrs. Rand. You are so transparent.

Camille's mother once had a collection of board games no one ever played. And random, incomplete sets of game board pieces. She was partial to puzzles that were incompletable, nonplussed by a sale sticker that readily admitted something was missing. The game of Scrabble held no appeal to Cam. But being part of a foursome gathered around a four-legged table, with four-legged chairs and happy people on each side? Irresistible.

Lemon diffuser. Let's diffuse a few stray thoughts.

Her appointment with Nana was an exact duplicate of the others before it. Cam's overly bushy bush analogy resonated as more relevant than ever. Nana wouldn't let Cam near her with a kind word, much less a pair of branch loppers.

Did Nana have enough years left in her to find peace about what she'd been through, to dig at the roots of her impossible regrets? How could Camille help her see that her husband's hoarding was not her fault, or even hers to influence? She'd done all she could to love him well. She'd done all she knew to help him manage his addiction. No human could undo the tangle.

Eli had tried.

But his remorse tasted of something more.

She closed the door to Nana's wing and retreated down the

long hall and across the great room toward the kitchen. It was rare not to find Eli's mother there.

"Well, Mrs. Rand, I wish I could tell you that she responded to me this afternoon. But that woman knows how to do stock-still better than most."

The word *catatonic* flitted through Cam's brain. Nana was tottering close.

Eli's mother looked down at the countertop she was scrubbing. The sponge moved slowly but covered every inch of the surface. She'd somehow found a balance of clutter and clean, treasures that hadn't consumed her.

"Thank you for what you're doing, Camille. We may not see results, but things happen beneath the surface and then pop up to surprise us one day."

"I'm not giving up. But I hope your expectations aren't going to lead to disappointment."

"With my mother-in-law? No. Whatever's going on in there is beyond her control. With you? Never. It makes me sad that she's shut us out. Hope doesn't have to listen to a person's history though."

"Well said, Mom." Eli's presence filled the doorway. "Cam, are you staying for supper?"

"About that," his mom said. "I have a vegetable lasagna in the oven. But you know how your father feels about combining those two words. He insists on taking me to the fish fry at The Landing tonight. Claims he likes their cherry pie better than mine, but you know that can't be true." She removed her apron and hung it on the hook near the pantry. "You two are welcome to share the lasagna. Table's set."

She'd set a place for Cam. Made room for her. No one ever made room for her. Except Eli. The heart flip meant nothing more than gratitude, right?

"Cooper's working late tonight, so be a good brother and save him a little," Mrs. Rand said.

"I always do, Mom."

"And would you mind keeping an eye on Nana while we're gone, Eli?"

"I always do."

"It's settled then."

Camille opened her mouth. Then closed it. Thinking. She'd planned on a simple salad for supper, the ingredients of which she had yet to procure from the store.

And there it was. Eli's mom pulled a perfectly composed salad from the refrigerator and set it on the table by the window. Lakeside.

"Candles?" his mom asked, the match in her hand.

"No!" they answered in unison.

"Well," she said. "That's decisive. Okay then. No candles. It promises to be a beautiful sunset though. Just as good." She winked. "The lasagna needs a few more minutes, and your father's still changing clothes. Why don't you two walk the path along the water's edge? Help you drum up an appetite."

"Cam?" Eli looked to her for an answer. "I think Mom assumed you'd agreed to stay. Was she mistaken?"

"Veggie lasagna sounds great." *And a walk along the lake? Come on. Who turns that down?*

"It's a no-wake lake," Eli said a few steps into their walk. "Did I mention that before?"

"No." The view of the house from this vantage point competed with the water view that beckoned her. "No water-skiing boats?"

"Or wave runners. Electric motors only or throttled-down low-horsepower gas motors. Human-powered kayaks, canoes, foot-powered paddle boats, the occasional pontoon, but with—you know—wave and wake restrictions."

"Cuts down on the noise that usually accompanies a popular lake."

"It does. Cuts down on prospective buyers for the properties for sale too. No noisy families looking to make a splash, if you know what I mean."

"I'd find the quiet more appealing. Would pay extra for it. Not that I'm looking to purchase anytime soon."

"It's a beautiful spot," Eli said, matching his pace to hers.

"It must have made it all the more difficult for your family with your grandfather's disorder. Or is that subject off-limits?"

"I'm open to talking about almost anything."

Not true, Eli. You're still hoarding—

Maybe that was the best term for it. He was hoarding stories he hadn't been willing to divulge. "Do you know the wound that launched the disorder for your papaw?"

"I think I do. He spent more than a year as a prisoner of war in Vietnam. He was an officer, so the treatment was probably even rougher."

"How awful. Most who come home from a situation like that suffer untold emotional damage."

"He so rarely talked about it. Rarely as in never. Kept most of it from Nana too. Man!" He rubbed his hand through his hair. "She's been coping with his fears since she was a young bride. I never thought about it that way. Their whole marriage was stained with the secrets he kept and the demons he fought. Great people. The best. But how many years did I live without understanding the kind of pressures they were both under?"

"It's likely his deprivations as a POW triggered his insatiable appetite for accumulating."

"Makes sense. Where were you," he said, a hint of teasing in his voice, "fifteen years ago when there might still have been time to reach him?"

Fighting my own demons, Eli.

"Never mind," he said. "That was thoughtless. I know where you were. And I wish you wouldn't have had to go through it."

"Invisible entry wound." If she made light of it, maybe they could move on to other topics. Like the weather or the price of gas or Eli's deepest regrets.

"Not so invisible," he said.

"What does that mean?"

"It shows. In kind of an extreme anti-hoarding way."

"I've made intentional choices to live more simply, to not allow myself to fall into a trap of drawing things around me just because my parents chose to support my mother's addiction even if it meant abandoning me."

He stopped walking. What could she do but face him? She turned her back to the serene lake.

"Did that feel good, to say it aloud?" he asked, his voice tinged with kindness.

"You already know my parents' story, Eli."

"I hadn't heard you use the word *abandonment*. That they *chose* to *abandon* you. Or as you say, that the addiction dictated their choices. And now, you shun things like they embraced them."

You apparently don't understand minimalism. "I'm selective about what I allow in my apartment."

"And how long it stays. And you believe efficient and comfortable can never share the same space."

"How is that a problem?"

"Maybe it isn't. Unless it consumes you."

"I'll have you know I bought two throw pillows recently. Red ones. Warmth. Online. They're staying."

"Look, Cam, I'm not judging. Goodness knows I have no right to do that. It's an observation. You won't ever take leftovers home from a restaurant."

"I'm opposed to the concept."

"You can't leave a cup or spoon on the coffee table until your guest leaves."

"Which is why I have few guests."

"Exactly."

"Oh."

"You've stripped your life to the bare minimum, on the surface." Eli rested his hands on her shoulders. "But I think you're successfully hiding a hoard of emotions."

That's not who I am.

The long pause did nothing to convince her.

It's not who I want to be.

They walked a few paces in silence.

"And do you know what I've observed, Eli?"

"What?"

"You've let a few clues leak that you've had an issue with hoarding. But you carefully tiptoe around telling me about it. You keep saying you're 'processing' your feelings about it."

"You doubt that?"

"No. But you do know whatever you'd say is safe with me, right?"

"Except for one thing."

"What's that?"

He stared across the water. "I don't want to risk your walking away from me."

Boom. Cannonball landed in the center of her chest. He cared more than he was letting on. It wouldn't have been a problem if she hadn't felt the same fear. The idea of being as open as she wanted to be—exposing her heart to the light—pierced her with fear that he would walk away. *What a pair they made.*

She'd been disappointed before. Gravely disappointed. What would happen if she risked imagining more than a working relationship with this man? He feared her walking away. She feared *he* would. What if one of them faced their fear head on, stared it down, refused to let it keep them from something that could be very good? What if *she* did?

Or what if it was a complete disaster?

"Do you want to turn back?" she said.

"No. Oh, you mean, back to the house? Sure, if you want."

"Eli."

"Hmm?"

"I think you'd better spill it all." *It's time, Camille. Time to let a little light into the possibility that someone might actually choose to be near you, with you, consider a future that included you.*

"Camille, I—"

"Because if you don't uncover what you've buried, we won't be able to take this relationship any further."

"Further? Relationship? You're not talking about our working relationship only, are you?"

"I was"—she reached for his hand—"hoping you meant you wanted to explore why you drive me crazy but I'd rather be with you—working or playing Scrabble or discussing low-throttle gasoline motors—than with anyone else I know." Somehow, exposed to the air, the words didn't seem as frightening as she'd feared. But he hadn't responded.

It would be okay. She might have misread what he was saying. She'd embarrassed herself before and lived through it. Cam would backpedal and reestablish the boundaries of their working relationship and his role as the podcast sponsor and—

"Cam?"

"Yes?"

He tugged on her hand. "Look at that."

"What?"

"Nana's standing at the window. Hands pressed against the glass."

"What do we do? Wave at her?"

"Wish we could, but it's a waveless lake."

"Eli Rand."

"Let's try this. I'll apologize later, if I need to." He cupped her head in his hands and kissed her on the forehead. Not the lips. Her forehead.

It was a start. "What's Nana doing now?"

"I can't see clearly, but it looks for all the world like she's smiling."

"We should probably get back to the house."

"Yes. Good idea. Lasagna and all."

How long had it been since her heart felt this warm? This full, but not in a *conflagration of meaninglessness* way?

"Eli? No apology necessary. And I fully intend to keep the throw pillows. For the record."

"We're a mess," he said.

"That's what napkins are for." She tapped on the cloth napkin his mother had set on the table.

"I mean, we're—all of us—dealing with something."

"Some of us better than others."

"You mean, like your clients?"

"If that's what you want to think." She forked the last bite of her salad.

"About my mess . . ."

She leaned her elbows on the table, then opened and closed her upraised hands. "Step into the light, young man. Wakeless lake. Shame-free table."

chapter twenty-nine

A REN'T YOU ITCHING TO CLEAN these dishes?" Eli asked.
"Stall tactic?" She carefully refolded her napkin and
set it under her fork.

"Maybe a little."

"It's your parents' home. I thought you might be the one
to do the dishes tonight." She leaned back with arms crossed.

"Well, I would, but I know how much it means to you."

"Dishes? These are lovely, but . . ."

"Spotlessness. Perfectionism. Nothing out of order."

She stood and carried her dishes to the sink. "And that's
wrong?"

"No." He followed her with his own. "Unless it becomes
an obsession."

"Obsession? You're using that word with me?" This wasn't
how the conversation was supposed to go.

"If the dish soap fits . . ."

She put down the bottle of dish soap she'd been squirting

into the rising hot water in the sink. "I understand perfection-ism, Eli."

"I know. You studied it in school."

"I recognize it. But I'm also well aware of how imperfect life is. Sure, some of my minimalism and diligence with clean-liness is probably a throwback from what life was like during my childhood. But these are things I can control when there's so much I can't."

"Which, I believe you might say is at the heart of many an addiction." He took the dishrag from her and nudged her aside.

"Eli, I don't like where this is headed. We were supposed to be talking about you."

"I am. There was so little I could control in my childhood too. So I found a way. And I found something to collect that made me happy and, for a while, formed my reason for living. And the beauty of it was that it was socially acceptable behavior."

The clank of dishes and running water filled the space while she waited for him to say more.

"But it eventually did what all hoarder collections do. It consumed me. It decayed me."

"Eli?"

He set the last few pieces of silverware in the draining rack and wiped his hands on a towel. "I hoarded money, Cam."

"That's called saving."

"Not the way I did it. I was a savvy entrepreneur, even as a kid. Business after business that eventually led me to bulging bank accounts and an accumulation of both money and the things it could buy that I tripped over it. I let that drive dictate my decisions. It reshaped how I approached people—looking for what might be in it for me, watching for ways to turn a buck whether others got in the way or not."

Cam waited, the words sinking in. The remorse she saw on his face registered as tightness in her forehead. He called that a major flaw? Aggressive business practices? Looking out for his personal interests? He just described a cross section of corporate America, didn't he? Not necessarily admirable, but his expression remained as dark as Allison's back hallway.

"There was more." He leaned against the counter. "I put other people out of business, outbid them because I could afford to and they couldn't fight back."

"Eli . . ."

"For some, it was their family business. They were going through hard times, and I took advantage of the opportunity to snatch up the vulnerable. And it wasn't because I needed more. I get sick to my stomach saying it now, Cam, but I was a financial predator, preying on the weak so I could grow my . . ."

"Empire?"

"I hate that word now. But yes."

Nothing he was saying even remotely resembled what she'd seen in Eli day after day. The man he described was not the man she knew. Cam took the towel from him. "That's not who you are now."

"No. But it's taken a lot to pull free of my obsession with possessing. You could say I had an almost literal 'come to Jesus' moment. He didn't exactly smack me in the head, but a timber from one of my construction sites did."

"Eli!"

"I lived through it, obviously."

"Obviously."

"But it changed me."

"The concussion?"

"The three weeks in the hospital. I lay there with no power. None. No influence. Couldn't put two thoughts together much less swing a deal." He pushed away from where he'd been leaning. "You know when you shake the cloth bag of Scrabble pieces to make sure nothing's aligned like it was in the previous game? It was like that. God rearranged my brain, and my core too. What mattered. What mattered to him. The man I want to be and how I'm going to accomplish that, with his at-my-elbow counsel."

Eli's confession had been a long time coming. All signs showed it had cost him to bare his soul to her. But somehow it pulled at nerve endings around her own heart. She empathized with the drama of that hospital scene for him, not near death but more like drawing closer to what life was supposed to look like. Was that what had been going on in her mind lately?

Did her disgust with her parents' choices have both a positive and negative side? She'd fought fiercely—and still fought—to help others pull free from their hoarding compulsions, sometimes against conventional thought or—*yes, Greta*—protocol. But she'd also buried herself behind drawn and pinned-shut drapes to keep herself from noticing the toxic emotions piling up in her soul. Most days she could navigate around them. Ignore them. Pretend they were no big deal.

Eli had been there too. But it wasn't his common pain that drew her to him. It was the "after" picture of his life. He'd learned how to live again.

He stood at the window wall now, his silhouette against the almost-sunset sky and the expanse of lake revealing he was breathing more comfortably. *Unburdening one's heart will do that.*

"This isn't my parents' house, Cam. It's mine. The land is mine. Plus a lot more. My compulsion has changed. But like any compulsion, it will raise its head when I least expect it. So I make intentional decisions every day to live generously rather than . . ."

"Hoarding what you have?"

He turned to face her and nodded. "Nobody coasts in this life without the danger of falling back into old habits."

His words faded, but their imprint remained.

What was it that made her so comfortable despite his past? She'd benefited from his transformation in a hundred ways. And so had her clients. Maybe more than ever before, she believed a person could change because she saw the "after" with her own eyes, felt it with her heart.

"That's it," he said. "The story of me." He gazed at his feet, arms crossed. "Except for the part about accidentally setting our picnic table on fire with a magnifying glass and a pile of kindling when I was eight."

Warm honey flowed over the raw emotions his story had exposed in Camille. "Wait a minute. The word *kindling* removes it from the *accidentally* category, doesn't it?"

"In my defense," he said, sounding more like his healed self with every word, "how does a kid know that Fourth of July parade confetti makes great kindling?"

Cam laughed, expelling far more than used air. "Want to sit again now that the table's cleared?"

"How about on the deck?"

"Great idea." She followed as he led the way to a coral-cushioned set of patio furniture. The sun was a half hour or more from setting, but the air had already started to cool.

"We keep a couple of blankets inside that end table, if you're cold," he said.

"Was I shivering?"

"No. I was anticipating."

"Eli, it's not that I don't believe what you're telling me about the sins of your past. But who I see before me today is kind and generous and if anything, *overly* thoughtful of others. Genuinely, I've assumed." She retraced their walk along the lake in her mind. Had she been misguided in thinking she could give her heart permission to even entertain the idea of a real relationship?

"I am genuine about it. New life goal. And God's holding my feet to the fire." He looked stricken. "I'm so sorry, Cam. Bad analogy. That's twice now."

She expected to smell a puff of acrid smoke, a familiar reminder only her mind had ever known. She'd been so far away, unreachable, when her family perished. Now, in Eli's presence, with the unpinning of what she'd kept hidden even from herself, she smelled only the lake air. A faint scent of lemon from the dish soap. And plums. For some reason, plums.

"Tell me about the transition."

"Are you asking as a psychologist, Dr. Brooks?"

"As your friend."

He stretched his legs out on the ottoman between them and laced his fingers behind his neck. "When Peg—Cooper—got tied up in drugs, some nasty stuff, I tried to help him, of course. I threw money at the problem, because that's what I had. But as you know well, money doesn't go deep enough. It never can. So I started to listen to him instead of preach at him or push him into one treatment center after another."

"And he responded?"

"Not right away." He lowered his feet to the deck and leaned forward. "But I did. It was so clear all of a sudden. His motivations were my motivations—the high, the numbing of pain, the euphoria, temporary as it always was. And the pull, the endless pull into a stronger rush. I saw me in him."

"Different consequences."

"In some ways. But we were both rotting inside."

"You know how un-American it sounds to disparage accumulating money?" Solar lights began to glow along the edges of the deck. Light. Just enough.

"Goes against the grain of our cultural narrative, doesn't it? And it's necessary for survival. But for me it had a grip that dragged me to a dark place."

"So you gave it all away?"

"Doing my best. But no. Not quite. I'm using it differently now so it doesn't use me. I think it was Eugene Cho who said, 'Generosity is what keeps the things we own from owning us.' Generosity."

"You're not a garbage man."

"I haul trash. I dig ditches. I volunteer at a daycare for senior citizens. If I notice a need, I feel not a compulsion but a privilege to help meet it. Scholarships for young people who will use it wisely, as opposed to how I used mine. Taking meals to the homeless and listening to their stories." He paused. "I support a really fine podcast that's just now exploding on the scene."

An elderly couple in matching work-out clothes power walked along the lake in front of them, chatting as their arms pumped. Not far behind was a young man and woman pushing a double jogging stroller, trailing a leash belonging to a short-legged puppy working hard to keep up. Life. Imperfect as it was. Going on in front of them.

"This was your confession, Eli? That you have this uncontrollable habit of generosity?" She shook her head.

"I almost lost myself to a cause that had no more merit than accumulating soggy magazines or garbage bags full of twist ties or broken coffee carafes, Cam. Just as damaging to my soul. I thought you deserved to know. But it's still hard for me to admit. And I don't want to get lost again."

"We're all hoarding something," Eli told me a few weeks ago. He's more right about that than I gave him credit for.

"And," he said, standing, "my parents are home. No. False alarm. Not my parents. That's Peg's noisy muffler."

Within minutes Cooper had found the leftover lasagna and joined them on the deck. "Great evening, huh?"

"Beautiful weather," Camille said. "The Coop going well?"

"Oh man," he said between bites, "once we got hooked up with Special Olympics, we're busier than ever. Well-run local program. Happy to partner with them."

"I made another phone call to the Wounded Warriors and another start-up ministry with the same kind of focus," Eli said. He flicked a lightning bug off his pant leg where it had landed. "If you're interested in those contacts—"

"Definitely. Thanks."

"I'll arm-wrestle you for an extra dessert," Eli said.

Cooper didn't flinch. "You know I always win."

"Rock, paper, scissors?"

"As long as I can use my feet," Cooper said.

Cam observed the interchange with a mix of joy and

longing. The brothers had been through a few things. More than a few. But the camaraderie they shared was enviable.

"I need to go check on Nana," Eli said. "Do you want to come, Camille?"

That iconic image of Eli's grandmother's nose and hands pressed against the glass, smiling at them from her window as they walked. The kiss. "It might be good for you to see her alone, Eli. She might just open up to you."

Cooper looked from Eli to Cam and back again. "Something happen I don't know about? A breakthrough?"

"Breakthrough in the making, maybe," Eli said on his way into the house.

"What did he mean by that?"

Camille adjusted her position so she could face Cooper more directly. "You know your brother."

"A nonanswer, if I ever heard one." He scooped up the last of the lasagna. "There's dessert?"

"Your parents went out for supper. Fish fry. The Landing?"

"Their favorite."

"Eli figured they were bringing home cherry pie for everyone." All her diligence to eat clean and healthy—except for the now nonexistent Jenx cupcakes—and she hoped Eli was right. Tomorrow she'd set her alarm early enough for a serious workout.

"You and Eli getting along okay?" Cooper asked. "Never mind answering. I can see it in your eyes."

"I pride myself on not being transparent, Cooper."

"There's that word. Pride. It'll get you every time."

She laughed. "I suppose you're right."

"Oh, I know I'm right." He tugged at his empty sleeve. "Pride almost cost me my life. I'm grateful all I lost was a limb."

The Rand boys were especially chatty today. Not that they weren't always. But Cam wasn't sure she could bear the weight of hearing both their guarded stories in one day. She let her gaze drift to the lake. Constant but ever changing. Welcoming or risky, depending on the weather's mood. Serene, like now, but with depths few had fully explored.

"Not many are grateful for losing a limb, Cooper. Must have been pretty traumatic for you."

The solar lights glowed brighter as the evening deepened. Cam tugged a blanket around her shoulders.

"I'd been considering getting a tattoo removed," he said, "that was right about here." He pointed to the spot where he would have had a bicep on that side if he'd had an arm. "No longer an issue."

"Eli said you were a radio operator in Afghanistan?"

"Communications. Few positions are considered safe desk jobs over there. I'd gotten cocky. Started taking risks. Thought I was immune to consequences. Not unlike the path that I took in my teens."

Was he aware how much Eli had told her about that season of his life?

"You'd once said your accident was Eli's fault. His doing." She watched his face for signs she'd ventured too far.

"It was his *doing* that I didn't bleed to death and that I'm a one-armed man rather than a dead man. He'd been home—I don't know—a couple of weeks from his tour of duty. Said he was overcome with this crushing need to pray for me. You know how people wake up in the middle of the night with someone's name on their mind, can't get back to sleep, start praying, and then later find out why?"

It hadn't happened to her, but she'd heard of it. Wait. She'd woken up the night her parents died. But that nightmare wasn't uncommon. She hadn't even thought about praying. What if she had?

"Ten and a half hours' time difference between here and where I was stationed," Cooper said. "It was predawn. Something like four in the afternoon back here. Eli was wide awake, but he had this weird ache in his left arm and said he couldn't shake the sensation that he needed to pray for me."

An in-line skater rumbled past them, the sound interrupting a story Cam leaned closer to hear. "What happened?"

"We were heading out on assignment. After I strapped my comm transponder onto my back, I hoofed it toward the ground vehicles with the rest of the men in my unit. Tired of the war, tired of predawn missions that rarely netted us results, tired of taking orders. I jogged ahead of the pack, turned around, and walked backward, making some kind of inane speech about how those of us in communications were the real soldiers. Where would the rest of them be without us?"

"And . . ."

"And"—he shook his head—"Eli came to mind. He'd been there with me through so much of my garbage. Invested in me. I wanted to be like him. Not like the pseudo-man I was at the moment. I stopped in my tracks, which meant all the brothers I was facing had to. IED went off just a dozen feet behind me. Lit up the sky like it was midday. I went flying. Most of me. The comm unit protected me some, but my arm ended up in another village, I suppose. Somebody's souvenir."

"Oh, Cooper."

"If I'd taken another few steps, it would have been a different story, and for more than just me."

"I am so sorry that happened to you."

"Changed my life. Most of it for the better. You know how an angry mom might drag a screaming toddler away from danger and the kid thinks his arm will fall off? God dragged me by my arm until it did."

"You don't think God caused that IED to—"

"No. I just meant that he can use anything to get our attention. Anything. Plus," he said, stretching his neck and shoulders, "I saved a fortune on tattoo removal."

"His favorite way to end that story," Eli said, carrying a pie, five plates, and five forks.

And an endless supply, Cam thought, *of his brother's gratitude.*

chapter thirty

RYAN AND NICOLE MADE IT a point to connect with Camille after they'd returned home from visiting Allison. Ryan's relationship with his mother wasn't by any stretch healed, but healing. And Camille was learning to be content with the difference.

When their name popped up again in caller ID, a jolt shot through Cam. Something was wrong. She could feel it before hearing a word.

"Dr. Brooks? Are you at Mom's or at your office?"

"My home office. Paperwork. What's up?"

"I've been in contact with Lia."

"Ryan, I'm glad to hear you're communicating with your sister. Does she know about your visit?" Camille clicked to speakerphone and leaned against the back of the sofa.

"Yes. She thinks I'm a fool and used another word with it."

"Oh."

"But there's . . . more. She wasn't feeling right, postpartum."

"It's hard on any new mom, and the mom's body."

"Yeah, this was more than that. The doctors did pretty

thorough testing. She has ovarian cancer. None of them can explain why they wouldn't have seen that on ultrasounds while she was pregnant. But from what they say, it's not in its earliest stages."

Cam buckled over at the thought. "Ryan, what a blow for all of you." What hollowing news for them all.

"I'm worried about Mom too. If we keep this from her, that doesn't seem right. But if we tell her, it might kill her. They were so close at one time."

"Are you looking for my advice?"

"Please."

"I'm frankly not sure what to say. Let me think about it. See how your mother's doing. The visit took a lot out of her, even though it was so necessary."

"Nicole and I thought we'd better let you know and tell you that we'll wait until we hear from you before doing anything. I tried to get Lia to call Mom. She won't. Says she can't. And I get that. I get it."

Camille searched the ceiling for answers. Nothing was written there. "Ryan, thank you for informing me. I don't have an answer for you right now."

"Understood. You'll be in touch?"

"Certainly. And keep me updated please."

"We will. Thank you for all you're doing."

If only what she was doing could ever, once, be enough.

At one time Camille thought she might get Allison interested in a cooking class. Or in Eli's mom's book club. Common interest in literature. A safer environment discussing books than discussing children or decorating tips or resourceful ways to maintain personal hygiene when living in a house without running water. But Allison hadn't left the house since their ankles-in-the-water park excursion. And two brief trips to her own front porch. Oh, and the dumpster-diving episode at the neighbor's curb.

Who would have thought Cam would be the one attending

the book club? Eli's mom had asked. Cam had accepted, admittedly as another excuse to cross paths with the book club coordinator's son.

The book they'd be discussing in a few weeks stared at her from her iPad Kindle app. Not her usual fare. Intriguing premise though—that our natural resistance to suffering can keep us from the help we need. But embracing suffering as one of many vital life experiences can change our fear response.

With Lia and Allison heavy on her heart, she flipped to the introduction and began to read. Avoidance? She sensed instead that she was on a quest for a broader language base to use regarding the topic. Research. And it couldn't come too soon.

She was forty pages into the book—and an hour behind in her official work schedule—when a text came through from Eli.

"Have you heard from Chester? He's not answering his phone. Dad caught him a mess of fish."

Cam texted back: "Mess is a word we try to avoid in this business. Haven't heard from him. Will try calling."

"He'll answer for you but not me? Pouting."

"Get over yourself."

"I'm trying."

A few minutes later she called Eli.

"I can't reach him either. That's curious. Can you picture that man going for a walk or puttering in his yard?"

"No," Eli said. "We were supposed to work on that final storage tomorrow."

"Right."

"And I'd planned to get his opinion on something I've been developing for him. That can wait. But . . . I think I'll head over there and check. Probably nothing to worry about."

"Probably." But the dangers of his health history and his past suicide attempts didn't boost her confidence level, despite the inroads he'd made. The mind was a fickle master. Emotions, even more fickle. "Call me when you get there?"

"I will."

Her two key clients—Allison and Chester—in more potential trouble than they already faced? "Eli, I'm going to head over there too. Can't sit here and wonder."

"Don't blame you."

⌐

How had Cam beaten Eli to Chester's house? Having a car that responded to depressing the accelerator helped. She'd entertained random thoughts like that during the drive to keep herself from imagining the worst. It had been weeks since she'd felt even a hint of remorse over giving up Old Unreliable. Couldn't call a car like that Old Faithful. She'd managed to hold on to—no longer hoard—the memories of how freer her parents had been in a car that color, that model, if not that year. Freer with conversation, interaction, breaks in the clouds that hovered over them in the house, and what felt like normalcy. No wonder she'd been willing to put up with her nonfunctioning car for too long.

Her bartered vehicle from the Rands had gotten her this far in record time—in front of Chester's rented house. Her feet were going to have to take her to the answers she needed.

Camille knocked on the front door as usual. Called his name. No response.

The drapes in the front window were wide open, a new habit for Chester. Major breakthrough. Breathing more heavily than the physical exertion required, she fought her way through the still-tangled shrubbery in front of the window and peeked in.

From behind her, she heard Eli's brother's bad muffler and a car door slam.

"Cam? Is he there?"

She nodded. In his favorite chair. With his favorite Marlene mug clutched to his chest. And a contented smile on his face.

"Is he going to let us in?"

"I don't believe that's possible, Eli."

He stepped closer to the window and peered in. Eli pounded on the window with an open palm. "Chester! Chester? Wake up and let us in."

"Eli, that's not the face of a man napping."

"I'll call 911."

"Yes." She backed away through the shrubbery, her arms wrapped around her middle, heart pounding in a way she suspected Chester's never would again.

Eli made the quick call, then headed for the front door. He tried busting into the house with his shoulder. Unsuccessfully.

"I think I can get us in through the back door. It doesn't have this many security locks. He never did give you a key, did he?" The emotion in Eli's words rang unmistakably clear.

⌐

Chester's funeral would be far less complex than his life of the last several years. Nothing extraneous would clutter it. Random thoughts again dominated as she and Eli stood back while the EMTs removed his shell of a body from the home. A clear path led from Chester's chair to the front door. It was as if in some way he'd been waiting for a clear path.

Cam would not have been able to see in, to discover what had happened, if Chester hadn't pulled the drapes open. She could see in because he'd let in the light. But it didn't keep his body from giving up on him.

The professional side of her had been on high alert for evidence that he'd *chosen* that moment to die. Eli must have been tormented by the same thought. Gloved, in case a police investigation was needed, he'd ignored her warning, peeked into the medicine cabinet in the bathroom, and sniffed Eli's electric stove for a whiff of gas. Yeah, neither one of them were thinking clearheadedly.

They'd talked little while waiting inside for the EMTs.

Cam had noticed first that a wide damp spot trailed down Chester's shirt from chin to waistband. It looked and smelled like coffee, as if his heart had given out mid-sip. Still damp. He hadn't sat with his feet up in that recliner for days, as some recluses might. They'd found him early. Not soon enough.

But the smile on his face. Undeniable.

"Tell me we did all we could, Eli."

"We did all we could."

"And you believe that?"

"Have to. I think what we did was offer him hope he hadn't known for a very long time. We helped him reconsider what was truly important. And we loved him. We cared and listened and treated him with the respect any human would deserve."

"You were especially good at that," she said.

"Don't underestimate your influence on him, Camille."

"In the end, though, I couldn't save him."

"That's not our job. But I know he reconnected with the One who can."

The EMTs were kind and efficient. When the body was wheeled out on the gurney, Cam sensed it was like a military escort of honor. How different that journey would have been if the way hadn't already been cleared.

━━

"I need to pay a visit to Allison," Cam told Eli when the house was closed up, the back door nailed shut pending a permanent repair of the break-in damage Eli had caused, and conversations completed with the police and Chester's landlord.

They stood in front of the house, staring as if it might start breathing again. It didn't.

"Right now?" He hadn't broken his gaze with the house.

"Soon. I'll need a little time to decompress."

"Alone?"

"I was hoping not."

"Your favorite coffee shop?"

"Could we take the coffee to go? Do you have time for a side trip to a quiet spot?"

Eli's smile did more to warm her than any since Chester's. "The beauty of being self-employed. Sure. Let's do that. Quiet is appealing right now."

At the word *self-employed*, Cam felt a surge of hope. The idea grew more appealing by the hour. She had a final incident report to file on Chester, and no one in the office would comprehend what she and Eli knew—that he'd died drinking more deeply and fully from life than he had in a long time.

"Can we leave one of the vehicles—like Cooper's belching exhaust machine perhaps—at the coffee shop so we can ride together?"

"I'd like that."

Within twenty minutes, the distance bridged, Cam pulled her car into the parking area of the small county park she and Allison had visited weeks ago. It wasn't as empty as it had been that day. But it offered quiet places to walk and talk or sit at picnic tables near the creek.

This late in the season, the creek was so low that the water danced around the pebbles on the bottom rather than rushing over them. Different, but beautiful and mesmerizing in its own way.

Allison wouldn't be able to stand ankle deep in the water today. She wouldn't be able to let the water lap above the scar on her ankle.

"What are you thinking about, Camille?" Eli climbed onto the bench on one side of a rustic picnic table.

She sat opposite him, her hands spread on the table's surface. "Allison. And Chester. And failure. And lost opportunity. The usual." Even she knew her smile wasn't convincing.

"You're so skilled at showing compassion to others," he said.

"Haven't quite conquered the need to show yourself the same compassion. Correct me if I'm wrong."

She toyed with a twig with two leaves attached that had dropped from above and landed on the table. "Not wrong."

"So that's your hoard?" he asked.

"What is?"

"Emotions? You can't afford to let others see what you've accumulated, even though the volume of it gets in the way and is so easy to trip over."

"I didn't used to think I hoarded emotions."

His eyebrows lifted at that.

"You've seen me express my emotions." This wasn't the path she hoped their quiet, conversation-less "I need a moment to compose myself" time at the park would take.

"I wonder if for years you haven't been resistant to open the door more than just a crack. What's built up beyond the door, behind the closed curtain, is so much more than anyone would know. And I—"

She bristled. "Eli. Please stop with the homegrown analysis."

"One more sentence? I was going to say that I'm privileged that you've let me see bits and pieces of what you've been through, what you've endured, and what still echoes inside of you."

She studied his hands, now holding hers. "Hoarder spaces don't usually echo. Not even emotional hoarding." Judging by the look on his face, she'd made her point.

The breeze couldn't ruffle hair as short as his, but it certainly tried.

Eli let a moment of silence pass. But no more than that. "I'm asking myself a tough question these days. Maybe you are too. How many people do you have to help before you'll give yourself permission to forgive?"

"Forgive who? My parents?"

"Everyone. Your extended family who didn't try to step in, if that would have helped early on."

"They gave up long before I did."

"Did you have a church family? What did they do? They had to have noticed something about the way your mom was living, the pain she was in."

"People—even people from the church we once attended—kept their distance. Nobody knows what to do with a mental disorder."

"Should be one of the safest places to discuss it."

Cam couldn't disagree with that. Her faith in God had reignited. But some of his people had yet to catch the vision of the role of a faith community in the lives of those dealing with mental illnesses. She couldn't blame them for not knowing what to do. But she wrestled with some people's unwillingness to become informed.

"What would happen, what would you have to risk, if you forgave your father for running back into the flames?" Eli asked. "Or forgave him for giving in to your mother's compulsions many years ago when they began to take over?"

"Forgive my mother for setting the fire?"

She could almost hear his heart beating.

"You're convinced she did?" That tender tone in his voice always did her in.

"I think she deeply believed there was no other way out but to allow what had consumed her to . . . ultimately consume her. She was wrong. So wrong. And I didn't know enough to help her. I was determined to help *others*. That was my goal. I gave her up as a lost cause."

"Lost causes are among God's favorite causes."

"Eli. You might want to quit talking before—"

"So was Papaw—wrong. He'd been through horrors I can't bring myself to consider too deeply. And deprivations unlike any we'll ever know. He was wrong in thinking that drawing *things* tight around him would protect him from or erase those past horrors. It eventually led him to live a different kind of horror story." Eli picked at a splinter in his finger from the picnic table.

"And you've been able to forgive your papaw? Even for the distress he caused your nana?"

He took the twig she'd been absently twirling, watching the two leaves become a single umbrella of green. He traced the outline of a leaf on the table. "I thought I had. Took it to a different level when I started listening to your podcast. When I started listening to you."

"But he loved you and you knew it."

"If your parents didn't love you . . . No, I can't even say that. What's not to love?"

"Excuse me?"

The tan on his cheeks took on a deeper hue. "Isn't it more likely that as the addiction grabbed hold, it's not that they didn't love you but that they didn't know how? They couldn't see past the towers they'd built around themselves."

A breeze lifted the hair falling around her face and cooled her forehead. "My father used to say, 'I'm sorry, Camy.' A lot. 'I'm so sorry.'" She grabbed for a deep enough breath. "He must have said other things to me. We had lots of conversations. Some of them almost normal. But what I still hear in my ears are his apologies."

She pulled her hands onto her lap. Time to refocus. "How did we get so far afield? We came here to process the fact that Chester's gone. That all our work, all those hours, all the investment gave him only a few weeks of happiness and peace. Just the kind of thing Greta will love to get her claws into."

"Greta?"

"My supervisor. The person who ultimately determines whether I'll have a paying job at the end of the year." *Unless I pull my own plug.*

"There's a lot to be said for turning independent contractor. Self-employed. I can help you with the tax ramifications."

There's a word for people who irritatingly read your mind when you don't want them to. She couldn't think of the term at the moment. "Eli, Chester died today! Hours or minutes before we got there. Whatever phrase you want to use for it, I brought him too little too late."

"On the podcast, you could use that as an example of a faulty thought pattern. Cam, because of you, he ended strong. A lot of people would love to be able to say that."

She left the table and stood on the low bank of the creek. At flood stage in spring, this section of the bank was probably under water. But it was a new season. Wildflowers bloomed among the grasses. Dragonflies darted in zigzags across her field of vision. Beyond the creek, another bank. Another world.

She slipped off her sandals and waded in, as her still-hurting client had. *Allison, I can't afford to fail you.*

chapter thirty-one

AN UNFAMILIAR SMELL GREETED CAMILLE when she stepped into Allison's house an hour later. It smelled like home, or like Camille's imagination envisioned a home should. She still had to dodge teetering stacks, but there were fewer of them. As she followed Allison into her kitchen, the stark lines on the faded carpeting showed the aisle was wider now than it had been.

"What have you been up to, Allison?"

"Baking."

"You've been baking? That's wonderful. Smells like molasses ginger cookies."

"They're Ryan's favorite. And they keep well. I thought I'd freeze some. In case they come back."

Cam took a seat at the cookie-filled kitchen table. The whiplash of the day's emotions had somehow affected the muscles in her legs too. "These look beautiful."

"I used to cook and bake a lot."

"These are the work of an expert," Camille said.

"Try one, if you'd like. I'm . . . saving them for . . ." Allison pulled another pan from the oven and set it on the stovetop. "I'm saving some for Ryan and Nicole."

"So you said. Trust me. I won't eat them all. But I'd love a taste. Mmm. Oh, Allison"—she swallowed—"you have a gift."

"Do you think it would be okay if I sent a box of them to Ryan?"

"I think they'd appreciate it."

"Nicole doesn't look like she eats much," Allison said.

"Even if that were true, she'll likely make an exception for a taste of these. That's a lovely thing for you to do."

Allison removed her oven mitts and took one of the other chairs. "If I box them up, would you mind taking them to the post office for me?"

"It would be my joy. Consider it done." Where did Allison intend to get a suitable box? "I could get some food-safe bubble wrap and pack the cookies in one of those Priority boxes the post office has available. Good, sturdy boxes. And they'll arrive within a couple of days. Still fresh."

"Good idea. I wonder . . ."

"What do you wonder?"

"Ryan and Nicole wouldn't say much, but I gathered that Lia isn't ready to talk to me. It hurts, but I understand. Or I'm trying to."

You don't know the half of it, Allison.

"I wonder if she'd mind if a box of cookies showed up in her mailbox too. I wouldn't expect anything of her. And I won't even ask her to visit sometime until I've gotten more done. That ankle-deep-in-the-water picture?"

"Yes?"

"I hung it in the library. I'd like her to see that."

Camille swallowed the last of her cookie and most of the rest of her fear. "We need to talk."

"Should I make coffee? Or tea?"

"Allison, Lia hasn't been feeling well. For a long time."

"Headaches? She used to get a lot of headaches. The doctor

claimed it was from dust mite allergies, but I know it had to be stress."

"Lia has ovarian cancer."

Allison palmed the base of her throat. "No, she doesn't. She can't."

"The doctors somehow missed it during the pregnancy. It's still a mystery how."

"Pregnancy?"

Cam scooted her chair closer to Allison. "Hon, you're a grandmother. Lia had a baby boy several weeks ago."

Allison's eyes filled with tears faster than a watering can sitting under an overachieving outdoor spigot. "Keep breathing. Keep breathing. Keep breathing," Allison chanted.

"I got a text message from Ryan a few minutes ago. She's scheduled for surgery tomorrow morning. Depending on how the surgery goes, they'll establish further treatment plans after that."

"I didn't know she'd gotten married."

"She's not married, Allison. She's on her own. But she's doing the best she can. And from what Ryan says, the baby's doing well."

"What's his name?"

Had Lia told her? Had she remembered to ask? "I'll have to check. My mind's been muddied by this news too."

"When did you find out?"

"Just this morning. I had another client with a . . . need that couldn't wait. I know this is a lot to take in, Allison. Where are your thoughts headed?"

Allison stood. "I need to find her hair ties."

"What?"

"I saved all her hair ties and bows from when she was a little girl. They're here somewhere. I have to find them." She left the kitchen before Cam could push her chair from the table.

"Allison, let's talk about this."

"I know they're here."

"Lia doesn't need her hair ties right now. She needs to know you love her."

"I might have put them in my bedroom. Help me look. Why won't you help me look?" Panic made caves of her eyes.

What, Lord? What do I do? "I'll help you look if you agree to talk to me."

Allison scratched at her forearm. "Maybe in the second bedroom. If you made me throw them away—"

"I haven't made you throw anything away, Allison. You made the decisions. These are your things."

"What if *I* threw them away? I'll never be able to live with myself."

Spiraling. Imploding. Self-sabotage. A setback of epic proportions. How could news like this not rock a woman with Allison's anxieties? "Lia's a grown woman. And a mother of a little boy. Hon, she needs her mother. She doesn't need those hair ties and bows right now."

Allison sank to the floor. "But I do."

━━

It was long after dark before Camille felt comfortable leaving Allison's home. Comfortable was an exaggeration. Allison had tamed her frantic search, but her eyes darted everywhere. Cam had pulled all the resources she knew to help cushion the blow of the news she'd had to tell her client. Was it enough?

Interesting. Compulsive collectors never saw a collection—whether trash or treasures—as enough. Emotionally healthy collectors said the same thing. So did Camille. All her efforts—never enough. Her education? Never enough. Her caring? Not enough. As if it were possible to complete a collection or fulfill the requirements of adequate investment in another's pain.

The goal couldn't be to reach the always elusive *enough*. Did she have to revise her own language, her own thinking? Was Eli right? Hadn't she too long been accumulating emotions, stuffing them into every available space except where they belonged, making rooms of her heart inaccessible for their intended purpose?

Had she walled off her faith too? It could come this far, no further. It was allowed to walk a narrow tunnel through the debris of her life. Eli had thrown the door wide open.

Was that why she'd been so resistant to believing Eli could be real, authentic, and relationship friendly? *And I just described him as "relationship friendly."* She well knew who she was as a psychologist. Who was she as a woman, a person? A wounded veteran of what hoarding could do, reaching a hand out to others? Was that it? Eli saw in her something more, he said.

She'd seen glimpses of it.

Was she as afraid of the light as the clients she worked with?

She'd made a conscious decision to keep her emotional environment compartmentalized, organized, everything put away in order when she was finished with it. But on closer inspection, she was constantly tripping over stacks of emotions she didn't realize were there.

Living behind heavy curtains or drapes is a barrier both ways, both directions. No one can see in. But no one inside can see out either. And light can't penetrate.

Cam set her alarm for five. She needed to run. Not away from, but toward. And she needed to get back to Allison before her curtains closed any tighter.

⌒

"Ivan, I didn't expect to see you here this morning." Camille approached the spot where the older gentleman stood near one of Allison's window boxes. "You work wonders with those flowers, Ivan."

"They needed deadheading," he said. "If you don't get rid

of the spent blossoms, they won't bloom again. There's more life in them yet."

"Good gardening advice. Thanks for the wisdom too." She stood at Allison's door, hope dim that it would open to her today. Ready to knock. Not sure she was ready for what she'd find inside if allowed entrance.

"Dr. Brooks?"

"Yes, Ivan?"

"I went around back to leave her some tomatoes I found at the farmer's market. Beauties."

"That's so thoughtful of you."

"Her kitchen window . . ." He gestured with his garden-gloved hands, but she couldn't read his personalized sign language. "It's boarded up from the inside. Like it used to be. Cardboard. I checked a few minutes ago. The tomatoes are still sitting there on the back stoop."

"Ivan, she's had some hard news."

"Anything I can do to help? Don't answer that. I should know better than to ask. I need to give it more time."

"How long does it take from a seed to a plant to a flower to a bee collecting pollen to honeycomb to honey?"

He nodded. He understood.

"Your faithfulness is important to Allison, whether she responds to you or not."

"As is yours, I suspect."

Cam looked into the well-lined eyes of the gardener, lawn-care expert, gift giver with the face of an ordinary man and the heart of the extraordinary. "I needed that more than you know, Ivan. Thank you."

"I live to bless," he said, and returned to deadheading tired memories of once-vital blossoms.

The door opened a crack without Camille needing to knock. Allison's hand emerged and waved her in. As soon as Camille slipped through, Allison slammed the door behind them.

"What were you two talking about?" Allison's eyes flashed fire.

"There are tomatoes on your back stoop," Cam said, not biting on her client's anger bait.

"Don't you think I know that?"

"Are you going to bring them in before the sun gets hot?"

"Not much sunlight back there." She wove her way toward her glider rocker, which was surrounded by magazines and magazine clippings. "I'll wait until he's gone."

"What's the project you're working on?"

"My nosey neighbor won't even notice this time that I took some of her magazines from her recycling bin. Nobody was awake at that hour."

Regression. With a capital *R*.

"Why did you feel the need for more magazines, Allison?"

"Clipping pictures of babies." She settled in the chair and grabbed a pair of scissors with the protective plastic finger hole missing on one side. Each cut must have bitten into Allison's flesh with the cold metal of the handle.

"Babies?"

"Imagining which of these faces might look like my grandson, or the other grandchildren I'll probably never see."

The stack of images was significant. Allison must have been at it most of the night.

"Today's Lia's surgery." Cam braced for any number of potential reactions.

The scissors stilled for a moment. "I am aware."

Cam could be fired for what she was about to say. But so be it if she was. It would save her the work of creating a resignation letter. It had to be said. "Allison, I know you're a woman of faith. I wondered if you wanted to pray with me for your daughter."

Allison set the scissors and magazine on the stack beside her. "I didn't take you for a praying woman."

"In my professional role, I'm not free to—"

"That's too bad," Allison said. "I haven't always known what to do with my faith. Where to put it, considering . . . I've begged God to fix me. I don't know why he keeps saying no."

"Does he tell you no? Or are his answers muffled by all this?"

"Might be it." Tears formed. The gentle kind. The ones that started at the outer corners of the eyes and traced a slow path over cheekbones, jaw, chin. "You'd pray with me for Lia?"

"It would be an honor."

"And you think Jesus will listen to someone like me? A mess like me?"

Cam patted the hand that looked so much like her mother's, the one she wished she'd patted with tender understanding years ago. Maybe somehow this moment could be commuted retroactively back to another house, another hoarder, a long-ago time. "I've had to be reminded lately, but yes. He's a champion mess fixer."

chapter thirty-two

W HEN PAIN IS MORE FAMILIAR *than freedom, its pull is like the difference between a child's horseshoe magnet—or a fashion magnet that holds a cardigan closed—and an electromagnet that picks up heavy loads of scrap metal.*

The tug, the attraction is exponentially stronger.

Those who have weathered extreme pain without the complication of addiction know where the switch is that disables the electric component. But addiction fogs visibility, forces the addict to paw around in the dark. Many never find the switch.

And those who do locate the switch—one that may take years to engage—experience both the euphoria of release and the lingering fear that any escape from the pull is temporary.

Cam stopped writing.

She could no longer separate the concept of freedom from the Freedom-Giver. She'd seen Allison's hopelessness respond more strongly to the Hope-Bringer than to the list of cognitive-behavioral modification techniques. She'd realized—through the words of her own podcast—that she offered listeners partial hope at best if she stopped shy of addressing the spiritual resources God offered. Her education was not wasted. But it was incomplete. The restrictions placed on her by those who valued a faith-neutral approach to treatment had grown too confining.

She'd watched Allison's countenance change as they prayed together. Was she suddenly freed of all that bound her? No. Was she changed by a power greater than good intentions? Yes.

Ankle deep in a pool of peace. Cam's growing arsenal of methods didn't follow a prescribed protocol of behavioral treatment she could document on paper. But for this client in this circumstance with that level of trust between them, it was right.

And so wrong. So antithetical to what she'd been taught, instructed, to what those who hired her would approve.

Cam too stood ankle deep in a pool of unexplainable peace. They didn't yet know the outcome of Lia's surgery. No sudden healing loomed that they knew of. Allison did not open her eyes to a well-organized, clutter-free home. And Cam's job was no longer merely at risk. It had moved to high risk teetering on the edge of done.

She'd found the switch that dropped the heavy conglomeration of scrap metal. She'd resign before they had a chance to fire her.

She'd have to go rogue.

⌒

If Camille were looking for a sign about the depth of Allison's regression, she found it in what emerged from the side door of the UPS truck blocking her route to Allison's front door. Boxes. Purchases. Items Allison couldn't possibly need. More fodder for the chaos.

Camille skirted past the UPS worker to arrive at the door before he did. She knocked and called out Allison's name. The door opened half a crack.

"Did you order something, Allison? Several somethings?"

"I may have. Yes. Essentials. You won't fault me for essentials, will you?"

The UPS worker had apparently driven this route before. He didn't even attempt to ask Allison to open the door wide enough for him to set the boxes inside. Instead he left the three stacked on a low table on the porch, nodded greetings to Camille, and returned to his truck, his route, his usual customers.

Cam calculated the mathematical impossibilities of shoving the cardboard cubes through the narrow opening. "Allison, do you want to step onto the porch to open these out here?"

"They're personal."

That could mean so many things. One distinct option was that Allison didn't want Cam to see what was inside, shrouded in bubble wrap or cushioned by crumpled wads of paper her client would also find appealing and savable.

"I'll tend to them after you leave," Allison said. "Did you hear anything about Lia?"

"Not yet."

"Then why are you here?"

The edge in Allison's voice and the fact that she hadn't yet allowed Cam entrance ratcheted Cam's concern.

"Allison, let me help you."

A songbird in a far-off tree tweeted a five-note echo. Another mimicked the first's tune.

"Let me help you." As the words fell from Camille's lips, they landed on her own heart. How long had she held Help at arm's length, assuring her Helper that she could handle it, all of it? A childhood that disappeared into the encroaching crowd of things. Hoisting anger and resentment onto her shoulders like a teen slips arms through backpack straps. Determined to—and successful at—escape from what should have been the place to which she ran, flailing at arms that longed to embrace her.

They'd loved her. Her parents had loved her. Like Allison loved Lia and Ryan but couldn't show it. Cam's mother had been no more able to pull herself from the quicksand that trapped her than Allison was. And each stab of pain, each new disappointment—even in herself—had dragged her mother further into the inescapable muck.

Let me help you, Camille had told her mother more times than she could count. But Cam had meant to help by filling garbage bags and hauling them to the curb. Or purging the house one shovelful at a time. Or shaming her mother into changing the unchangeable.

If she'd known what kind of help her mother and father needed, and if she'd known the difference love could make . . . love without conditions. *I'd love you if you'd pay more attention to me than to your accumulation.* No. Love without conditions, without qualifiers.

"Allison, please let me help you."

The woman opened the door to her. "I ordered a case of pacifiers," she confessed, her forehead deeply creased with the effort of speaking the truth. "I didn't know you could order cases of pacifiers, did you?"

Ache's fingers tightened around Cam's heart. "No."

"And formula. For all the grandbabies I'll never see. For the child I'll never hold."

"What was her name?" Cam put an arm around Allison, who shivered as if in postpartum shock.

"She died inside me. At eight months. My doctor said it would be best if we let her be born naturally rather than go in and . . . retrieve her. I carried her two more weeks. Neither of us had a heartbeat. But I had to keep living anyway."

Allison turned out of Cam's embrace and headed for her glider rocker. She sank into it as if thirty years older than her true age.

"What was her name?"

The broken one looked up into Cam's face. "My husband wouldn't let me name her. He said it would hurt more. Her birth and death certificate were practically the same document."

"Do Lia and Ryan know about that child?"

Allison's eyes widened. Had she ever been asked that before?

"No. They were toddlers. How do you tell a toddler about that kind of thing?"

Cam felt the familiar tingling riding the backs of her arms. "Allison, tell me her name."

Nearly a full minute passed. "Jolee." Tears coursed down the soft cheeks of a woman who bore so many of Cam's mother's features. "Dr. Brooks, how did you know she had a name?"

"I imagine that in a way, you're still carrying her inside of you, and her name is embossed on your heart."

"She's buried in the church cemetery."

"Her tiny body is buried there. But who she is, who she would have been, never left you, did she?"

Allison swiped at her eyes with the back of her sweatshirt sleeve. "No."

"And none of this"—Camille gestured toward the piles that seemed never to shrink no matter how much effort they'd exerted—"succeeded in pacifying the pain of losing her, did it?"

"But it did. For a flash of a moment. When I was scrounging through other people's garbage for bits that might be useful someday or pawing through the clearance bins in the days when I still left the house, or scrolling online and stumbling onto a must-have, for that flash of a moment, my attention was diverted."

"But the high never lasted long, and soon you needed more, stronger, a more powerful hit." Camille was rehearsing for herself as much as for Allison.

"What's wrong with my mind, Dr. Brooks? I'm smarter than that, smart enough to know nothing can take the place of . . . Jolee Ann."

Camille swiped at her own tears. "It's not about intelligence, Allison. It's not about weak will or insanity."

"It's not? There aren't many days I don't wonder if I'm sane. Or if I might be sane and the rest of the world is delusional."

"What you're dealing with is so much more complicated than a simple diagnosis or a trigger that was pulled when the doctor told you your baby no longer had a heartbeat."

The two sat in claustrophobic silence.

Cam's phone thrummed.

"Is it about Lia?" Allison asked, hand pressed to her heart.

Cam barely glanced at the caller ID before accepting the call. "Ryan?"

Allison tipped her head back in her chair as if that could stop tears from spilling down her cheeks.

"Ryan, do you have word about Lia?"

"I do," he said. "The hospital just called. She came through the surgery, but there have been some complications. She's in ICU right now."

"Oh—" Cam kept herself from finishing her sentence—*Oh no!*—and left only the first word floating on the dust motes in Allison's home.

"They don't expect her to stay there long," Ryan said. "I think they're being extra cautious because of how long the cancer had a foothold before they discovered it and because of her body having gone through delivering her son not that long ago."

"Thank you for letting us know."

"Us?"

"I'm here with your mother."

Ryan hesitated. He cleared his throat. "I can't talk to her right now without breaking down."

"Understood."

"Would you tell her I love her?"

"Of course."

"I'll call her in a day or two to talk."

"I'll pass that on to her."

He cleared his throat again. "Thank you for being there for her."

Cam looked at the woman now leaning forward, eager to know the other side of the conversation. "It's an honor."

"I gave the hospital your number for updates. I hope that was okay. It seemed too risky to have Mom hear news that might tip her over the edge."

"Yes, that's fine, Ryan. I appreciate that." *And I have a case of pacifiers and formula sitting here to show you how wise a move that is.* "We'll talk to you soon. Thanks for the update."

Cam read the strain in Allison's whole body as the woman waited for the news.

"Lia came through the surgery. A few complications."

"Oh dear."

"She's in ICU so they can keep a close eye on her, but Ryan said they didn't expect her to be there long before they can move her to a regular room."

"I wish I could have talked to him."

I wish you could have too. "Ryan said he'd call you in a couple of days."

Allison nodded. "Rebuilding takes time."

"Very insightful of you."

The room grew quiet again. Too quiet. For all her training, Camille could only guess what might be going on in Allison's mind. Was she sliding deeper into depression? Running toward it? Was she considering what life might have been like for her family if compulsive hoarding hadn't set up camp in their home? Was she contemplating her next purchase or itching for Camille to leave so she could resume her fruitless search for her grown daughter's hair ties, the ribbons of a different life?

The thought that flitted through Cam's mind was too ridiculous to consider, too outrageous to allow it a voice. She shoved it out of the valleys of gray matter it was attempting to inhabit and slammed the mental door as firmly as Allison would against an unwanted visitor.

To Allison, they were all unwanted.

Which made the idea Cam fought against all the more bizarre and impossible.

And impossible to hold back.

"Allison, I'd like to take you to Stafford to visit Lia in the hospital. She needs to know you love her."

"I've told her I love her."

Cam filled her lungs with air, then let it out slowly. "There's a difference between telling it and showing it."

Flinching, screaming, clawing, fleeing, throwing things, showing Cam to the door . . . Of all the probable reactions she might have anticipated from her client, a quiet nod of Allison's head was not on the list.

"My words didn't mean much," she said, "when I couldn't show her that she matters to me. She matters."

"Today would be too soon."

"Yes."

"The second day after surgery is usually the roughest for the patient."

"I remember."

"We'll plan on the day after tomorrow then?" Cam waited for the flip-flop sure to come.

Allison straightened her posture. "Day after tomorrow."

"I won't leave your side during the trip, Allison." Even a Great White Shark truck couldn't hold the amount of courage it was going to take to propel Allison from wanting to visit her daughter to doing it. Leaving her house. The car ride. Being thrust into an unfamiliar environment. Entering a hospital—a symbol of more than one of her life's darkest moments. Surrounded by strangers. Crossing the threshold into the room of a daughter who was expected to reject her . . .

"Won't leave your side."

Allison's face paled. "We won't have to stay overnight somewhere, will we?"

Major courage strain. "It's four hours each way. But we will leave early enough that you can have a nice visit"—*God, please help it be a nice visit*—"and then we'll drive back the same day. If that's what you want."

"I need some time alone to make cookies for her."

"Okay."

"Now. I need time now. By myself. To make cookies."

"Understood." Cam gathered her thoughts and her things and made her way to the front door. "I'll call tomorrow to see how you're doing and to make plans for what time we'll leave."

Allison was already in the kitchen.

chapter thirty-three

COOPER WAVED HIS HAND AND brought Camille's sentence to a halt midstream. "Let's try that again."

She removed her headphones and leaned back from the microphone. "What did I do wrong?"

"Not wrong, per se. I thought you might want an opportunity to adjust your pronunciation of placating."

"What did I say?"

"Well . . ." Cooper chewed on a corner of his lip. "Lactating. Unless you *meant* lactating."

"Cooper! I said that?" Ever since handing in her resignation, she'd been plagued by doubts and lapses in concentration.

"Not to worry. I caught it. We'll redo. All is well."

Camille repositioned her headphones and sighed. *Get your head in the game, girl.* She skimmed her script. Ah, there was the offending sentence. "Starting over at 'Our efforts to appease'?"

"In three . . . two . . . one . . ." Cooper pointed at her, then returned his attention to the sound board in front of him.

If you've been listening to this podcast, then you likely know it's titled Let In the Light. *But you may not know—I didn't until recently—that there's more than a grammatical reason why* Light *is spelled with a capital* L.

It's not uncommon for a hoarder household to be markedly dark. Windows may be completely covered with makeshift curtains, quilts—more protection from prying eyes, cardboard, heavy drapes, or plywood. Light can't get in. Light can't get out.

The symbolism is as heavy as the drapes. We've spoken about that on air in the past. But I beg your indulgence as I share a personal story about that capital L.

We can use all our hard-won wisdom and insight, our years of experience, even the depth of our relationships to attempt to mitigate, appease, and assuage the anger and angst of a compulsive hoarder. I have tried. Often with at least a measure of success. But too often I've done it staring in the face of my limitations, science's limitations, research limitations.

Only recently did I realize that the best I can do is pull back a curtain, and only then after months' or years' worth of investing in a client. I can sometimes succeed in encouraging a client to let in the light. But I am not a light source. I'm a drape puller. We're all drape pullers, those of us who care about, love, work with, or reach out to a compulsive hoarder.

The light source is Jesus.

You can disagree with me, argue with me, or debate until sunrise. But the sun will rise because of God the Creator. And the Light—capital L—*that dispels darkness is his Son, Jesus.*

I realize that I may be risking everything to share this very personal story. In fact, I have risked it all. In order to have the freedom to tell you the truth—that Jesus brings light to darkness—I needed to break some ties that were like a security blanket for me, or like the important but comes-with-a-price items to which a hoarder clings.

You, listener, may choose to unsubscribe to this podcast. I understand that. But I urge you to keep listening. I'm on the near edge of this revelation—that even if I manage to convince someone to fling open their tightly closed drapes of secrecy and shame, it does no good if Light is not waiting on the other side. I'm still exploring what it means and how it fits in the realm of mental disorders like those you or a family member may be battling. And I would appreciate it if you would please continue to accompany me on this journey.

Imagine yourself completely exposed and vulnerable to the Light. But rather than finding that Light harsh and penetrating and blinding, it is instead protective, embracing, warming, healing.

Imagine—as I have—the wonder of this timeless truth from 1 John 1:5—"God is pure light. You will never find even a trace of darkness in him."

"What's this?" Eli asked, opening the envelope Camille slid toward him across the table at the coffee shop not far from Allison's home.

"It's a partial refund," she said, her breathing more even than she'd expected it to be.

"For what?"

"Your sponsorship money. I intend to get you the rest, but it may be a while." She stirred the foam on her coffee until it deflated into a mere skin of white on its surface. "It may be a long while."

Eli stilled her wrist with his solid but kind grip. "Cam, what's going on? I thought we'd dispelled all that conflict-of-interest nonsense. I'm not profiting from advertising on your podcast. I'm not being paid for working with your clients. I drew a clear line there. If I do gain any business from the ads, it will be freelance projects for people who are *not* your clients."

"That's not it."

"And I didn't offer sponsorship to drum up income for myself anyway. I did it because I believe in what you're doing."

"But that has changed, Eli."

"What do you mean? Should I have ordered an extra shot of espresso? For both of us?"

She dug in her purse for the object she was looking for and positioned it on top of her head.

Eli's eyebrows raced toward his hairline. "You're not—"

"Yes. I'm repenting in dust and ashes for not telling you sooner."

"You can't quit helping people, Camille. You can't."

"I'm not quitting. I'm . . . retooling."

"What does that mean?" He sat back in his coffee shop–worthy chair.

"In essence"—she sighed—"it means I lost my day job."

"Lost as in fired?" His face wore a mask of confusion. "Lost as in you don't remember where you put it?"

"Very funny."

"Then what?"

"Lost as in I let it go. I am now self-employed." The statement almost sounded adventuresome when she said it, which screamed at the reality of the loss of her paycheck, benefits, security . . .

"Good for you. It's about time." Eli raised his hands in the air, clearly not caring if anyone noticed.

"Don't you want to know why I made that move?"

"Hard to take you seriously with dryer lint on your head."

She snatched it from her hair and stuffed it back into her purse. "Eli, I owe you an explanation."

"You don't owe me anything, Cam, much less an explanation. Unless, you know, you wanted to tell someone. Everybody says I'm a good listener." He folded his hands on the table and stared without blinking, as if he couldn't until she spoke.

He'd obviously underestimated her ability at staring contests. But she acquiesced for the sake of time. "The podcast has changed. And it couldn't unless I separated myself from being paid by the county. My whole approach to coaching my clients is changing."

"Oh." He drained his coffee.

"That's it? *Oh*?"

"Actually, I'm happy dancing inside." He shoved the envelope toward her. "It's not obvious, is it? I mean, I wouldn't want to make a fool of myself in public."

Uh-huh. She slid the envelope closer to him. He slid it back.

"I think you made a wise decision, Cam." His eyes showed nothing but seriousness now.

"You do? I haven't even told you why I made it."

"So you can operate from a position of freedom, free to work outside of conventional expectations if wisdom runs contrary to your gut, or your soul."

"Huh. Wish I'd had those words when I talked to Greta."

"If only you'd asked me. And I'm kidding. I know you needed to do this on your own, without my excessively exuberant help."

"You know this about yourself? I thought we were going to have to have an intervention." She allowed herself another sip of coffee, then dabbed at the foam that clung to her upper lip.

"I'm so stinkin' proud of you."

"The man with the silver tongue." She chuckled and crumpled her napkin into a ball.

"I mean it, Cam. You're so gifted. But you've been handicapped from doing what your heart knew it needed to do."

"Story of my life, actually."

"You're writing new chapters. I like them. They make a good read."

"The podcast is taking a new direction. I suppose some would call it faith-based counseling."

He nodded.

"You're considering what that means or you're nodding in agreement?"

"Both," he said. "You didn't think I never talk to my brother, did you?"

"Didn't I have him sign a confidentiality agreement? I don't think I did." She shook her head and thumbed a note to herself on her phone.

Eli's face revealed his approval of what she'd done. And maybe more than a hint of approval for who she was. She couldn't afford to consider that for long, or she'd never find her way out of the labyrinth of conversation.

"I'm not going all woo-woo with heavy spiritual teaching or anything. I still see the value in all the neurological research, the cognitive-behavioral therapy techniques, and I still need to keep my license and my credentials. I know how many people they are affecting for good."

"Understood."

"But on the podcast, and in person, when I see an open door, I can no longer stop shy of the truth I know."

"Preach it, sister."

"That's what Shyla used to say. Or rather, 'That'll preach.' But I don't want to preach. That's someone else's gift. I do, however, want to be free to talk about the source of Light when appropriate."

Eli dropped his gaze. "I have a confession too."

Another one? This can't be good. "What is it?"

"I'd like to increase my sponsorship level. What was that, gold level? I'd like to increase to the platinum level. That's the one that comes with a *Let In the Light* mug, right?"

"Eli."

"Camille."

What was happening to her? Delirium from being her own boss for the first time? A brain squeeze from the burden of financial pressures like she'd never known before? "You can have the *Let In the Light* mug. And the glow-in-the-dark pen too."

He leaned forward. "You have one of those?"

"No, Eli. I don't. And no mug. Possibly no audience. I may have lost my entire audience. Just so you know, partner."

"That word has a certain ring to it, doesn't it?"

"Eli, it was a joke. The partner part. Not the audience part. It may be gone within minutes of that first naming-the-Light podcast's airing."

"Then we'll build a new one."

She nudged her coffee cup closer to the center of the table. "Have you ever made a decision so radical, so risky, that your heart kept flipping from elation to—"

"Yes," he said. "I have."

"How did it turn out?"

"I don't know yet."

"Big help." She pulled her coffee closer and pushed the envelope his direction.

"Are you free for dinner tonight at the house? Mom's making bean and bacon soup."

Cam wrinkled her nose. "No offense to your mother, Eli, but if I never ate bean and bacon soup again, I'd be okay with that."

"Me too. That's why I was hoping you'd give me an excuse not to be home during the dinner hour. I thought we could visit a new seafood place that just opened in Hillsboro."

"I have to pass, Eli."

"It's important to me."

What was that look? It took a lot to disappoint Eli Rand, but she clearly had. "I'm calling it an early night tonight. Leaving not long after dawn and will be out of town all day tomorrow. That's the hope, anyway."

"Can't be for a client. The people you specialize in helping rarely leave their homes."

He'd already crossed way too many boundaries regarding patient privacy. It had always worked to the patient's advantage, but despite Cam's aversion to rules and restrictions, she did have professional and ethical standards to uphold. And if Allison backed out or regressed even further, it would be chalked up as one more failure in a long list of Cam's risks. She trusted Eli, more than she'd ever trusted anyone. But a road trip with Allison that might not happen? He'd said she didn't owe him anything, including an explanation.

This time she'd have to take him up on that.

chapter thirty-four

FOR A GARBAGE TRUCK DRIVER—no offense to all the garbage truck drivers in the world—Eli Rand had uncanny— also no offense or pun intended—insights about human beings. He'd connected with Chester in a remarkable way that, even without Cam's work with her client, changed the trajectory of his last days on earth.

Eli had found a way into Allison's good graces. And for as much as Cam doubted his authenticity in the early days of their working together, it had all proven to emanate from a heart that oozed kindness and generosity.

He also had an uncanny ability to worm his way into Camille's thoughts. For much of the night, she mentally carried on two conversations—one with Allison, fending off imaginary excuses that might keep the woman from following through on her commitment to the road trip, and one with Eli, testing the waters of both options.

If she'd told him where she was going with Allison, he would have volunteered to drive. That was way out of the protocol box. The whole trip was. But ruining her reputation within the counseling community—despite her new status as a freelancer—was a risk she felt compelled to take. She couldn't risk dragging Eli into a situation that might destroy his future work as part of the cleanup team for other psychologists specializing in hoarding disorders.

He had a business to run and a professional reputation to protect. Hers was already toast.

But Eli also had uncanny timing. His text message arrived just as she finished her morning smoothie, which she hoped would carry her through for the whole trip to Stafford.

"Missed you last night. Mom's bean soup was atrocious. Dad loved it. I washed mine down with an extra helping of Mom's world-famous mocha chocolate cake and fudge frosting, which u do need to try sometime. Tonight?"

Cam stared at the remnants of her blueberry-kale-celery smoothie and considered the exceptional benefits of fudge frosting. "Not sure when I'll be home. Will call later."

She watched the three little gray dots on the screen that indicated he was keying in words, apparently lots of words that he wrote and then deleted. Nothing came through for the longest time. Then . . .

"Whatever it is, wherever you're headed, I'm going with you . . . vicariously. Praying for you."

If Eli ever came to his senses and realized she wasn't worth it, she hoped he'd let her down gently. *Because you are so worth it, Eli Rand.*

Wonder of wonders, Allison was not only still on board with the idea, she was waiting in one of the patio chairs on her front porch, purse in her lap. She'd dressed in crisp black slacks and a black-and-red geometric print top that looked brand new. *Oh dear.*

"You look so nice, Allison."

"Did the wrinkles come out?" She brushed her hands down the front of the blouse. "I must have had this for years. Don't even remember buying it. But the tags were still on it."

"They still are." Cam tugged at a clearance designer tag hanging from a plastic thread near the collar.

"I know. I couldn't find a pair of scissors." Allison frowned. "I probably own twenty pair of scissors. Today I couldn't find even one."

Cam smiled. "I have one in my manicure kit in my purse." She dug until she found it. "Hold still. I don't want to mess up that beautiful top."

"Having a hard time holding still. It'll get worse the longer the trip drags on. How fast can we go on the interstate?"

Camille returned her scissors to the scissor-shaped depression in her miniature manicure kit and slipped it into its zippered pouch in her purse. "The speed limit. That's how fast we can go." *See? I do sometimes follow the rules.*

"I find that answer disappointing," Allison said, her eyes bright but her hands clenching and unclenching.

"And I find it the best way to stay on the good side of the law. Did you bring your antianxiety medications, Allison?"

"I don't leave home without them, as they say."

You don't leave home.

This was nothing short of a miracle, a miracle of a mother's overcoming love.

Mom, it's okay. I survived. I get it. You didn't have anyone walking you through what I didn't know way back then. All the Allisons of the world will receive my best attention, Mom, in your honor.

"Ready?" Cam slipped her purse strap over her shoulder.

"Not quite," Allison said.

You can't back out now.

Allison disappeared into the house and emerged with two white bakery boxes. She locked the door behind her and rejoined Cam.

"Where . . . where did you get the boxes, Allison? And what's in them?"

"This one's a care package of my cookies for Lia. This one's a mix of fruit and veggies and cookies for you and me on the trip. And I know what you're thinking. The boxes came from the bakery at the grocery store. I . . ."

"What?"

"I called Ivan and asked if he'd pick them up for me."

Cam drew a sharp breath.

"I know. You're proud of me. I'm proud of me too."

"Ivan is a faithful friend."

"Yes." Allison stared at the boxes. "Let's hope he's a faithful date too. I told him I'd go for coffee with him someday soon. He's only been asking for eight years."

It started with a podcast. Then a response to Allison's chat question. Then a tentative knock at her door. No, it had all started a lot longer ago than that, with the persistent kindness of a friend from church who brought strawberries and tomatoes, petunias and plum honey, who shoveled sidewalks and cleaned leaves from the downspout whether Allison wanted him to or not. Persistent, insistent caring.

No shaming. No nagging. Ivan Probst had shown up and showed he cared, rejected for every act of kindness day after day, year after year. For almost a decade, Allison had denied it mattered. But it did.

"You did mean we'd get to see Lia today, right?"

Cam looked up to see Allison standing by the front passenger door. "Yes. It's time. Let me get the door for you. You really brought veggies?"

"Carrot cake is considered a vegetable, right?"

"Allison, this is going to be a fun trip. I'm looking forward to spending time with you." She started the engine and secured her seat belt.

"I wouldn't be doing this if you weren't just a few inches

away from me. I can't pretend I'm not already so far out of my comfort zone that I'm unsure I'll ever be able to find it again."

"Ankles in the water?"

"That one day. I had that one day. Oh! We have to turn around!"

"Allison, keep breathing," Cam said. "This wave of fear will pass."

"I have to go back! I forgot the picture for Lia. The one with me with my ankles—"

Cam chose the first driveway wide enough to turn around safely. "I'm glad you thought of it now. We wouldn't have wanted to miss giving her that gift today. She may need her own ankles-in-the-water reminder."

Allison sniffed twice, then again.

Buckle up, Allison. It could be a bumpy ride.

⌒

"I'm afraid I can't let you in." The nurse's tone grew rougher each time she said it.

"But this is Lia's mother, as I explained," Cam said, leaving her professional credentials card visible on the visitor check-in desk.

"And as *I* explained," the nurse said, "the patient's records indicate that her mother is deceased."

Allison leaned over Camille's shoulder and whispered, "In some ways I was."

Camille patted Allison's hand. "We'll get this cleared up. We didn't come this far to be turned away."

The nurse raised her eyebrows.

"Could I speak with your supervisor?"

After a long sigh, the nurse said, "Yes, of course. Dr. Brooks, I'm not insensitive. In your line of work, you must be well versed in HIPPA regulations and how it's changed visitation policies. Although, the ICU, step-down, and the psych departments have their distinctions in that regard."

Cam glanced at Allison. Had she stepped back farther from the desk at the nurse's use of the word *psych*? Cam clasped her hands together. "I do understand. I'd still like to speak with your supervisor and attempt to clear up this misunderstanding. Lia's mother is, as you can see, very much alive."

Ten minutes later, they had an answer. Not the one they hoped for, but an answer nonetheless.

The nursing supervisor stepped into Lia's room to ask for clarification. The success or failure of the trip, and the state of Allison's broken heart, now rested in Lia's hands and words.

When the supervisor returned, she cocked her head and said, "The patient is not convinced that her mother is here, but she did admit that her mother is alive. Do you have any ID?"

"Here." Allison opened the white bakery box. "Take her one of these. She'll recognize it. Me."

"I was thinking," the supervisor said, "of something more on the order of a photo ID? Driver's license? Passport? And the patient is on a restrictive diet, as you can imagine."

Camille stepped forward. "She doesn't have to eat the cookie. Just recognize it."

"This is so far away from normal *protocol*." The veins in the supervisor's neck throbbed visibly.

Cam smiled, well familiar with that phrase. "Please just try it," Cam said. "My client hasn't driven for years. She's had no need for a passport. But she knows her daughter. And her daughter knows her."

"I have photo ID." Allison pulled a picture frame from under the bakery box.

"What's this?"

Allison lifted her chin. "I'm a bit surprised you don't recognize an ankle, ma'am. It's my ankle. Lia will know that scar."

"And the shade of toenail polish," Cam added. *Completely*

professional. My calling card. I'm always the consummate profes-sional. Toenail polish?

The supervisor seemed to study the ceiling tiles for a sign. She held out her hand to receive the photograph of Allison's ankle in the creek water. "I'll be right back."

Cam and Allison looked at each other without speaking, as if one or the other were about to be called into the principal's office. What was taking so long?

"Mrs. Rand?" The supervisor, sans photograph, waved Allison over.

Camille followed. "I need to accompany my client," she said. "At least for the initial part of the visit."

"Of *course* you do," the woman said, a quarter inch shy of what qualified as rolling her eyes.

Lia had been crying, the framed photo clutched to her chest. Fresh tears still spilled down her cheeks. Allison stood just inside the door, Cam beside her.

"Mom, I can't believe you're here."

"I can hardly believe it myself," Allison said.

Lia's brief burst of laughter made Allison cringe.

"Don't bust open your stitches, Lia. Not for me."

"Oh, Mom." Lia spread her arms wide, IV tubing swinging with the motion. "You came."

"Oh, Lia," Allison said, burying her face in Lia's shoulder, "you let me in."

Camille lowered herself to a chair near the door. The scene belonged to the two of them, not her. But somehow she could imagine herself in Lia's place and her mother dressed in a black-and-red geometric print with one tag still hanging from a sleeve.

⟞

Allison's anxieties rose closer to the surface several times during the visit. But each time, Camille watched her client rein them in for the sake of her daughter. Lia had to have noticed. Tensions weren't instantly healed between them. But they'd made significant headway.

Allison explained the story behind the ankles picture. Lia pulled up images of Allison's grandson.

A nurse stopped in to check Lia's vitals but left without comment except to mention that Lia had been cleared to return to her normal diet, should she want a snack. "A homemade cookie, for instance," she said, tapping the top of the bakery box on her way out the door.

"Are you staying overnight, Mom?" Lia asked, a yawn punctuating her question.

Cam pocketed her phone and leaned forward. "Not this time, Lia. I . . . I have responsibilities I need to attend to. But we can come back, if you'd like."

"After I get released?" she said to Allison. "I'd like you to meet your grandson."

"It's a good thing," Allison said, "that he's too young to have heard about me. How I've not created the legacy I want to leave in anyone's mind."

"He's a snuggly baby, Mom. You two will get along just fine."

Way to go, Lia. You could have said so many other things. At your age, I would have. She'd just checked her messages and dealt with a few emails. *Now* her phone thrummed. She retrieved it from the pocket of her jacket. A text from Eli.

More than once in the last couple of hours, she'd wished he could have been there to witness what she was watching. She and Eli cared about so many of the same things. As she reached to open the text, it occurred to her that she no longer felt compelled to steel her heart against getting involved with someone like Eli. Correction. Not "someone like." With Eli.

The message read, "Is it wrong to miss you this much? And to wonder where you are and what you're doing?"

She texted back, "No." Enough for now.

"And is it wrong to say I can't wait until you get back because I have two important pieces of information that I can't withhold from you anymore? They're eating me up inside."

"What? That is unfair, cruel, and a whole lot of other words."

"Then, come home. I'm praying you home."

"We're on our way." Oops. she should have edited that before she'd hit Send.

"We?"

"Explain later. If I can."

"Can I call you?"

"No."

"I'm going to call."

"I won't answer." Not in a good place for a phone conversation.

"You're in jail, aren't you? They finally arrested you for obstructing injustice."

"Nice one, Eli. Now, stop texting so I can get on the road."

"Over and out."

chapter thirty-five

*S*TORIES DON'T START AND END *on the first page. The story of a hoarder's journey toward freedom could fill a library, not one book. I often ask my clients to start a journal of the whys behind the purchases they make, the items they scavenge, the pain that drives their obsession. Those willing to participate fill that journal and ask for another. When they're honest with themselves, when we're honest with ourselves, the pain pages—tear stained and ink smudged—tell the truest stories.*

Allison was safely home but bearing a new pain—distance from a daughter who was willing to walk gently into a future that had her mother in it. She hadn't yet told Lia or Ryan about Jolee and how their unknown stillborn sister played into Allison's condition. She hadn't yet cleared her home of even half of the excess. But Camille believed she would, no matter the cost. It wouldn't be today or next week or next month. But she'd exchanged addiction for determination. Setbacks no longer spelled defeat for her. The enormity of the task ahead of her—once paralyzing—took on a new name: Challenge.

Their discussions in the car on the way home had reassured

Camille that hope had gained a foothold and it wasn't about to give up territory it had reclaimed from the rubble. For two hours of the four-hour road trip home, they'd played Situations. Cam threw out a variety of situations and asked Allison to form an alternate plan for how she'd handle it—an arsenal of coping mechanisms that were health- and life-giving.

"You're home alone," Cam had started.

"I'm always home alone," Allison answered.

"Play along with me, please?"

"Okay."

"And you're watching a favorite sitcom."

"Not fond of sitcoms."

"A movie then." Cam let her left brain drive and focused her right brain on engaging her client in the exercise. "During a commercial break, you see an advertisement for fabulous new pots and pans that never scratch, never stick, and come with a second set for only $19.99 more, plus free shipping. What do you do?"

"Eat six cookies until the feeling passes."

"Is that your final answer?" Cam shook her head.

"I would . . . pause the TV and get a drink of water. Then I'd fast forward through the commercial and go back to watching the movie."

"That's a great solution, Allison. Now try this one."

Two hours of tool building marked the miles to set Allison up for success. Eventually she wouldn't have to think about it. Like muscle memory, she would react with positive choices rather than the destructive ones that had ruled her life for so long.

Cam had promised Allison that yes, she would stop by the next afternoon. Cam read between the lines. She didn't yet trust herself. She needed the accountability Camille offered. It was late.

She climbed the stairs from the parking garage to her

eighth-floor apartment, wondering if it were too decadent to set her alarm for noon.

Cam's adrenaline kicked in as she reached for the Emergency button on her phone. A man sat slumped on the floor in front of her door.

Eli?

"What are you doing here at this hour?" Cam punched the keycode for her apartment security system and opened the door.

He rose stiffly and said, "Waiting for you."

"I hadn't told you what time I'd be home." She dropped her purse on the coffee table and kicked off her shoes.

"Yeah. I hoped you weren't driving home from Hawaii or something."

"Hawaii?"

He sat on one end of the couch. "Cut me some slack. I haven't eaten since you left."

She flicked on another light and sat next to him. It was almost midnight. He hadn't eaten all day? "Can I fix you a sandwich or something?" Did she have anything in the house with which she could make a sandwich?

His eyes showed more than fatigue. Something else was going on.

"You can fix me." He slouched and dropped his head back until his neck was supported by the back of the couch.

"What are you talking about? The two important things you've been withholding?"

He pushed himself upright again. "Cam, I know you're new to the idea of working independently, and it must all sound invigorating and exciting to you."

"And scary and terrifying and a lot like walking across the Grand Canyon on a tightrope, with the wind blowing, and sleet falling, and I forgot my shoes."

"I know it's probably the worst time in the world to ask, but would you consider taking on a partner?"

That word again. Something must have changed inside her. She didn't taste bile.

"We've been over this territory before, Eli."

"Yes, but I didn't have my credentials before."

"What do you mean?"

He rubbed his palms on his thighs—a nervous tic. "Those two important things? One is that I . . . I know how hard you worked to get your PhD."

"That's news? That's it's-midnight-but-I-just-have-to-tell-you news?"

"I k-n-o-w."

"Eli . . ."

"I know because I had to work that hard too." He didn't raise his head but peered up at her like an octogenarian professor might peer over half-glasses.

"What are you saying?" *There* was the expected heartburn.

"Awe-Done? That's a side gig."

She breathed a little easier. "You have a lot of irons in the fire. That's no deep, dark secret."

"Camille, I'm a clinical psychologist. I just got word yesterday that I passed my boards."

She stuck a thumbnail in the narrow gap between her two front teeth, the ones her parents couldn't afford to have looked at by an orthodontist because their money went to other things, worthless—in her mind—things.

"I know," he said. "It wasn't fair of me to keep that from you."

"You've been stalking me all this time? Pretending to be someone you weren't? Checking up on me?" *What if . . .* "Were you working for Greta? Tattling on me to her? Eli!" She stood, blood draining from her head to her toes.

He stood too. "No. Not at all. That's not it. If anything, I was shadowing you. I admire you. I admired you before I ever made the sponsorship offer. From the beginning I've wanted to"—his hands moved as if grasping for words in the air—"seriously, I've wanted to partner with you. I like everything about you. What you say on the podcast. The way you approach your clients. The passion you express in what you do and how you do it. The distrust you have for a treatment modality that doesn't allow for the faith factor."

Blood rushed noisily close to her eardrums. "Eli, I don't understand. Modality. You used the word *modality*." She tented her fingers on her forehead. It was unlikely to keep her head from exploding, but nothing would. "Who *are* you?"

"A fan."

"I've driven eight hours today and wrestled with an alligator pretending to be a nursing supervisor. I am way too tired to— Oh! Every stupid move I've made, you've seen! You noticed. And you processed it not as the friend I thought you were but as a colleague waiting for me to mess up!"

"None of that is true."

"What, then?"

"I've viewed it as someone who highly respects you and would consider it an honor to work with you to help others like the people I've watched you serve. That's what I want to do with my life—what you're doing."

"So you disguised yourself as a garbage man?"

"No." His voice grew quiet. "I *became* a garbage man so I could understand the challenge from all sides. So I could see if there was anything of value I could offer to the process. I'm content to drive a garbage truck the rest of my life if it helps people heal. But, as you pointed out so clearly, the one who hauls the garbage isn't supposed to have the kind of access to clients that a counselor has."

"You decided to get your PhD in your spare time?" Her voice ricocheted around the sparsely furnished room.

"I've been working on it for years. All I had left when I met you was my boards. And I . . ."

"What?"

"I passed. Not that it matters anymore. I guessed wrong.

I thought there was hope that we could work together." He walked to the door and paused with his hand on the knob. "I wanted to be part of what you're doing. Like always, I apparently went about it all wrong."

"Eli? What was your second big important thing you wanted to share with me?"

His shoulders lifted, then dropped. He still hadn't turned to face her. "It's of no consequence now."

"I'd like to know." Thoughts collided against one another like bumper cars. He was a good man. This should have been news worth celebrating. What was she supposed to feel? Whatever it was didn't come naturally. She'd often wondered if her mother's mental disorders would one day show up in her. Apparently, today was the day. She couldn't think straight, couldn't make sense of what she was hearing. "Eli, I'd like to know."

He removed something from his shirt pocket and hung it on one of the empty coat hooks by the door. "It was . . . kind of a dual partnership idea. Gone awry. Good night, Dr. Brooks."

The door closed behind him before she could say, "Good night, Dr. Rand."

She locked the door and reached for the object hanging on the coat hook. A ring. Like, a fourth-finger-of-the-left-hand kind of ring. Her sanity was secure. *He* was the crazy one.

She hadn't used the word *crazy* since before college. Not intentionally, anyway. Mental disorders were serious business. No laughing matter, as she'd said more than once.

Who did that? Who met a woman and decided within a couple of months that he wanted to marry her for her mind? And her heart? Wait. That was what she'd always wanted.

Who made a fortune, then felt bad about it and decided to give it all away? Who enlisted to make sure his brother found his way back from the brink of self-destruction? Who would ignore his degrees and drive a garbage truck for the rest of his life if that helped more people?

Who bled to convince an old man to give up what could hurt him?

Eli was certifiably crazy.

But he had excellent taste in rings.

She left it on the coat hook but had a hard time ignoring it. She'd turned off the ceiling light and the end table lamps. But even the blue light on the stove face and the lit clock on the microwave and the city lights that stole through the thin slit where the two halves of the draperies came together made the thing sparkle as if it were lit from within.

Light had a way of piercing all kinds of darkness.

The hour of random thoughts and brilliant ideas, of problems solved and problems introduced, of hearing voices and hearing from God—3:00 a.m.

Why was it always three in the morning?

And why these thoughts? A poster had hung in her dorm room her freshman year. She'd memorized its message:

Hawking: "Religion is a fairy story for people afraid of the dark."
Lennox: "Atheism is a fairy story for people afraid of the light."
—Don Sweeting

Early in her practice, she'd observed that more people were afraid of the light than of the dark. Could it be that she was one of them? Had she resisted happiness as if it were too precious a gift for someone like her? Had she pushed aside Eli's affection because she was afraid of being loved? Why did his admiration frighten her? Was it so uncommon in her life that it felt like a language she couldn't understand much less interpret?

She'd been alone. Somewhere in the years between her

parents' death and now, she'd told herself, convincingly, that alone was safer than together. But in her practice, she'd promoted the opposite.

Eli had—until her meltdown at midnight—apparently wanted to express his desire to share life with her and share her life's work. And other than the suddenness of the idea, she couldn't think of a single reason to fault his logic. No excuse for pushing away his affection survived long in the light.

But the risk. Oh, the risk of pulling back the curtains that shielded her heart and letting another in. Not merely another. Eli.

She grabbed her phone from the bedside stand. He wouldn't see her text until morning, but if she didn't send it now, she'd become the person Shyla said she was. The first gift Shyla had ever given her was a dish towel that said, "Give me a minute so I can overthink this."

"Eli, can two people build a relationship on pain?"

She slid the phone back onto the bedside stand and turned her back to it.

It pinged within seconds. He wasn't sleeping either.

"Cam, the answer is no."

Her heart sank. Her reaction had erected an impenetrable wall between her and the one man whom she could imagine spending the rest of her life with . . . the one who carried light with him like others carried emotional baggage. Broken, like she was. Not healed, but healing.

Another ping followed the first. "But we can build a relationship on redeemed pain."

chapter thirty-six

THE DAYS ARE GETTING SHORTER." Cam tugged her Sherpa shawl tighter around her as she watched hooded, fleeced, and gloved kayakers milk all they could from the remaining days of open water on the lake.

"No stopping that," Eli said, wrapping an arm around her. The warmth of his touch penetrated through shawl and sweater, clear to her marrow.

"Want me to build a fire in the fire pit?" Eli didn't move.

"Maybe later. I don't want to lose this." She pulled at his hand so his embrace tightened around her.

"Your fingers are cold," he said. "Here." He took both her hands, tucked them inside his jacket, and pressed them against his chest. "Better?"

"Better. How's Nana? Should we check on her?"

"Mom's with her. Doing her nails, I think. Who knew that would be something they could share together? Glad you suggested it."

"Whatever works."

Eli's breaths were steady and strong. Steadying. "Nana asked me if I'd proposed to you yet."

"Did she now? What did you tell her?"

"The truth. Nine times, if you don't count the ring-on-the-coat-hook attempt."

"I hope she understands why I keep turning you down."

"Not a bit. In her opinion we're perfect for each other."

With her hands trapped inside Eli's coat, what could she do but lay her head on his chest? "I don't disagree."

"I know. I know. It was too soon. Too sudden. Too out of the blue. Too much to take in. I get it. I don't like it, but I get it."

The solar lights edging the deck began to glow with their stored energy. Pinpricks of light dotted the darkening sky.

"You're shivering, Cam. Do you want to go inside?"

She shook her head. "No." How far they'd come in the last weeks. Tag-teaming on the podcast opened more time for her to devote to her clients. Their clients. The practice was building slowly. They hadn't lost the vast numbers of listeners she'd feared, but had gained significant numbers of followers. The way they'd always dovetailed their skill sets and specialties enhanced their work with people in need. What she didn't think of, he did. What he missed, she didn't.

Having the freedom to discuss once-privileged information and background histories of the clients brought both relief and the benefit of their brainstorming innovative methods. She was no longer alone.

Allison had reserved a beach cottage for Thanksgiving with her family. She'd spent days preparing menus for multiple meals and small gifts for each of them. Ryan was handling travel arrangements. He and Nicole had moved closer to Lia to help with the baby and Lia's recovery. Cam had suggested Allison compile her menu ideas into a from-the-heart cookbook for her children. With so much progress made on her cleanup, and with other projects to hold her attention, Allison said she had never been more content.

Eli's parents had treated Cam like a daughter they'd never had. She belonged. She knew what acceptance and sacrifice and commitment looked like in healthy relationships.

"I don't want to go inside yet, Eli. I want you to ask me again. On second thought, I'll ask you."

Plums. I get it now.
I understand how fruit can grow in an overgrown,
overtrashed yard.
Some fruit is tenacious like that,
not needing perfect conditions.
And sometimes the refuse
decaying at the tree's feet
feeds the tree
that forms the blossoms
that draw the bees
that make plum honey
that drips from the fingers
of a less-than-perfect life.

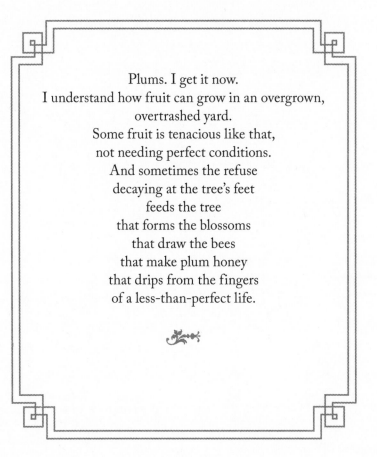

Author's Note

A novel like this owes a great deal to the people who live with its themes every day, those whose stories I've heard about at a distance and those I've heard face-to-face as individuals and families dealing with hoarding disorders and addictions have confessed their struggles. I'm grateful to each one who offered insights, talked about the fallout, or expressed their renewed hope that someone would listen and would treat their unique but too-common distress kindly.

Dr. Barbara Wilson, licensed clinical psychologist, author, speaker, and friend, provided key guidance from her professional perspective, letting me know which elements of the main characters' behavior would require a disclaimer in the book to cover when they veered from standard protocol or expected practices. Their "veering" was important to the story and to the eventual conclusion. Dr. Wilson's knowledge and insights were invaluable as I walked that fine line.

Wendy Lawton, my agent and cheerleader, rallied hard for this book, believing in its importance for readers and its place on bookshelves. As always, Wendy, I wouldn't want to do this without you by my side. If anyone walks away from this book with a sense of readerly satisfaction, or with a heart tenderized to the unique challenges of hoarders and their families, or with the confidence that they are better equipped to reach out in love to those whose emotional hoarding has crippled them, know that they wouldn't have without you.

I remember the day I sat beside Catherine DeVries as we chatted with the rest of the team at Kregel Publications about *Afraid of the Light*. The feedback told me the story line was resonating with that conference room full of people—marketing, sales, editorial, design, the executive team . . . Before the book was in print, it spoke to those hearts. And that moment will forever be etched in my memory. Thank you, Kregel team, for believing in the project and for blessing me from minute one.

No book makes it to readers without the influence of those who pray for me as I write. May God reward you for your diligence in prayer for me, for my imagination, and for the readers who now hold this book in their hands or read it on their devices.

To the guy I live with—the man I married after only nine years of dating him (when you fall in love at eleven and twelve, that time span makes more sense). Thank you, Bill, for understanding book deadlines better now and always gracing me with your blessing on my stories. Thanks for your inexpressibly meaningful prayers for me.

Thank you to the Author of Hope, without whom I would have no stories to tell.

And, reader, please know you are on my heart. May you be hemmed in and overflow with hope (Romans 15:13).

Discussion Questions

1. What made the partnership between Camille and Shyla work so well?
2. Camille claimed to be able to keep a distance between herself and other people's pain. Could she? What makes you answer that way?
3. How did Camille's mother's disorder affect Camille in unexpected ways? We know the toll it might exact on Camille, but what strengths did it build in her?
4. In the early days of the story, Camille and Eli seemed to be the unlikeliest pair. Initially, what common bond(s) kept them from bailing on each other? Later in the story, did your understanding of their bond(s) change? How?
5. Some people might find Chester and Allison hard to love—or to empathize with—in the beginning. If that was you, did your attitude shift somewhere during their journey? What rearranged your thinking?
6. What critical but unspoken role did Eli's brother play in Camille's life? In the friendship between Eli and Camille?
7. In the movie *Schindler's List*, the sight of a little girl's

red coat—the only spot of color in an otherwise dark, gray world—raked the souls of viewers, as it did that of the author of *Afraid of the Light*. What moments in this novel showed that a flash of color changed things for the characters?

8. Some of Camille's techniques with her clients lie outside the boundaries of accepted practice and standard protocol, including Eli's developing involvement with Camille's clients. Whose example in history, or from your life, did Camille and Eli seem to mirror when they opted for untraditional and unexpected yet effective methods?

9. It's been said that we're all hoarding something, even if it hasn't reached disorder or addiction levels. If it's not possessions, it's emotions, resentments, bitterness, memory-tripping hazards, and so on. What were the secondary characters in the novel hanging on to that should have been discarded long ago? How about Eli's parents? What had they carried, and how were they managing it?

10. We're not told, but what do you think compelled Eli to begin listening to the *Let In the Light* podcast?

11. Why do you think the author chose to allow the characters moments of humor? What role did humor play in the story?

12. Authors know readers often create a "What comes next?" scenario in their minds. Imagine Eli and Camille a year after the story concludes. What do you think life would look like for them? For Shyla and Jenx? Eli's brother? Allison and her family? How does the gift of imagination give you hope for your own life's circumstances?